"I found it a fast read and kept thinking I had the ending figured out. Of course I was never close to figuring it out but found it a fascinating, humorous read!"

— Cathy B., alpha reader

"A rollicking romp through the lingering stench of the wretched refuse of human civilization. I really enjoyed it. I read it straight through. You should consider this an extreme compliment – rarely happens... bloody brilliant."

— Chris B., alpha reader

"Enjoyed the book! Much sillier tone than MSD, it was a fun read"

— Bobby R., alpha reader

I0601110

X. HO YEN

CUSTODIANS
OF THE FUTURE

Published on Earth by Grand Unification Monastery, Colorado, USA
https://GrandUnificationMonastery.com

ISBN 978-0-9766158-5-9 (ebook)
ISBN 978-0-9766158-6-6 (soft cover)

Cover design by MiblArt.com   Blue Gold

https://XHoYenAuthor.com

Acknowledgements

Many thanks to my alpha readers who provided notes: Cathy B., Chris B., and Bobby R. Thanks also to Debora W. and author William Marshall. As always, your support and feedback is priceless.

Thanks to Sasha L. and Christian R. for your help with some of the Swedish language bits.

Thanks to The Blues Brothers, The Great Birds of the Galaxy, Rob Grant and Doug Naylor, James S.A. Corey, and all the other creatives who built the numerous works to which I've dropped loving nods herein.

Thanks to Sweden for the 'Sweden Sans' font, and to Glen Jan for the free 'Sreda' font, both of which give a nice yet subtle Swedish feel to the titling.

Perpetual thanks to LB, who always has my back.

For Dr. Priya G. – whose heart knows no bounds even though she's been through much worse than this book's MC.

Chapter 1

FNG

7:03 AM, Thursday, December 31st, 2099
Östnoraberget Waste Processing and Power Production
Station of Stockholm Vatten och Avfall (SVOA,
Stockholm Water and Waste), Sweden
Global Waste BV's mobile technical team 18819-FUJ

"Everyone remember where we parked, check?" Keiok said as Janitor Squad Fuj ("fooj") walked the short distance from their tall, grey, rented utility van to the mostly underground facility's mid-level entrance. Everyone in Janitor Squad Fuj spoke English, mostly for the sake of the former American on the team, Nycci. English had become the lowest common denominator language across the globe anyway.

The facility's small parking lot was below ground level on three sides. The side farthest from the facility was ten meters above the downhill terrain in the direction of the sea. The whole facility was a multi-step, gravity-driven "waterfall" of wastewater.

So, the dim, morning twilight caused the grey van to blend into the background of the grey, rock wall beyond it and the shadowed surface of the parking lot beneath it. Nevertheless, what Keiok said was pointless. There was no way to lose the van in that small lot only a short distance from the facility entrance.

"Right," said Irena, the team's FNG ("Focking New Guy").

After only a few steps, their wristcomps beeped and flashed.

"You are a vital component of Global Waste," began the

motivational company email Irena and her teammates had received on their wristcomps, written in English but with other language option buttons along the top of the message.

"No shit," Uncle Bode and Nycci both mumbled to themselves, deleting the email.

"Merde," mumbled Cosmo, also deleting it.

As they approached the entrance, everyone eyeballed their official team leader, Keiok, as he started mumbling an "additional log" into his wristcomp. Somehow, Keiok had seniority.

"Guess what, guys?" Irena said. She used her wristcomp to send the work order access code to unlock the windowless, metal door. She held it open for her teammates.

"We are a vital component of global waste," Uncle Bode said with a voice and face so straight it could calibrate a laser. Bode (pronounced like "ode", short for Bodhi) had picked up the nickname "Uncle" years ago. He was older than the others, very experienced, and had an uncle-like manner, the good kind of uncle, not the bad kind.

They all chuckled except Keiok, who was off in his own world as usual.

Irena was new to the team, assigned only a week ago. She had been on a few jobs with them already, but had never spoken out of turn, and certainly not informally. Trying to break the ice with a little sarcasm, she blurted, "'Smell the world', they said. 'Keep civilization moving,' they said. 'Be part of a crack team of technicians'."

Nycci tried to sound playful, but there was an undertone of contempt in her response. "What's a fancy lunar habitation engineer doing in a janitor squad, anyway, princess?" she said more than asked.

Irena didn't like being called 'princess'. She was 42! And this was her third career (attempt). But she knew she had to ignore it, at least for now. As the newest member of this janitor squad, she faced an uphill battle for acceptance. And her educational creds worked against her.

"After my sister's accident, I needed all this travel pay and overtime to help with her medical expenses," Irena explained, hoping to appeal to the group's sympathy.

She was lying, or at least exaggerating. Sure, her sister could use the financial help during her recovery from the accident, but it wasn't absolutely necessary for Irena to take a higher-paying job. The plain reality was that she didn't just want acceptance in the group, she needed it, both professionally and personally.

At her job on Luna, she had become a social outcast. Well, okay, she had been fired for not being able to get along with her teammates. It became dangerous. On the Moon, team cohesion is crucial.

But she also had a long history of not being able to fit in. It was taking a toll on her.

She needed a fresh start, and Global Waste was always hiring for their janitor squads. But she wasn't about to reveal that her job is actually probationary and contingent upon good reviews by teammates. This could be her last chance to stay in a technical career. The engineering industry is brutal about firings and rapid job changes. If she failed here, she'd probably end up in Rust, Germany, operating the 'Flying Carpet' ride at Europapark.

But it was more than that. She needed a sense of belonging. It had been too long since she'd had that.

Not wanting anyone to smell her neediness, Irena shook her head to clear it and avoid getting maudlin. Then she tried adding some counterbalancing humor. "But whenever I see these company-approved puns, I think 'I should've stayed on the Moon'."

"Yeah," said Nycci, being intentionally ambiguous.

Irena thought, *I knew she was gonna be a problem. I should've kept my mouth shut.* She realized too late that bringing up her engineering gig on the Moon again wasn't

helpful.

As the janitor squad shuffled into the tall, dank, mid-stage, underground waste processing chamber, banging their bulging toolbags with dull thuds against the metal door and frame at the service entrance, Uncle Bode stopped and cleared his throat.

"Again, Uncle Bode?" Nycci said more than asked.

"I can't help it," Uncle Bode explained. "It's a genetic memory of dysentery." He turned down a short corridor leading to the lavatory.

"I heard it's the company food packets," Nycci said. "If you don't nuke 'em long enough they give you the runs. There were complaints about that below the latest company blog."

"That's what happens if you don't follow the cooking directions," Irena whispered sarcastically. Then, to change the subject, she switched back to her outside voice and declared, "This place stinks."

"Yahuh," Cosmo agreed.

"Exactly," Uncle Bode said, opening the lavatory door.'

Chapter 2

The Great Ostriching

*H*alf *a century into the Anthropocene Era, as the global population reached eight billion, the ice caps and permafrost melted, and the long-predicted pandemics repeatedly swept across the global village, people started to yearn for a more hopeful time.*

So, publishing and marketing AIs started screening for positive works and rejecting the dystopian, dark, or cerebral. Soon a global positivity took hold.

By a century into the Anthropocene, following viral pandemics and pandemics of anti-intellectualism, tribalism, sexism, creedism, racism, jingoism, pretty much all the -isms, that policy of screening for 'happy' public-facing works led to the happy future everyone wanted for everyone's grandchildren.

"Just Believe," went the mantra.

This kickstarted a new era of learning how to profit from egalitarian practices and forethought. Corporations began screening their officers for sociopathic personality disorder, and then voluntarily switched from the extremely short-sighted quarterly earnings reporting schedule to triennial reporting. They stopped marketing to children, restored net neutrality, and ended the practice of Big Data espionage perpetrated on the public for decades.

Even though it seriously reduced profits, they even paid for parks, pools, and playgrounds, roads, bridges, and mass transit, environmental protection, work safety, food safety, education, and social safety net services, and all the other things that used to require dues-driven unions and tax-driven governments of, by, and for the People. There was goodness for everyone on the planet as well as the biosphere.

They even started to refreeze the polar ice sheets.

Every industry voluntarily retooled, refit, and revamped. Atmospheric greenhouse gas levels dropped precipitously and sustainably. Ocean pollutant levels did, too, so the ocean stopped dying, and fish populations rebounded with negligible toxin content.

But the whales didn't make it. Fortunately, their mothership hasn't come looking for them.

Religions stopped becoming evangelical/jihadist. With "Just Believe" as their mantra, the zealots regained faith and no longer needed to murder infidels in order to feel their god's love. Religious institutions stopped dividing and polarizing everyone and stopped trying to kill science. Education finally experienced a Renaissance. Peace came organically to regions historically fraught with religious violence, and the rest of the world sighed with a relieved, collective "finally!"

Mafia states like Russia, apotheosis autocracies like Turkmenistan, and other kleptocracies like the PRC and the US voluntarily transformed into representative democracies with full transparency and real checks and balances. Russia ceased production of AK-47s and broke the mold, ending the pipeline of cheap weaponry to warlords across the world, effectively ending the war profiteering industry. Turkmenistan ousted its latest self-apotheosized leader and took down all the gigantic gold statues of him and his predecessors. Turkmenistan also finally sealed the 'Door To Hell' burning methane vein, which had been glowing aflame since 1971 C.E. And those warlords? They became schoolteachers.

Widespread genetic ancestry information finally convinced everyone to accept that there's only one human race.

Women the world over were now considered people, each

new generation allowed to attend school and to be or not to be wives or mothers, at their own discretion.

Revitalized, reunionized, and re-allied, the world took up peaceful space exploration again.

People even stopped talking at the theater.

And it was all thanks to that screening for 'happy' works a few decades earlier, known as "The Great Self-Censorship." Or "The Great Ostriching" among those happy to both commit doublespeak and perpetuate that myth about ostriches.

Well, actually, none of those things happened. But the privileged masses across the "developed" (user-economy) world, accustomed to having their stuff made for them by wage slaves in distant countries and pretending it isn't so, bought the rose-colored spectacles pushed by those same publishing and marketing AIs, and declared everything to be perfect. At least for a while they did – almost two decades, enough time to raise children in that delusion.

Then scratches began to appear on those rose-colored spectacles. The world is an imperfect place.

For the sake of the historical record, it is into this world that we plunge.

'Splishoop-splishoop-splishoop', went Uncle Bode's plunger.

"Damn, whoever uses this toilet needs to flush it completely between uses," he muttered from inside the lavatory. Despite the stink of someone else's biowaste decimeters away, there wasn't a hint of anger or even annoyance in Uncle Bode's voice. He was simply commenting on an operational matter.

From the other side of the lavatory door, Cosmo agreed.

 13

"Yahuh."

"I'll bet they chose the wrong flush timing for this bowl," Uncle Bode said.

His words echoed off the dank lavatory's cold, hard walls.

"I heard you can get Narcissistic Personality Disorder from a toilet seat," said Nycci, standing in the short corridor outside the lavatory, reading the e-bulletin board full of notices and SOP posters.

"Is that what you heard, Sparkles?" asked Uncle Bode rhetorically, his splishooping coming to an end.

Irena wondered if his use of 'sparkles' was a way to re-level the playing field after Nycci's rude use of 'princess'.

"I heard that a bunch of people saw it posted on multiple platforms, so," Nycci replied, but then she became distracted by noticing and touching the moisture condensing on the light blue painted concrete wall. Somewhere in the dark corner farther along that wall, a cockroach hissed.

Keiok was near Irena on the main walkway, still near the entrance to this Waste Processing and Power Production Station (WPPPS, pronounced "whoops", like the mistake). He continued to say strange things to imaginary people as he moved his hands along the WPPPS's electrical conduits. They ran down from the cable trays overhead and into several junction boxes at waist-level on the wall.

Irena had seen Keiok at each of their job sites pretending that he was leading an imaginary team of space explorers, and that the WPPPS they were sent to repair (or clean) was a fantastical space vessel, space station, or alien facility in urgent need of repair, hacking, or paradoxing into submission. There was a rumor that he'd picked up the nickname "Cap'n Kirok" from a previous team, but no one on Team Fuj got the reference. They usually just shortened it to "Cap'n" if they were in a mocking mood. Mostly they ignored him. No one wanted to think about how working this job could break someone that badly.

"Execute your prime function!" Keiok said to a junction box at the end of the 'foyer' wall.

Uncle Bode replied from inside the lavatory. "Alright, alright, I just need to use this thing! That's why I took this detour in the first place, remember?" The toilet flushed once more, and the team could hear Uncle Bode tapping the plunger on the toilet to dry it a bit.

Irena deleted the company motivational email she'd just finished reading in full and rolled her eyes, partly in self-mockery for doing so. Then she scanned around the vast, unevenly lit chamber before them.

Pipes containing half-processed waste slurry entered this mid-chamber near the top at the back of the cavern, gently whooshing as they fed huge staging tanks along the back wall. A spaghetti of smaller pipes exited the staging tanks at valves, distributing the slurry to various chemical injection cisterns, testing equipment, and power extraction machines before passing it along to the huge Membrane BioReactor pools under the floor. One of those spaghetti lines led to a lab somewhere back in the shadows. That was their destination.

There was a platform against that back chamber wall that provided access to those valves. In the center of that platform was a ladder going up to a rounded cutout in the rocky ceiling.

Equipment droned and occasionally pinged or popped in thermal adjustment. Despite over a century of experience with this sort of plant, human ingenuity had yet to find a way to make a WPPPS not stink.

"This place stinks," she said again, but quietly this time. She glanced at the others to confirm they weren't annoyed by her repeat statement.

"Yahuh," said Cosmo.

"I heard if you inhale ammonia fumes every day, you'll train your nose to stop smelling poop," Nycci said.

"Uh," said Cosmo.

That's because eventually you'll be dead, and while no scientific studies have been done to prove it, I think it's safe to say you can't smell poop if you're dead, Irena thought. She ran another glance at the others as if checking that no one had overheard her sharp thoughts. *Uncle Bode would agree with me, wouldn't he? And Cosmo?*

"Let me know how that works out," Irena said instead of speaking her mind, trying to sound composed. She immediately regretted saying anything.

But then, as she moved her eyes across the far end of the chamber, Irena spotted something. "Wait, there it is."

She pointed across the chamber to a platform one flight up, partially obscured by a giant chemical injection vat and the pipes that fed it from above. The lab door would be in that blind spot behind the vat's feed pipes.

"Yahuh," said Cosmo, seeing the platform.

Exiting the lavatory and seeing Irena and Cosmo's focus, Uncle Bode caught on. "Let's go fix a bioreactor."

"So we can get paid," said Nycci.

"Yahuh," said Cosmo.

"Landing party, with me," said the Cap'n to his imaginary crew, following his real crew as they moved deeper into the chamber toward their destination.

Chapter 3

Zeitgeist

*W*hen the fast-moving, rogue megaplanet WISE3R-13061-Zeitgeist zoomed through the inner solar system a few decades ago at a steep angle relative to the plane of the ecliptic, it gravitationally perturbed hundreds of thousands of the dirty ice chunks known as Kuiper Belt objects. That sent tens of thousands of them plummeting toward the inner solar system, many thousands of which might survive the journey and could eventually blast Earth.

But they won't get close enough to be a threat for thousands of years, so nobody cares. That wasn't the problem.

Gravity goes both ways. Our Kuiper Belt objects yanked back. As a result, Zeitgeist's lone moon was pulled out of orbit and began tumbling into our Kuiper Belt. The moon had been dubbed Eisbergspitze ("tip of the iceberg") because when the rogue planet was finally imaged by telescopes shortly before its closest approach, its bright moon looked like a pointy bulge on the side of the cold megaplanet's dim, fuzzy dot.

Thusly plunging down the gravity well, Eisbergspitze could eventually hit a Kuiper Belt object and go splat. Nobody cared about that, either, at first.

But shortly after this mutual orbital disturbance began to play out, thousands of small objects were observed leaving Eisbergspitze, on their own power and with impressive acceleration. These could only be spacecraft of a technologically superior alien species, dubbed the Eisbergspitzisch, or Icebergers.

They zoomed down the gravity well, occasionally zigging

and zagging to avoid Kuiper Belt objects, and soon (after a couple of years of observation) it became clear they were heading for the nearest gas giant, Uranus, which was not so different from Zeitgeist, although smaller. They all settled on the moon Umbriel.

Radio messages were independently sent from multiple Earth nations.

"Greetings. We're humans on the planet Earth, from which these signals are emanating. Sorry about your planet. Who are you?" That sort of thing.

"We've seen your alien invasion movies!" came the reply. "Leave us alone! We do NOT want to invade. We just want to get high and watch tv. And **don't** try to invade **us**!"

Subsequent requests for communication with the Icebergers were met with silence.

Owing to the blissful attitude about the future which had been inculcated into the populace in The Great Ostriching, humanity collectively shrugged and continued with its daily affairs.

But some years later, an Icebergian object sped down the gravity well unannounced, arriving at Earth and slowing itself for a reasonably gentle splashdown in the Labrador Sea.

The problem was that no one ever heard from it or found it after splashdown.

As blithe humanity prepared to celebrate the turn of another century, it was common, at least among middle-aged and older adults who'd instituted The Great Ostriching, to willfully relegate the mystery of the Iceberger spacecraft to a blind spot in the back of their minds.

"I need the urine sampler," said Uncle Bode, leaning over the open bank of bioreactor power cells. His gaze was firmly fixed on several cells near the urine distribution feed at the center of the cell vat. His left arm was outstretched, hand open, awaiting the sterile sampling device. Those central cells were more red-orange than the expected yellowish-green.

"It still stinks in here," said Irena with a scrunched face as she handed him the tool. She cast furtive glances at everyone.

"Yahuh," said Cosmo.

"Would you like cheese with that whine, princess?" said Nycci.

Irena scrunched her face more, but this time because she was berating herself for whining.

"Helm, routine orbit," said Keiok, who was sitting in a desk chair on one side of the room, leaning forward and staring dramatically at the digital whiteboard on the other side of the room. He was using his wristcomp to feed the display a computer-generated, orbital view of some unknown planet.

Nycci looked over Irena's shoulder at the cell voltages display she was checking. It showed the history of generated voltages of each cell in the bioreactor cell bank Bode had opened. The central cells had started to decay a few days ago, and the ones immediately surrounding those had started to decay yesterday. Something was wrong with the biochemistry, and it was getting worse.

"Interesting coincidence that it's happening right under the feed," Irena said to herself, and then cringed when she realized she'd expressed it that way aloud, using the 'c' word.

"Syllojizm says there are no coincidences," Nycci added. The wildly popular Syllojizm web site was both a random opinion generator and an online community of consensus seekers on those random opinions.

That's right, attribute magical agency to simple pattern recognition, Irena thought, but stopped herself from going further into a distracting internal rant. She glanced at Uncle Bode and Cosmo to see if they were reacting to the conversation.

"Full sensor sweep. Scanners to maximum," said Keiok in the background.

"Okay, I have a good sample," said Uncle Bode, climbing off the bioreactor bank with the sampler in hand. "Let's see what's in it." He transferred the sample to a sterile test tube and inserted the tube into the lab's urine feed quality analyzer. It began to whir and chirp to indicate its progress.

"Okay, all the stuff you'd expect," said Uncle Bode as the output came up on the analyzer's screen, "but... there's some other stuff, enough to matter."

Significant glances were exchanged, except between Irena and Nycci.

Cosmo transferred some of the sample to the centrifuge, started it spinning, then paced the room. By the time it was done, Irena and Uncle Bode had worked out how they would extract a subsample of the mystery material from the stratified sample in the test tube that would be coming out of the centrifuge.

"It could be almost anything," Irena said, trying to keep it to herself.

"Yahuh," said Cosmo. Irena noticed Cosmo agreeing.

Uncle Bode just maintained his mellow countenance, drew the sub-sample from the target density layer, and moved half of it to the molecular analyzer and half to the electron microscope. He pressed the "Go" buttons on the two devices.

"On screen," said Keiok.

"What kind of a name is 'Keiok', anyway?" asked Nycci. "I've never heard anything like it."

"I'm from Makkovik, but now I work in space," Keiok

said as the fictional planet on the digital whiteboard was replaced by the analysis output. One side showed the electron microscope view, the other the molecular analyzer's tabular report.

Nycci made a half-squint "whatever" face at Keiok, shook her head, and added, "as a space janitor."

Irena looked up Makkovik, found it in northeast Canada, and convinced herself that she could imagine Keiok being part or even full Inuit.

After Uncle Bode tweaked the electron microscope's position and zoom settings, the view showed a polygonal structure at the end of a tube, and gripper 'legs' coming out of the bottom of the tube.

"That's one of many in this sample alone," he said.

"That's some kind of virus, right?" asked Nycci.

Keiok walked up to the digital whiteboard and stood with arms akimbo beside the image. He pointed to a pattern of molecules on the side of the thing's polygonal 'head' and said something that Irena couldn't quite hear, then, "...what do you make of this?"

"X...D...S...9...TM," Irena read. The 'TM' was smaller than the other characters. "It's trademarked."

"This smells fishy," Nycci commented.

"Yahuh," said Cosmo. Irena noted Cosmo's quick agreement with Nycci.

Uncle Bode pointed at one sublisting from the molecular analyzer report. "This part of the report shows what's inside the 'head'. With a virus like this, the proteins of the gripper legs and central tube latch onto a cell wall and pierce it, and then the stuff in the 'head' floats into the attached cell. I think. If I remember correctly."

"That's not DNA or RNA," said Irena. "Wetware isn't my thing, but don't viruses inject genetic material into host cells?"

"It looks like a hunk of metal," said Nycci.

"Here it is, down here in the list," said Uncle Bode. "Shows up as 'various Thallium compounds.' Doesn't Thallium cause nerve damage?"

"Yahuh," said Cosmo, who drifted to the far side of the room and started fidgeting with the equipment there.

"All of those artificial viruses contain Thallium?" Irena asked.

"Probably," said Uncle Bode, "based on the molecular analyzer report."

"It's in the waste stream," said Nycci. "The locals will be dying in days to weeks. Who would do such a thing?"

Irena thought, *Now hold on, we don't actually know anything about this situation.* But she kept it to herself. She'd already asserted herself more than usual at this job site, and it hadn't gone well.

"This is above our pay grade," said Uncle Bode.

When no one said otherwise, he placed a call to their SVOA contract supervisor.

Chapter 4

The Borg Identity

*T*he *Great Ostriching finally made America great again. The pro-corporate, pro-gun, old-testament, jihadist-evangelical-although-nominally-christian bloc took over. The Constitution was mostly revoked on the grounds it was anti-state and anti-corporate. Gun manufacturers convinced the bloc to replace the second amendment's "A well regulated militia" with "A well-armed militia". Old-testament-christianity became the official and exclusive national religion, kicking off decades of well-armed, bloody conflict over whose interpretation of christianity would hold power. As far as anyone knows, those clashes continue to this day.*

Now officially "Murrica", it severed ties with the rest of the world, put domestic journalism out of business (i.e. executed all proper journalists), ended science research (i.e. executed everyone with a Ph.D.), and nuked Hollywood, San Francisco, Portland, New York City, Washington, D.C., and much of Mexico. Many argued for Boulder, Colorado, too, but even the new administration didn't want to detonate a nuke that far inland, that close to the heartland. The glorious mushroom clouds full of vaporized lefty actors, hippies, freaks, refuge seekers, and cartel workers were "great", certain witnesses said. "Everything will be better now. I believe!" they declared.

All government regulation of businesses ceased, allowing the international conglomerate Koche Industries with its ALECH lobbying front to save billions in lobbying and propaganda expenses. That was great, it said. But then it lost a huge fraction of its market when, only a few years later, Murricans could no longer afford its products. When the internet collapsed, Koche moved its headquarters from Wichita, Kansas, to Chongqing, China, as did Herkshire Bathaway.

The new CEO of Murrica set up the new capital/headquarters in St. Louis. It was supposed to be in Miami, but Miami was fast becoming Miami Shoals. Shortly afterward, the big one hit, and St. Louis was flattened. Then the newer new CEO of Murrica set up shop in Oklahoma City. But the big twister hit, and OK City was flattened. With great fanfare, the newest CEO of Murrica, a Texan, established the new capital in the Alamo, but radioactive fallout from Mexico and Los Angeles made that location too cancerous. He moved the new capital to Boise, but the same thing happened with radioactive fallout from San Francisco and Portland.

After outlawing the prevailing westerlies, he established the new capital in Nashville. Everyone slapped their foreheads — of course, Nashville! They set it up in the Nashville Public Library Central Library building, which had been shuttered since The Great Book Banning and Lynching nationwide event years earlier. But then a clash between Brooksites and Churchites ended in a great fire. The CEO lost his entire collection of autographed Hank Williams, Jr. bobbleheads in the fire and was so angry that he moved the new capital to Charlotte, North Carolina.

Though everyone knew the last of the Mooreites had been burned alive years earlier, Buckites in Charlotte soon accused some of the CEO's female staff of being Mooreites. Their skirts were just above the knee, and they objected to being groped. Following summary lynchings of those staff members and their defenders, the CEO took the advice of Mormon leaders in Utah and moved the new HQ to Salt Lake City, where it remains to this day, as far as anyone knows.

The Brits joined in, having already severed as many ties as possible with the outside world by the time of the Great Ostriching. Now Murrica technically spans the Atlantic Ocean and there are millions of Murricans who eat marmite and say "trousers" instead of "pants", and "wiff" instead of "with". But both still say "Eye ran" instead of "Ihrrahn", although in recent decades that country's name had all but disappeared from their shared vocabulary anyway.

They don't communicate with each other though, being isolationist, and the spiritual void left by not maintaining contact with the newly great mainland Murrica has kept England in a funk for the entire latter half of the century. It replaced the funk that was driven by the loss of Empire, which had run out of steam early in the century and needed replacing. The lynchpin of the economy became lager, which many described as 'great' after consuming several pints.

Canada finally put up a wall on their southern border. They found it worked better if they painted "666" on its southern face every hundred meters or so (and on maritime interdiction vessels), and better still if they painted "$1^6 - 2^6 + 3^6 = 666$". In cases where fear of the 'mark of the devil' didn't keep Murricans out, math did the trick. If those didn't work, the "Canadian Socialism Wants You" immigration kiosks were a solid tertiary strategy on the Murrica side of the moats, electric fences, and snipers.

Scotland and Ireland did something similar, but they used billboards depicting brown-skinned people happily mingling at famous Irish and Scottish locales. It worked like a charm is supposed to but doesn't because magic doesn't exist.

"Twenty minutes," Uncle Bode reported. "They said to wait here."

Everyone stared at the walls, occasionally taking sips from their water bottles.

Keiok said to his imaginary crew, "It's a mystery. I don't like mysteries. They give me a headache." Then he walked over to the lab door and stood staring through the glass out at the broad, stinky wastewater processing cavern.

Uncle Bode and Nycci briefly speculated about how the bioreactor could damage the virus' protein shell and the Thallium would then chemically alter the reactor cell walls. It seemed like a good explanation of the damage they were seeing in the bioreactor.

Irena wasn't convinced they knew what was going on, let alone that someone had done this intentionally.

She imagined herself making an impassioned speech about due diligence which convinces everyone to stop and check their work. In the vision, everyone nodded and agreed, pulling out manuals and working the equipment correctly.

Trying to sound neutral rather than antagonistic, she asked the room, "Why would anyone bother using an expensive, manufactured virus to poison people with Thallium? Why not just find a way to dump a bunch of Thallium directly into the water supply?"

They thought about it for a few moments.

Uncle Bode started and stopped talking a few times, clearly was considering the question, and then said, "I think Thallium would precipitate out of rivers and streams fairly quickly, being as heavy as it is. They'd have to add it into the water supply very late, near Stockholm, and that would be noticed."

"So," Irena said, thinking aloud, "these viruses prevent it from precipitating out? If you're gonna poison people, why use very expensive, manufactured viruses and a slow poison that's likely to be detected before it works?"

"It's diabolical!" said Nycci, completely ignoring Irena's question.

Irena stewed, exasperated. The others apparently considered her question rhetorical, which to them apparently means irrelevant. They went quiet.

Irena walked to the far, dark corner of the lab, behind storage tanks full of cleaners and reactants. Feeling her isolation, she recorded a quick vidmail for Kekoa, her last friend on Luna, the vac suit checker at the Kyrgyz Moon Landing Museum.

"'Loha, Ke," she started, not knowing what else to say. "I guess, I guess I'm missing you. Not sure about this new job." Something was happening behind her, so she cut it short. "I'll keep you posted. Please stay in touch." She pushed 'send' and returned to the others, trying to count the weeks since Kekoa's last message.

The metal stairs outside the bioreactor room were thumping with footfalls.

A figure appeared on the platform, the door opened, and a statuesque woman in a power suit entered the lab. Not a black vinyl or high-tech-kitted power suit, not an armored war machine power suit, but a very-short-skirted, well-fitted, business-like power suit, making very prominent the ins and outs of her shapely physicality. In concert with her chic coif and perfect skin, her presentation did what it was meant to do — distract, disarm, and discombobulate everyone in the room. You wouldn't be surprised to see her partying on a billionaire's superyacht, although she'd be wearing something different on a superyacht.

How manipulative, thought Irena.

Cosmo had turned to look. *Holy shit, rockin' legs*, was written all over Cosmo and Uncle Bode's faces. Their stomachs pulled in a little, their postures rose a little.

Keiok remained at his captain's (desk) chair along the side of the room, speaking quietly into his wristcomp.

"Hej, everyone," the woman said with a lovely voice and a disarming Swedish accent. "I'm Annika Borg, your contract supervisor at SVOA. Normally I focus on the Fågelöudde and Erstavik facilities, but I was in the area when you called."

"Hej," said the younger man who stood behind and to her left, "I'm Hugh Borg, her cousin. I work in the Technology Division."

"And before you ask," Annika continued, "no, we are not related to the famous tennis player, nor to the famous singer and winner of *Idol*."

Keiok said to his wristcomp in a whisper-shout, "Throw the switch!"

"What's the concern?" Annika asked the center of the room while side-eyeing Keiok.

Heads swiveled but quickly settled on Uncle Bode. Everyone pointed to the digital whiteboard and let Uncle Bode explain their discovery of the trademarked, manufactured virus containing Thallium.

"We think that's what started damaging this urine bioreactor a few days ago," Uncle Bode said, pointing to it. "That establishes the timing."

Annika was unfazed.

Nycci continued, "So, someone is poisoning the people of Stockholm. They dumped this virus into the water a few days ago, and soon people will start losing their hair, getting the shakes, and dying."

We don't actually know that, thought Irena, clenching her jaw, furrowing her brow, and looking down at the floor.

"Days to weeks," Cosmo added, still fiddling with equipment on the far side of the room.

"You have to *do* something!" said Nycci.

Keiok, in his own world as usual, whisper-shouted, "Fire torpedoes! Full spread!"

Side-eyeing Keiok again, Annika said, "Okay, listen to me

carefully. It's nyårsfirandet, New Year's Eve. Tonight there will be celebrations, and most people will not be drinking water. I will handle this. You have done your job, you've found the cause of the power production problem, you've informed me of your finding. Our techs will see to the equipment, and our government will investigate these viruses and address the public safety threat."

Cousin Hugh nodded and said with a smile, "Just believe."

"You have fulfilled your contract," Annika continued, "and will be paid. You may now return to Global Waste. Have a nice flight!"

She smiled an earnest-looking business smile and ever so gently shook her head back and forth, causing her wavy brown hair to assert itself in league with the rest of her physicality. Cosmo and Uncle Bode blankly blinked at her.

Sexual manipulation disgusted Irena, but she stood up and started collecting her toolbag, hoping to get the others to start packing up, too. She just wanted them to let it go and pursue their own, separate treatments for whatever was in their blood, if treatments were really needed.

Seeing the rest of the team stationary, Annika lowered her nose and raised her eyebrows in a distinct "What are you waiting for?" look.

"Yes, ma'am," said Uncle Bode, taking a deep breath. "We just need to collect our things."

"Very good, you do that. Happy New Year." Turning toward the door, Annika glanced at Hugh. He opened the door, let her pass, then fell in behind her. The Borg disappeared, thumping down the platform's metal staircase. They were halfway across the chamber before the janitor squad had processed what was happening.

"How does she walk so fast in those heels?" Uncle Bode mused, watching Annika go.

Nycci said, "I guess I expected some more information, you know, on the plan." She was tapping on her wristcomp.

"I wonder what Syllojizm says about this Thallium virus."

Cosmo turned away from whatever he was doing on the other side of the room. The squad could now see a microscope where he stood, its soft, plastic cover in a heap behind it on the lab table.

"I have those things in my blood." Cosmo held up his pricked finger, a tiny drop of blood drying on it. "You probably do, too," Cosmo said.

"Well, I'm wearing wrist and ankle bands infused with both copper and extract of nettles, and every day I drink a shot of my own pee, so I should be fine," said Nycci.

Everyone turned to look at her. Irena's mouth opened a bit.

"Medical emergency on the bridge," said Keiok.

"Hey, a bunch of people saw it posted on multiple platforms, so… And I haven't been sick in months." She changed her voice to match that of an online ad to which everyone had been subjected. "Fabulosa Narcissus insists it works," Nycci carefully enunciated.

"And bring Dr. McKenna," Keiok said into his imaginary intercom.

Irena inhaled, closed her eyes, and imagined her hand slapping her forehead. Then she used her wristcomp to start researching Thallium poisoning and manufactured viruses.

Cosmo beckoned the others to join him at the microscope.

Keiok stroked his chin and watched intently as the planet spun once again on the digital whiteboard. Occasionally he rocked as if experiencing turbulence. He pressed an imaginary button on the chair's arm, and said, "Precautionary measures — dispatch recorder buoy, and broadcast the past week's log entries."

Chapter 5

It's Canadian Bacon To Me

*B*efore The Great Ostriching, the Moon had been *colonized and industrialized by several superpowers, such as Saudi Aramco, General Electric, Royal Dutch Shell, and PetroChina. Generally speaking, inhabitants of Luna, as it's now commonly known, were selected for a few key traits: safety-mindedness, a broad education (not just STEM), and team focus. But they also self-selected. Most had a strong desire to get the hell away from the rest of crazy humanity.*

In this regard, the volunteers in that relatively minor migration resembled migrants throughout human history and prehistory. From the first ones who left the Great Rift Valley to found Babylon, getting the hell away from the rest of crazy humanity was a common characteristic. It was the same with those who left the Fertile Crescent and Central Asia to found India, Indochina, China, Europe, and Polynesia.

Oh, how the future Europeans must have wanted to get away from the rest of humanity, enough to eat lichen and live in ice and freezing rain with no citrus fruits or scantily clad people.

Oh, how the Polynesians must have wanted to get away from the rest of humanity, enough to jump into small boats and ride for weeks over the horizon into the deep, dark waves and storms, guided by mysterious lights above their heads, and then to remain on tiny islands whipped by typhoons and smashed by tsunamis.

Those who left Central Asia to become 'white' people in Europe and also to cross the Bering Strait and become 'red' people in North and South America regretted not going far enough after they ran into each other again centuries later.

Humanity's quest to escape itself came full circle with those who moved back to Africa from comfortable developed nations in temperate zones, as with the Ghanaian Revival. People have always been willing to leave comfortable places to get away from other people.

So the migration to Luna, a radiation-beaten vacuum hellscape, came as a surprise only to those who knew little about humanity's nature and past. The earthbound called the migrants lunatics, yet the migrants were already in the habit of referring to everyone else back on earth the same way.

In reality, lunar migrants were barely aware of The Great Ostriching when it happened. It was far too abstract a philosophy for them, being laser focused as they were on the practical challenges of survival and productivity in said hellscape. Not only had they no need for the "Just Believe" motto, but it was, in fact, a lethal mindset to adopt. The vague, essentially religious notion that self-censorship would make the world a better place was no substitute for rigorous, disciplined maintenance of vac suits, facilities, and vehicles, adherence to thoughtfully developed checklists, and knowing the chemical engineering that underpinned everything they worked to achieve and which kept them alive.

Back on Earth, The Great Ostriching led to a resurgence in STEM, except STEM had been re-defined to mean "Social Media", "Trolls", "Eat", and "Me" for many, "Stop", "Teaching", "Everything", and "to My children" for others (admittedly a stretch, but somehow it caught on in Murrica, and may still be used there, as far as anyone knows), and "Sleeping", "Tranquillising", "Eating", and "Mimicking" for still others, words popularized in the lyrics of a platinum-selling song by the band "Elephant

Ride Mumpsimus." The lyrics were meant to be sardonic and ironic, but after a campaign of subtle co-opting ads by the recreational self-medication industries and related pro-consumerism lobbies, they were adopted as the mantra of a 'rebellious surrender' movement. Profits jumped, starting with alcohol, of course.

Problems on Luna were all too common, though, mostly because of supply chain and quality issues among earthbound suppliers. For key manufactured goods, medical products, most arts, and nice foods and luxuries, lunar workers remained woefully reliant on the lackadaisical adherents to the "Just Believe" motto back on Earth. As a result, accidents happened far more often than they should.

The same could be said of the human and material supply chains that underpinned operations on Global Waste Space Station.

Keiok couldn't be drawn away from his imaginary world, but Cosmo showed that everyone else had the Thallium-carrying viruses in their blood.

"I don't trust that Borg woman," said Nycci. "She was too laid-back about this."

Uncle Bode, the eldest of the group, said with a shrug, "You young people are so negative. She's been informed and said it would be taken care of. Everything's fine. Just Believe. That's how we reversed climate change," he said, his wristcomp's default screen displaying the 20 to 30 C weather forecast for the first week of January in Stockholm, Sweden.

"Oh, yeah? Look at this." Nycci swiped her wristcomp toward the display screen, overriding Keiok's feed. The screen showed the Syllojizm website, Nycci's favorite rumor mill.

The site had entries on a variety of topics, each one beginning with "Isn't it interesting that…" Nycci highlighted one that read, "Isn't it interesting that sales of manufactured viruses reached record levels shortly before reported illnesses skyrocketed?"

"See that?" she said. "Coincidence? I don't think so."

Irena cringed and subvocalized, "Post hoc ergo propter hoc." Even her quick, initial research showed a plethora of medical uses for manufactured viruses. And the date on that entry was in the middle of the annual flu season, so of course, illness reports would've spiked around the same time. But she didn't want to get into a debate, let alone an argument. She was on thin ice already.

But Nycci had the attention of Cosmo and Uncle Bode.

"And this," Nycci continued, highlighting an entry that read, "Isn't it interesting that polls in Canada show a strong increase in anti-Sweden sentiment?"

Wait, what? thought Irena. *What is she overinterpreting now?* She opened a new window on her wristcomp and did some quick research on the same subject. She quickly discovered that the so-called strong increase in anti-Sweden sentiment in Canada not only was well within the long-term noise, but it also correlated to a particularly egregious foul perpetrated by a player on the Swedish national hockey team. It was essentially a meaningless, short-term data blip.

Nycci was already showing her next highlight.

"Isn't it interesting that the CSA buys manufactured viruses?" Nycci read.

Irena noticed Uncle Bode perk up with interest. *This is not good*, she thought.

"And this," Nycci continued, reaching a presentational crescendo. She read the final highlighted entry. "Isn't it interesting that there's now a CSA office in Stockholm?"

"Holy shit," Cosmo said slowly.

"The goddamn CSA," said Uncle Bode. "I read blogs last month about their Big Lie. It broke my heart." A deep furrow between his eyebrows transformed his normally placid countenance.

"Wait," said Irena. "What's the CSA? Something 'Security Administration'?"

"The Canadian Space Agency," Nycci said with bile in her voice.

"It was fake news, all those decades," Uncle Bode said. "I grew up building models of the International Space Station and our beloved Canadarm2. But recently I found out they never actually built it. All those decades they said they built the Canadarm2 and used it on the ISS, but it was all a lie. And now this."

"But" Irena couldn't help herself, "there are decades of videos showing the Canadarm2 in use, and astronauts talking about it, and them attached to it for EVAs. You've all seen it forty million times. A cover-up like that would require tens of thousands of civilians from many countries to collaborate on such a lie..."

"All CG. Never happened," Nycci said, then took a sip of water.

"...including deep fake video artists," Irena continued, "and accountants hiding CSA expenditures on those deep fake video artists, and, and...," Irena knew such a conspiracy would require countless others, vendors, journalists, and so on, people not necessarily driven by whatever Nycci believed could drive all those people to create and cover such a lie, but she couldn't work out the whole list on the spot. She switched gears.

"...and such a conspiracy would have to last for decades," she huffed, exasperated. "Try getting *ten* people to all agree on picnic arrangements." Irena had blown her wad on conflict. She took a deep breath and felt her jaw and lips clamp.

"Hey, they did it with the Moon landings, they can do it with the Canadarm," Nycci said. "And now this," she pointed accusingly at the screen. "The CSA has a liaison in Stockholm, Sweden, of all places. Coincidence? There *are* no coincidences!"

Uncle Bode fumed. Cosmo was getting wound up, too.

Irena found it difficult to breathe. She went limp, dropping her shoulders and her toolbag. Irrational behavior always threw her into a fit. It's probably why she couldn't get along with her coworkers on Luna.

Nycci saw Irena's reaction and pressed. "Connect the dots, princess," she said. "It's plain to see if you just open your eyes and look. Manufactured viruses cause illness. Canada hates Sweden. The CSA is all about lies. The CSA buys manufactured viruses. There's a new CSA office in Stockholm. And now there are manufactured viruses here poisoning everyone with Thallium."

Nycci pointed her upturned hand at the screen. Shortly after Nycci highlighted those entries, the site added a new comment. "Is Canada waging war on Sweden?" it asked with no fanfare. "You decide," it suggested in its calm, easy-to-read font. An ad popped up. Nycci read it for a moment, then dismissed it.

"The friggin' Canadian Space Agency is waging a secret war on Stockholm," she said. "Look. It already has almost sixteen thousand likes. It has to be right. We gotta do something!"

Uncle Bode slammed his hand on the table. "I hate the CSA. Lying bastards stole my childhood." Irena had never seen him like this.

Nycci addressed everyone but Irena, "We need to let the public know who's behind this and warn everyone of the danger." Uncle Bode and Cosmo had their backs to Irena.

Uncle Bode said, "And I want that CSA 'liaison'," he did

air quotes, "on camera when we do it."

Irena mindlessly cleared her wristcomp's screen. She was in a tizzy. Her squadmates were on a "mission from god" and there was nothing she could do about it.

On her wristcomp, just below the story about the Swedish hockey player's egregious foul, had been another story about a recent party on the superyacht of Swedish gajillionaire "Ronja." There might have been a pic of Ronja and several other young, attractive people, including Annika Borg in a stunning swimsuit, but Irena was in such a tizzy that she didn't process any of it before clearing the screen.

Chapter 6

Prime Function

B<i>y the final decade of the 21st century, the youngest generation in the developed nations was growing cynical again. STEMing wasn't making their lives better. The Great Ostriching had given the banks an excuse to cancel all savings-based services and switch to an entirely debt-based business model. It had given the insurance industry an excuse to remove all prevention-based services and shift healthcare to an entirely emergency-response-based model. It had given employers the power to remove all benefits and tell employees to "Just Believe" in their safety, health, and long-term future.*

These young folk had seen firsthand what those changes did to their parents' lives upon reaching upper middle age. They had seen people save their money at home, only to become victims of life-ruining theft. They had seen egregious work accidents take lives, preventable diseases treated all too late in emergency rooms, worn down employees being fired due to disability, with no public safety nets.

And somehow, word began to spread about something people used to call "retirement." They had found mocking references to it in old writings by people in the underdeveloped, over-enslaved world. Such people never had job benefits or the luxury of retirement, so they mocked the sense of entitlement amongst those in the developed nations who dreamt of retirement. But, being steeped in mockery, the youngest generation in the developed nations skimmed right over the mockery and took away from those writings the realization that there used to be things called job benefits, savings plans, collective public safety nets, and retirement for those who had worked hard for many years and smartly invested a portion of their earnings all those years. These ideas stuck with them. They no longer blindly followed the "Just Believe" mindset of their parents, who called them spoiled, misguided troublemakers, or worse, even as those parents suffocated in the "employer's market" wage slavery establishment they helped create by Just Believing.

After decades of dealing with violent extremists, police forces across the planet had started to look more like police forces in 'Murrica and Myanmar. It was a natural evolution, with hiring practices and workforce retention selecting for ever more violent police officers in places like Denmark just as racism and the police-vs-civilians corruption culture had done so in 'Murrica. Body cams proved an insufficient check. Police violence and murder in turn converted ordinary moderates and just-want-to-be-left-alones into violent, anti-police mobs, which reinforced that selection effect and amplified the problem.

The situation became untenable, but a compromise solution first used in Denmark spread quickly. It involved creating a third branch of the police, to create a three-point system of checks and balances. Now, in addition to Enforcement and Internal Affairs branches, there was a new field branch acting in parallel with Enforcement and with jurisdiction only over Enforcers, not civilians. The new field branch was required to shadow all Enforcers in the field, albeit separately to avoid collusion. These "Watcher" units were separately deployed, with their own vehicles, assets, and even a separate communication system. In this model, the Watcher branch was just as public as the Enforcer branch.

Nominally, the Watchers were all about making the world more like the Great Ostriching fantasy world.

Often, their uniforms had "smiley face" patches on the shoulders or emblems on vehicles. Enforcers, on the other hand, tasked with directly chasing criminals and fighting violent extremists, dug deeper into skull-and-crossbones motifs and tattoos. Both branches attracted ever harder-nosed proponents who were energized by a good fight.

Thus, in the final decades of the century, public protests by the younger generations calling for the reinstatement of job benefits, savings accounts, etc., routinely devolved into police brutality against the protesters followed by police-on-police brutality when the Watchers got involved to stop the Enforcer-on-civilian brutality.

Video from one such protest in Malmö went viral after protesters fled the field, leaving only Enforcers and Watchers fighting each other, riot shields clashing against riot shields, rubber bullets and sandbag rounds knocking both sides down, tear gas filling the street.

Police haters called it The Pig Roast, the more cerebral called it The Ouroboros Riot, journalists called it a focking embarrassment, Internal Affairs called it a shit ton of paperwork, city officials called it the system working out its kinks, and the protesters were unhappy that the police were getting all the news coverage.

Afterward, police budgets were never expanded, resulting in fewer but more ardent Enforcers on the streets. This, plus the proliferation of self-driven vehicles, ended the practice of traffic enforcement. In the Great Ostriching world, locals often took criminal matters into their own hands. Frontier justice bloomed anew, sometimes with uniforms, sometimes with homemade strobe lights, but always with extrajudicial punishment.

The mid-late morning sky was a partial overcast, so the team's shadows were blurry at best.

"Please, just drop me off at the spaceport. I want nothing to do with this," Irena said as Nycci, Cosmo, and Uncle Bode marched toward their rental van, still alone in the small, empty WPPPS lot. Keiok lagged behind Irena despite not being burdened by a toolbag.

Nycci spun around and pointed an accusing finger at Irena. "Are you gonna be a coward about this? It's our chance to fight the bad guys, and you wanna ostrich like a geezer?"

"That's not," Irena tried to respond, but she was flustered by Nycci's force of will. "You guys are going to jail if you harass or attack that CSA liaison," she said, making sure to frame her objection as concern for the others. Irena's eyes frantically checked Cosmo and Uncle Bode for any sign of agreement, uncertainty, or hesitation.

Nada.

Nycci resumed her march toward the van. "I'll be proud to go to jail if it means saving Stockholm."

Irena frowned and her nostrils flared, but she had no comeback.

They all piled into the van. Cosmo was in the "driver's seat," setting up the navigation for the van's autopilot.

"Don't you understand the huge assumptions you're making?" Irena said, but she didn't have Nycci's ability to shout and bully. Judging from her accent, Nycci was an American, from somewhere in the northeast megalopolis.

Nycci engaged one last time. "It was all right there on the screen, princess. Open your eyes." Then the trio pulled up a Stockholm map on the van's display and started talking through how they were going to lure a news crew to the building where the CSA office was located.

Irena wondered why they stormed out to the van to do such planning. The wall display inside the plant was larger,

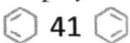 **41**

and the lab was more comfortable. *Maybe this feels more like action to them*, she thought. *Or maybe it was just the stink inside.*

Keiok sat in the righthand back corner of the utility van, on the other lengthwise bench seat across from Irena. He gave her a significant glance. It was a rare moment when Keiok seemed present and aware. Then he spoke softly to her, under the din of the others' planning session.

"Execute your prime function," he said, looking right into her eyes.

Irena's brow furrowed. *What the hell is he saying?*

Then Keiok pressed a button on his wristcomp. "Log entry, additional," he began, after which Irena lost track of his gibberish. She didn't have the time or patience to decrypt Keiok and his geeky weirdness. The others had found the CSA liaison office and were planning some sort of a caper.

What can I do? Irena seemed stuck in a loop. *No one listens to me.*

But they might listen to Monty, she thought. Monty Hogue was their Global Waste supervisor. *He might be able to talk some sense into them.*

The problem was that Monty Hogue was also the only supervisor on the hiring committee who'd voted not to hire Irena. Her job was probationary because of him.

Chapter 7

Supervisor Face

*A*t *the same time the younger folk were growing discontented with their lot, during the last decade of the century some of the oldest of the Great Ostriching generation were losing faith. Whisperings and old-school cover-your-ass maneuverings raised instinctive hackles and triggered suppressed suspicions and habits. Before anyone realized what was happening, secret slush funds were redirected into operational accounts, decommissioned operatives were brought in from the cold, and suddenly everyone was spying on and sabotaging each other again.*

And that was just in the fantasy futbol clubs, intoxication cliques, parent-teacher associations, e-sports leagues, quilting guilds, professional organizations, kaffeeklatschen, and local parishes. Things got a lot uglier at the corporate level.

Due to the lackadaisical "Just Believe" attitude spawned from the Great Ostriching cultural movement, poor quality in manufactured goods quickly became the norm. The world of the Great Ostriching was okay with dangerous and unreliable vehicles, appliances, electronics, medical equipment, processed foods, etc., as long as everyone's escapism was thorough and unchallenging. The alcohol industry loved the Great Ostriching.

Once the hackles went back up, though, corporate operatives were directed to make certain specific and difficult-to-detect quality failures happen in key manufactured goods of rival corporations. Such sabotage operations were mostly impossible in the pre-"Just Believe" era, due to stringent Quality Control processes rigorously applied by diligent QA departments. But almost overnight diligence went out the window like a Russian oligarch during Putin's mafia consolidation phase, because convenience-driven consumers accepted whatever was on the menu and didn't apply leverage with their money.

The new Hackles-Up era began when simple, but effective ad campaigns were launched featuring backhanded compliments of rival products.

The amusement park ride market had shrunk during the 21st century for a variety of reasons and therefore had become more competitive. The very first backhanded compliment ad campaign in the new Hackles-Up era was a simple message, perpetrated by Ermenswatz Excitations of Wank, Deutschland. "We, the Amusement Park Ride Operator's Union, stand by Apex's 'Flying Carpet' amusement park ride. Our thoughts and prayers are with the victims and their families. We're absolutely sure that future riders will be safe. Just Believe." The ad was widely distributed, despite there being no such thing as an Amusement Park Ride Operator's Union, nor a single accident on the mentioned ride. The language was carefully ambiguous, never actually stating that there had been accidents on the 'Flying Carpet' ride. To a credulous public, implied allegation was enough.

Amusement park ride operators were too busy struggling to make a living to look into it, or they adopted the low anxiety "Just Believe" attitude about it, or if all else failed, rebellious surrender. But the public and the amusement parks were also steeped in "Just Believe" bliss, so they reacted slowly and with less alarm than they would have in the pre-Great Ostriching era. Nonetheless, the impact on ridership was noticeable.

Banking on the public's blissful apathy, Apex (licensed as 'Apex School of Spiritualism and Guerrilla Design') did not take public, retaliatory legal action. The Wankers at Ermenswatz then saw a boost in sales of, and maintenance contracts for, their 'Frammis Duct' ride across the amusement park market. Apex's 'Flying Carpet' rides were being replaced by 'Frammis Duct' rides.

The happy mood at Ermenswatz lasted for weeks until suddenly several of them died or sustained life-altering injuries in freak accidents that somehow affected only the buses, rail cars, and lifts frequented by Ermenswatz executives during their daily commutes.

Within the fifteen minutes during which those deaths appeared in news feeds, the CEO of Apex, a former New Jerseyite who called himself 'The Yogi', issued a press release. It decried unnecessary commuting to workplaces as an environmentally unfriendly and completely obsolete practice that had contributed greatly to global warming. It also announced plans for a new amusement park ride, 'The Meditator,' which incorporated the latest safety features not found in other rides, such as Ermenswatz's 'Frammis Duct.' That press release kicked the new Hackles-Up mindset into a higher gear and also was the first widely covered mention of global warming in decades. Orders for 'Frammis Duct' rides were canceled, and 'Flying Carpet' rides were instead being replaced with 'The Meditator,' i.e. new sales for Apex.

In a fifteen-minute news cycle two weeks later, it was reported that 'The Yogi' was missing, presumed dead, during a trip to Rust, Deutschland, to attend the annual IAAPA Expo. The Spreuters coverage, and only the Spreuters coverage, of his disappearance included interviews with IAAPA attendees who alleged a variety of possible nefarious causes for The Yogi's disappearance. These included, but were not limited to, underworld dealings gone wrong, underage sex parlor escapades gone wrong, an autoerotic asphyxiation cover-up, and a *cover-up of his death on 'The Meditator' before its unveiling at the Expo. Suddenly, orders for 'The Meditator' were being replaced again with orders for the 'Frammis Duct' ride.*

Outside the Amusement Park Industry, the new era of open corporate warfare was nastier still.

"Mhmm. Mhmm." Supervisor Hogue seemed interested in Irena's whispered squealings. He seemed to be taking notes on his desktop. Irena saw the minor changes in brightness of his screen in the light reflecting off his brown-yellow anorak with the "Global Waste" logo on the upper left pocket.

Is this why the company insists that all remote communications between employees be video calls? Irena wondered. *So everyone can see everyone else's "Global Waste" logos? To give unengaged supervisors opportunities to seem engaged?*

Then Supervisor Hogue started jamming keys at a frantic pace. When the reflected light changed brightness and became more obviously green, he grimaced, dropped his hands to his lap, and slumped back in his chair. Now a scowling brownish pile in the back of the chair, Supervisor Hogue of Global Waste looked the part.

"You were playing a video game, weren't you?" Irena asked.

Monty's face loosened slightly, but he otherwise remained still.

"You didn't hear what I was saying, did you?" Irena asked, trying to keep her voice down.

Monty sat up and put on his supervisor face. "What janitor squad did you say you're with?"

"It's right there on your comm screen, I'm sure," she whisper-shouted. She was getting frustrated. "Eighteen eight nineteen fooj, foxtrot uniform juliet. This is Irena Żuraw."

"Oh, *Doctor* Żuraw." Monty's face changed from a practiced company supervisor facade to that of a relaxed but disinterested trade bureaucrat stonewalling an ivory tower prick.

"I don't have a Ph.D.," Irena protested. This was Monty's equivalent of calling her "princess" just because she had a few more years at Uni than her Global Waste coworkers, including him.

But he cut her off before she could repeat her account of the situation.

"Follow the chain of command, janitor. Follow your team leader. Hogue *out.*"

Irena's wristcomp screen went blank, but with the lingering stench of the wastewater treatment plant in her nose and the brown-green color that seemed to remain on her wristcomp's screen for a moment after the call ended, Irena had a brief sensation of having gotten something disgusting on her wrist. She felt a sudden urge to shake it off and spit something nasty out of her mouth. Fortunately, the delusion didn't last long.

She was back to square one. And, clearly, her supervisor was also a vital component of Global Waste.

"Yahuh!" said Cosmo, as the van turned onto northbound Riksväg 73, heading for Stockholm. Cosmo had rotated his seat to face the others. He'd long since finished entering the navigation plan into the autopilot.

"Yes!" followed Uncle Bode.

It sounded like the conspirators had arrived at an important decision.

Uncle Bode said, "He's probably drinking bottled water and doing other things to keep the virus out of his system. His behavior will stick out like a bad dog's John Thomas."

"What? Who's John Thomas?" Nycci asked.

"A bad dog's," Uncle Bode repeated, loudly and slowly as if the problem was the loudness of the road.

"What?" asked Nycci.

"His behavior will stick out like a bad dog's John Thomas," he enunciated slowly.

"We already found out his name is Hai Hernandez," Nycci said, exasperated.

Uncle Bode finished a sip of water and shook his head. "We will catch him with his trousers down," Uncle Bode said. "Because of the bottled water."

"John Thomas?" Nycci asked, shaking her head and shrugging.

"Yes, exactly," Uncle Bode said, pointing to the space between them.

Nycci said, "Whatever. Look, we need to get inside and stream video showing the liaison's extreme use of bottled water and probably hand sanitizer, maybe even a mask."

Uncle Bode and Cosmo nodded energetically.

"Everything else will become obvious when we show the water sample, the microscope images, and the analyzer results," Nycci continued. She tapped on her wristcomp. "There," she said. "I just put in a request for janitorial service on behalf of the Swedish space agency."

"Uniform," said Cosmo while tapping his coveralls just below the Global Waste logo on his chest.

"Exactly," said Nycci.

Irena couldn't stop the others, but maybe she could stay out of jail. All she had to do was not go with them. Irena looked back at Keiok. He was asleep. Maybe he'd stay with her in the van? She had to make good use of her time, so she started a search in earnest for the manufacturer of the XDS9 virus.

The clouds were breaking up after the forty-two-minute

ride to Stockholm. There they saw two new seawall construction sites in the downtown area. They'd heard about others not far from their destination. The new walls would be on both sides of the bay end of the Bällstaviken canal. The Swedes were especially keen to save Bromma Aerospaceport. Some years back the sea level rise rate had finally surpassed Scandinavia's post-glacial continental uplift rate, and now Stockholm was joining much of the world in dealing with the encroaching ocean.

"I wonder if that's why Canada is waging this stealth war against Sweden," said Uncle Bode. "Spiteful jealousy after Vancouver."

Fifteen percent of Vancouver had become sea floor over the 21st century. Half a million people were displaced or directly affected, and many others moved out. Infrastructure and transportation were a shambles. The economy still hadn't recovered. It was a case study. Everyone knew about it, at least in Irena's circles.

They're past wondering who's responsible, thought Irena, *and have moved on to imaginary motives*. She didn't want to face the reality that she'd landed in another group that she would never belong to, never belong in. She imagined herself making that impassioned speech about due diligence again. The dream was interrupted before anyone in it nodded in agreement.

Nycci said, "Cosmo, maybe you should program the van with navigation for when we're done. You know, speedy getaway."

"Yahuh," Cosmo said, turning back to the van's navigation touchscreen.

"After exposing the CSA, we can go to Bromma and catch the midday shuttle back to GW Station," she added like they were planning a picnic to follow today's assault.

Cosmo stopped what he was doing with the navigation interface and turned toward Nycci. "We can't leave," he

said, pushing his index finger into his arm like it was a phlebotomy needle.

"We need the cure first, Nycci," said Uncle Bode. "Not all of us wear copper bands and drink our own piss."

"Oh, yeah," said Nycci. "Well, maybe we can squeeze it out of that CSA lackey after we expose him."

"Yes, exactly," Uncle Bode said. "It'll work. It'll be fine," he said, with that same "Just Believe" tone of voice he'd expressed earlier.

Leaning over Cosmo's shoulder from his bench seat, Uncle Bode pointed at the map and started suggesting a route, which ended up at Vikdalen. "Just in case he doesn't have the cure, we can lay low in Vikdalen for a while and work out what to do next."

"And grab some lunch," said Nycci, again with the picnic planning voice. She started typing on her wristcomp. "I'm telling the local newsblogisphere about this."

"Oh, a Jula," Cosmo said, pointing at the marker on the map identifying the venerable home/garden/outfitter chain department store by that name in Vikdalen.

"Good, we can stock up there," said Uncle Bode, looking around the van. "Anyone low on solder? Fiber couplers? Sanitizer? Self-sealing stem bolts?"

Irena avoided eye contact and hunched deeper into her wristcomp, her search for the manufacturer of the XDS9 virus becoming more desperate. And for the hell of it, she also looked up the operating manual for that molecular analyzer they tried to use, plus some other miscellaneous things running through her mind.

Chapter 8

Crudité Theory

After leaving the E20 just past central Stockholm, the van negotiated two roundabouts, then swung north and south and north again on the Storgatan until it reached a 'T' intersection. The Swedish National Space Agency building was a few left turns ahead.

Rounding the final bend, they could hear the sounds of urgent seawall construction toward the southwest, on the other side of a tree-covered hill that partially concealed the district's cooling plant. The heating portions of the plant had been mothballed years ago.

The Rymdstyrelsen building was a bland, concrete-and-glass building like so many others that just kept surviving, decade after decade. Nycci had learned that the CSA office was on the top level, four staircases up.

Cosmo gave the van final site parking commands. The van crossed the sidewalk into the inner lot area and nestled up against the front of the building between two security bollards. In this post-solstice midday sun, they were in the building's shadow.

Irena imagined that back in the day this shadow-prone inner lot area must have had the building's custodians in constant warfare with ice at this time of year.

"Let's wait for those newsbloggers of yours," Uncle Bode said.

"If we use bodycams and set the VCC to record," Nycci said, "then when we come back out, we'll be able to share video with the newsbloggers whenever we want, even if they don't show up."

"Yahuh," said Cosmo.

Irena didn't know anything about bodycams or a "VCC."

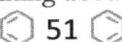

There was no mention of either during her brief training on GW Station, and she was never issued a bodycam.

"Oh, I like that plan," said Uncle Bode.

Nycci stood up and moved toward Irena. She took a knee, looked up at Irena, and said, "Okay, princess, time to spread your legs." She tilted her head, and with her hand made a back-and-forth pointing motion toward Irena's crotch.

"What is wrong with you?" Irena said. She pulled her legs together and her ankles back. She held her arms tightly against her belly. Just how sideways had all this gone?

"Open the pod bay doors, Hal," Nycci said with some menace. That line was commonly used among the Janitor Squads on Global Waste Space Station. They seemed to use it as a generic, standalone complaint about obstacles.

"I'm afraid I can't do that, Dave," Irena said. Just how criminally insane had her heretofore seemingly harmless coworkers become? She turned her knees to the side, putting her flank toward Nycci.

Nycci reached forward quickly, saying, "Thanks." Before Irena could properly flinch, Nycci had popped open a storage door under the bench seat and pulled out a thick, sturdy briefcase. Still kneeling, she closed the storage door and in one motion swung the briefcase away from Irena and up onto her small bench seat behind the passenger seat.

Irena sighed with embarrassment and some relief. Now she remembered that case among other supplies the crew had loaded into the rental van after their shuttle ride from the station.

Nycci opened the briefcase. Now Irena could see the "Video Command Center" label above a video screen set into the upright lid. Nycci started working the controls.

"Alright, bodycams on," she said. The others did something on the chest area of their work coveralls and the VCC screen lit up, showing four video feeds. The quadrants were labeled "Keiok", "Ozols", "Lachance", and "Grubble", the surnames of her squadmates.

"Record mode is on… now. Let's go, everybody!"

Irena realized this was a crucial moment. She imagined herself stopping them, chiding them for the intellectual and moral equivalent of crossing the tracks before checking for a train, and then thanking and praising them back after they thank and praise her for preventing them from crossing a line.

Instead, she panicked and covered her ass.

"I'm not going with you," she said. "This is crazy. You're all crazy." There. She had said it on record. Whatever happens next, maybe she won't go to jail. Maybe she'll be able to keep her job and continue supporting her sister. Maybe the team would forgive and accept her someday, when they got out of jail.

"Whatever," said Nycci. "Oh, wait, I did that wrong. There's no red light." She worked the controls. "Okay, *now* it's recording." Each video quadrant now showed a red dot in the upper left corner.

And they were clomping off the van with their toolbags and slamming the door shut before Irena could say anything that could be clearly picked up on their cams. She had failed to state her objection on the record. *Damn it!*

Irena looked around, blinking. She ended up staring at the far corner bench seat where Keiok had been sitting before he clomped off the van with the others. The sides of her mouth turned downward. Earlier, Keiok had seemed sane and maybe even an ally. But he went with them.

If only to save her job, she had to prove that they were chasing illusions. She had to figure out who bought and deployed these viruses, and why. So she pulled up her wristcomp and returned to her research.

When the janitor squad started interacting with the building's occupants, Irena realized the VCC was presenting both video and audio. She tried to ignore it, but it was too distracting. A brief visit to the VCC showed that she was locked out of the controls, and even the lid had some kind of lock keeping it open. She couldn't even mute the thing.

Irena returned to her bench and started launching automated queries. She wanted multiple lines of investigation running in parallel. Some would skip trying to find the manufacturer of the virus and would go straight to trying to find buyers in the Stockholm area.

Meanwhile, the team stepped off the lifts on the fourth storey, gathered themselves, and pressed the intercom button at the plexiglass security door that was the entrance to the top-floor offices. The security reception desk and agent were just inside.

"Hej," Nycci said. "Someone called for a Janitor Squad."

"Yes," came the reply, in English to match Nycci. "Your job order number, please?"

"Echo Oscar Four One Romeo," Nycci replied, reading off her wristcomp. Irena couldn't help but watch the four video feeds, piecing together who was seeing whom in the overlapping views.

The security locks on the door clicked. Squad Fuj entered. Irena's throat tightened. Whatever happened next, she would be considered an accessory.

When Nycci walked forward her camera feed became filled by the security reception desk's tall front wall. But Keiok's camera feed showed Cosmo and Uncle Bode standing behind Nycci at the desk, cubicles and glass-walled offices beyond. Obviously, Keiok was standing behind the others.

"The CSA office was the focus of the call," Nycci said. "Where's that?"

Damn, she's a good liar, Irena thought.

The security agent explained some of the rules of the facility and gave Nycci directions to the CSA office. Uncle Bode turned toward Cosmo's camera and Irena heard him say quietly, "How 'bout that Annika Borg, eh?"

Cosmo turned and said, "Sexyyy."

Keiok's feed showed Uncle Bode and Cosmo smirk as Uncle Bode said, "Ya*huh*," Cosmo style. Then they turned to follow Nycci already striding off toward the CSA office.

Irena thought she heard Keiok whisper something. It sounded like, "I said *dig*," for all the sense that made.

But now Irena's automated queries were showing some hits. She cross-fed the relevant hits to update the queries and leaned into her manual control over the search.

Apparently, the virus was not sold directly by the manufacturer, but by subsidiary medical sales companies. Those companies liked to boast about their various sales, so Irena built several new queries to search for those kinds of mentions. They were usually carefully worded to sound boastful while also sounding nonchalant.

And they invariably used generic, fancier-sounding terminology instead of specific chemical or product names. For example, BuckyPharmaTecLab boasted about global sales of "novel siRNA lipid complex for gene therapy" instead of just saying the brand name "Patirisan." So Irena widened her search to find generic descriptions of this XDS9 kind of manufactured virus.

Then she double-checked her mailbox. Still nada from Kekoa.

The live feeds on the VCC remained a distraction. Given directions, the team made a beeline for the CSA office, which was only two sections away down the main corridor. The VCC showed the corridor on the Grubble feed, Nycci's back on the Ozols and Lachance feeds, and the Keiok feed showed Nycci, Uncle Bode, and Cosmo walking in spearhead formation down the corridor. Employees who crossed paths with the squad said, "Good dog." Irena knew they were saying "good day" in Swedish. She didn't hear her squadmates say anything in reply.

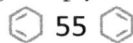

Irena's queries were making more progress just as the team entered the lone CSA office, which consisted of one large, glass-walled office with one desk. No one was present, but there were water bottles on the desk.

"I knew it!" Nycci said.

"Wow," said Uncle Bode.

"Everyone get good video," Nycci said.

"Oh, right," said Uncle Bode.

The three video feeds circled the desk, getting multiple angles on the several empty and full water bottles on the desk. Keiok stayed in the far corner, capturing the whole scene.

Then a new voice appeared on everyone's audio feeds.

"Excuse me, what exactly are you doing here? Ms. Hernandez is in a meeting." Someone else had entered the office, and it wasn't the CSA liaison. The video feeds turned toward the door to show someone wearing a business suit standing in the office doorway. He was most likely a manager, since most of the workers in the facility wore business casual.

"Let me show you," said Nycci. She moved forward, and the Rymdstyrelsen manager maintained distance, backing into the cubicle bullpen outside of the CSA office. Through Nycci's video feed, Irena saw Cosmo and Uncle Bode swing around and line up on the other side of the manager. Behind them, other space agency workers stood up and some slowly shuffled out of their cubicles to listen to the unusual conversation taking place. Keiok remained behind Nycci, seeing it all.

Nycci spoke quickly, showing her Syllojizm web page list to the manager. She went through the same spurious argument presented to Irena earlier, only this time she pointed backward at all the water bottles on the CSA liaison's desk.

"It's a crudité," Nycci concluded.

"Excuse me?"

"You know, a hostile takeover."

"…A coup d'état?"

"That's what I said. Well, okay, not a takeover, a, you know, an attack. To kill Swedes. Because of Vancouver." Cosmo's arms went akimbo. Uncle Bode nodded gravely.

Somehow the manager was still in professional mode. "A secret CSA crudité to kill Swedes with medical grade manufactured viruses carrying Thallium, because of Vancouver."

"Exactly. And the CSA rep's excessive use of bottled water is proof. He, she knows it's in the water. The whole conspiracy is clear as day!"

The manager's jaw clenched. "The potable water is down in the entire building," he explained. "We're *all* drinking bottled water." He waved his arm across the bullpen.

Nycci's body cam moved a step forward. Its view now showed that there were similar water bottles on most of the nearby desks. She turned toward a nearby recycling bin. It was almost full of the same water bottles.

Irena snickered, covering her mouth despite being alone in the van.

"It's the seawall construction," continued the manager. "And why exactly are you here?" His arms moved into a low akimbo as Cosmo's dropped. "Surely not because of your," he paused, "crudité theory."

Irena's wristcomp chimed and she lost interest in the squad's antics on the VCC. Her queries had found an XDS9 purchase in Sweden, and her heart jumped! She opened the related links, but the contract documents consisted mostly of unintelligible business and legal language.

If it's not one thing, it's two or more, she thought, as she canceled her running queries and began setting up new ones.

"We had a work order!" Nycci said as a security guard approached the manager.

"Ring polisen," said the manager, followed by faster Swedish words. Nycci started running down the corridor, backtracking, and Cosmo and Uncle Bode followed her. Keiok's unmoving video feed showed Cosmo shoulder-checking the security guard as they took off. The guard collected himself, then, with anger in his voice, he spoke Swedish into his shoulder microphone.

Nycci's camera feed showed her rapidly approaching the front desk, but guards could be seen approaching from the lifts on the other side of the transparent wall. Keiok's feed was now full of pinkish smoke. Nycci's feed turned around, revealing that the area they had just fled, down the corridor near the manager, was filled with that pinkish smoke. Coughing people were stumbling out of the smoke in every direction, and the guards and the manager were not visible. Maybe they were in the smoke trying to grab Keiok.

Then Keiok stepped out of the smoke, beckoning and pointing. The other three feeds fell in behind Keiok, who led them into new territory farther down that main corridor, beyond the pink smoke.

Irena's attention suddenly popped out of both her wristcomp and the VCC. Her eyes widened as she looked out the front and rear windows of the van. They would be coming for *her* soon, wouldn't they?

One last glance at the VCC revealed a simple display on the horizontal panel that was estimating the position of the others relative to the VCC case. There was one small, bright, red dot for each of them. They were moving away from the van and, Irena realized, toward the north end of the building.

Irena took the driver's seat and activated manual control, which wasn't truly manual. The heads-up display popped up, showing the inner lot ahead of the van overlain with drivable pathways and a little arrow marker. Irena pointed to move the arrow marker along the drivable path toward the far end of the building. When she pressed the 'go' button, the van started driving along the path she had specified.

It stopped almost immediately. A car farther along the inner lot was backing out of a parking spot, and the two vehicles had negotiated that the van should be the one to wait.

Irena huffed and scanned the van's camera displays showing views to the side and behind the van. No one was approaching yet, but her heart was racing. She could feel her skin grow hot.

But as quickly as the delay began, the other car was out of the way and exiting the lot at the far end. The van resumed its forward motion.

She drove it this way along the inner lot to the end of the building, turned the van left, toward the street, but then switched to reverse mode. The heads-up display opened a large overlay with a rear-facing view and showed the one selectable pathway behind the van. Irena told the van to back up to near a pair of exit doors she could see on the north side of the building.

Then she activated the van's flashers and returned to her seat, watching the VCC camera feeds as well as the position dots. The dots were now larger, indicating the others were closer to ground level. They were close now, nearing the center of the relative position display. Their video feeds showed them scurrying down an emergency exit stairwell. Now Keiok was behind the others again. His feed showed Cosmo's bag knock into Uncle Bode, nearly buckling his knee more than once.

They burst out of the building on the north end, although not through the double doors Irena had seen. It looked like maybe they were somewhere farther east, around the corner.

 59

Keiok quickly realized where they were and led them around the corner. Irena slid open the van's side door, leaned out, and waved. Over the top of the van, to her right, she noticed security guards exiting the building back at the security bollards, so she ducked down as Janitor Squad Fuj approached.

Chapter 9

Chicken Bones

*I*t had taken decades for self-driven ground vehicles to become reliable, efficient, and convenient enough to satisfy the general public. By mid-century they were still fairly rare.

But industry wanted them. Movement of cargo demanded reliable, efficient driving. And not only that, the holy grail of logistics had always been fleet-wide operational optimization beyond mere radio-dispatched scheduling and routing. Computerization begged for it.

Yet industry also relied on human drivers, who became less reliable in proportion to company reductions in wages and safety nets. Drivers became even less reliable after the mid-century Great Ostriching normalized a lackadaisical approach to life in general.

Collectively, industry said, "We're gonna have to take steps." So it found a way to make The Great Ostriching work in its favor. But it took a globally coordinated palm-greasing program to make it happen. Fortunately, industry had a lot of experience with palm greasing.

An apathetic public, either wearing rose-colored spectacles or descending fully into nihilistic surrender, allowed industry to get radical new pro-business laws passed. In 2062 and 2063, laws with names like "Protect the Public's Right to Efficient Business" were passed in legislatures across the industrialized world.

Among other things, they granted commercial self-driven vehicle owners immunity to moving violations, such as colliding with motorized vehicles, human-powered vehicles, or pedestrians. Commercial self-driven vehicles could commit a "hit and run" with immunity.

The rationale put forth in the law was that commercial self-driven vehicle systems were very reliable and were designed from the bottom up to prevent moving violations. Therefore, any moving violations involving a commercial self-driven vehicle would have to be caused by a rare operational parameter exceedance that was not attributable to insufficient maintenance, or by human (or other self-driven vehicle) decision making, such as placing oneself in front of a commercial self-driven vehicle at close range, within its response horizon.

It was legal mumbo jumbo for "if we hit you, it was your fault."

And the resulting flood of money into the commercial self-driven vehicle industry filled the streets with self-driving grey vans.

They did occasionally kill people, thousands across the world every year, because system reliability is a statistical thing, and no plan survives contact with reality. But now, with legal immunity, industry could relegate that public safety problem to their R&D departments while enjoying the benefits of real-time, fleet-wide, computerized operational optimization and reduced staffing and legal budgets.

Once the streets were filled with commercial self-driven vehicles, the general public gave up all pretenses of resistance and adopted self-driven vehicles for personal uses, without moving violations immunity. In fact, in the fine print, those commercial immunity laws specifically denied immunity to personally owned self-driven vehicles. Industry could not have personally owned self-driven vehicles colliding with commercial vehicles, interrupting the movement of cargo, and then getting away with it. Industry could recoup financial losses from such accidents from the general public, but not vice versa.

Police retained the right and ability to remotely shut

down or control self-driving vehicles. Enforcers loved remoting. It gave them a sense of control over the whole self-driven vehicle situation.

But the R&D departments of the cargo-moving industries had to balance their work on improving public safety against a parallel and very secret demand of their executives. They were to find ways to use their legally immune commercial self-driven vehicles to intentionally execute moving violations in order to disrupt the operations of their cargo-moving competitors. As long as the repair costs were outweighed by the market gains, it was a winning strategy.

Early deployments of such systems were flawed. There was the occasional incident. They usually occurred at night and in bad weather intentionally, to add plausible deniability under the "rare operational parameter exceedance" clause. These incidents involved grey vans marked FedX, IPS, and/or Scythian attempting to execute Tactical Fishtailing maneuvers on each other.

One would make the attempt, the other would thwart the attempt through preemptive, hard braking and avoidance steering. Then, finding itself near the rear end of the initial attacker, the initial defender would attempt Tactical Fishtailing in retaliation. The initial attacker would thwart that attempt through preemptive acceleration and avoidance steering. Eventually, both vehicles would end up at limiter speed again, but through steering optimizations and random environmental and traffic factors, they could end up in a position to repeat the exchange farther down the road, which they did. All night long. All night.

Once these incidents showed up in the newsblogisphere, the embarrassing controversy and mutual allegations became costly. So the automated retaliation response was quickly removed to prevent these road rage perpetual loops.

R&D was back on the hook to develop a viable strategy, both for offense and defense.

Soon enough they settled on a way to disrupt the operations of their cargo-moving competitors that didn't involve direct confrontation: they would disrupt non-commercial traffic in and around zones of operation dominated by their competitors, and with complete immunity. The key to this strategy was to secretly use unblockable police remoting technology. Their vehicle passing through a target area would cause non-commercial vehicles to collide with other non-commercial vehicles or with competitors' commercial vehicles, causing at least slowdowns. Two hours of slowdowns a day, every day, in multiple zones of operation, added up to a non-negligible loss in a competitor's profit margin, and some loss of their market share.

Of course, everyone was doing on average the same amount of damage to everyone else's profit margins and traffic was backing up everywhere. It took a few decades for industry to agree to end such practices in the name of collective optimization. After all, ever since the invention of the syndicate, businesses have understood collectivism.

But over the course of those decades, the general public lost thousands of lives and millions in liability losses. Words like "everything happens for a reason, it'll be okay, just believe" were often spoken by surviving family members.

By the end of the century, though, personal financial capacity was so decimated by radical pro-business laws and practices that the market for personal self-driven vehicles collapsed, leaving the roads mostly to commercial vehicles. This had the secondary effect of guaranteeing the survival and expansion of mass transit systems.

Their unmarked rental van drove them out of the area following the pre-programmed route Cosmo had entered earlier. No one seemed to be chasing them or attempting to override the van's control system.

They sat quietly as the Rymdstyrelsen building, the wooded hill, and the Norrenergi cooling plant receded behind them.

They shifted in their seats on the Huvudsta Bridge. Moments later they were crossing the centerline of the main runway at Bromma Aerospaceport, which was across the canal bay off to the right. Cosmo leaned forward, looked, and pointed upward. "Midday space shuttle," he said. They heard it pass right over them on final approach.

Nycci didn't look but got into her wristcomp.

"Okay, well," said Uncle Bode, trying to get the ball rolling again. "Maybe it wasn't the CSA after all. But it could still be the Canadians. It does make sense."

"No, it doesn't. It's not a Canadian plot," Irena said firmly, trying to cash in on her rescue of the squad. "The idea that the Canadians would spend their money on an elaborate mass murder scheme, and an expensive one at that, out of jealousy that the Swedes haven't had to worry much about sea level rise is… it's just absurd." Irena cringed about her voice squeaking at the end of her outburst.

"Yahuh," said Cosmo. Irena was surprised, but she persisted as the van negotiated the roundabout at the 279-275 intersection.

"And the fact is, we don't even know the danger posed by those viruses. We don't know anything about them," Irena said, but quickly realized it was a mistake. Everyone hates uncertainty and will do anything to end it, and she had just dumped them right back into it.

"You're right," said Nycci, looking intently at her wristcomp. Everyone looked at her. Cosmo and Uncle

Bode's eyebrows were up. Irena's were down.

"The Canadians were too obvious. That was a red herring."

Irena's head tilted forward, and she stared aghast at Nycci.

"It's the Buddhist monks," said Nycci.

Irena closed her mouth and eyes. She inhaled, trying to will herself out of the conversation, out of the van, and back to Luna. She accessed her wristcomp, but her finger froze in place, stopped by a morbid fascination with Nycci's new accusations.

"Here," Nycci tap-swiped her wristcomp toward the VCC. The lefthand side of its display showed a map of the central part of the Värmdö Kommun, a municipality east of Stockholm, with a marker labeled "Buddharamatemplet." The righthand side showed the Syllojizm website again, with another list of "Isn't it interesting?" murky coincidence-mongerings.

Nycci started reading. "Isn't it interesting that there have been over sixty civil suits against Buddhist temples alleging that they framed various defendants?"

Irena thought, *how does that compare to similar civil suits* not *against Buddhist temples? And how many were found to be frivolous?*

"Isn't it interesting that there have been over seventy civil suits filed *by* Buddhist temples against municipalities in Canada, and several right here in Värmdö?"

Similar questions about context ran through Irena's mind. *Plus, she's actually implying, using Syllojizm's selective statistics, that the local Buddhist temple has implicated Canada!*

"Isn't it interesting that throughout history Buddhist monks' protests have often taken the form of suicide?"

Wait, thought Irena. And then aloud, "Are you implying that the Buddhist temple here in Värmdö poisoned their own water supply in a suicidal protest of some kind? And are you using their history of non-violent protest as *supporting evidence*, because their temple is downstream? All while suggesting that they *also* poisoned the greater Stockholm area to accomplish this suicide? It's spurious, contradictory madness!"

"Big words don't prove anything," Nycci replied with a sneer. "This is convincing enough for us, right guys?" She looked at Cosmo and Uncle Bode, nodding in affirmation. They didn't give her much in return, so she pressed on.

"Everybody knows the Buddhists are hypocrites, liars, and con artists. They say they have no self, but they claim they reincarnate. If there's no self, what's being reincarnated? They say they reject the material world, but they have big temples and gold statues. They say to have a healthy mind you have a healthy body, but have you seen that Buddha? He's fat and bald! How could anyone worship that guy? He's obviously a false idol. The whole thing is a sham cult! And," she raised a finger, "the Mormons *proved* it fifty years ago."

"Whuh?" said Irena. "Huhwhuh?"

"That's right. It's been a meme on Syllojizm since I was a kid, so…"

"You've got it all wrong," Irena said, squeaking again. She drew upon both her education and her friendships with several Buddhists on Luna.

"First of all, only certain cultures believe in souls and reincarnation. That's a cultural thing, not strictly a Buddhist thing. Same with the temples and statues, some of which were created by misguided people trying to prove their piety or wow the masses. Buddhism is not about worshipping Buddha, either. You've just got it all wrong," she said, trying to stay calm.

"He's clearly a fat, bald cult leader," Nycci said, not giving a centimeter of ground.

"Oh, and about that," Irena said, "the fat, bald statue isn't the Buddha, it's a depiction from over a millennium after

Gautama. It reflects Chinese cultural norms of that era. They associated an ample body with wealth, good luck, and noble behavior. It's typically Western of you to jump to a literal interpretation."

"Go ahead, throw more big words at me, I'm not listening," Nycci said. "The evidence points right at the Buddhists."

"The *evidence!*" Irena said, barely able to shake her head while sending a pleading look at Cosmo and Uncle Bode.

"Oh, but there's more," Nycci said. "Lots more." She tap-swiped again.

The display updated with new entries.

"Isn't it interesting that the Thai Buddharam organization built five temples spread around Sweden, in an 'L' formation? See here, from Boden to Fredrika, Ragunda, Karlstad, and then over to Värmdö, see, forming an 'L'? The Thai alphabet has not one, not two, but three kinds of 'L' letters. Five times three is fifteen, and 'Stockholm virus' contains fifteen letters. It's just too coincidental!"

Again Irena was gobsmacked. The wind was out of her sails.

"How could anyone believe such a chain of so-called connections?" she managed to utter, more to herself and to the universe than to Nycci or the others. *I never should've left Luna*, she thought. *I should have taken that vac suit checker job at the museum.* She'd lost whatever speck of hope she might've had of actually influencing Nycci with her protestations.

"Hey, I've presented at least nine pieces of evidence and you've only been able to come up with one weak objection. Nine beats one," Nycci stated flatly, shooting daggers from her eyes. "And I'm not done yet," she continued, pointing at the screen.

Irena whimpered. She was folding inward. As the van approached Vikdalen, tears welled in her eyes, preventing

her from distracting herself with the research queries running on her wristcomp. She would go to jail, lose this job, and eventually end up repeating, "Es tut mir leid, Ihr Kind ist zu klein für diese Fahrt" before pressing the big, green "go" button on the amusement park ride's three-button control panel for the forty millionth time, and then someone would complain that "Fahrt" isn't the right word for an amusement park ride, and then she would argue that "Vergnügungsparkfahrt" is unnecessarily lengthy in this context, and then they would complain to her manager and get her fired from that job, too. More tears.

"Isn't it interesting," Nycci continued reading, "that approximately seven percent of all researchers who use artificial viruses are Buddhists?"

Irena didn't have the strength to ask if seven percent of *all* of humanity is Buddhist, which sounded about right, in which case that last Syllojizm bullet wasn't interesting at all.

"Isn't it interesting," Nycci read from another Syllojizm bullet, "that most people *assume* Buddhist monks are innocent pacifists?"

There was a distinct growl in Irena's rising stomach as she understood that Nycci was using the pacifism of Buddhist monks as an argument for their guilt in mass murder!

"*And* isn't it *interesting*," Nycci was emphasizing her final point in this new list of conflated coincidences, "that Thallium rat poison was common in Thailand long after it was banned in other countries? It makes perfect sense that the Thai Buddhists in Sweden would know more about Thallium poisoning and be more comfortable with it than both Swedes and Canadians."

Irena pinched her nose bridge, as if doing that was helpful.

"So that's means, motive, and opportunity, as 'Joe Sixpack: Biker Lawyer' used to say. And Joe always said, '*That means guilty*'," Nycci bellowed. She slammed shut the VCC case and tossed it on the floor in front of her, a 'mic drop' gesture. She leaned back, hands behind her head, crossing her legs and propping them up on the reinforced case.

Irena felt sick. The smug smile on Nycci's face punctuated the stark reality that Nycci had identified neither means, motive, nor opportunity in her case against the Buddhist monks of Sweden. And yet here they were, driving right past Vikdalen toward Värmdö and the nearest Buddharam monastery. The van drove past the 'Jula' store sign, following its programmed route.

"Twelve to one, princess. I win. It's obviously the Buddhists. I don't know how we missed it before. Maybe we were swayed by Uncle Bode's lifelong pain over the Canadarm2 cover-up, so we took the red herring bait that the Buddhists arranged for us to find." Nycci pursed her lips and tilted her head in an expression of sympathy aimed at Uncle Bode.

Uncle Bode nodded acknowledgment and looked intently at the floor of the van. Cosmo knee-jerked a quiet "Yahuh."

Nycci pointed at her wristcomp. "Oh, and this sequence now has over fourteen thousand likes, so." She clapped her hands like a stage magician signaling that the beautiful assistant, having been severed at the belly, remains alive despite her body being in two separate boxes.

Irena remained dumbfounded. Even after being so wrong about the Canadians, how could the others believe this insane chain of wispy implications just because there were more of them on the list?

One thing was obvious, though. The Syllojizm site was a brilliant clickbait machine. Whatever search criteria you entered, it would collect spuriously related statistics and present them as unlikely coincidences which the reader could feel smart about stringing together and adopting as dogma with the smug conviction of the insider-outsider. If the reader decided they were wrong about the first interpretation, they could abandon it in favor of the next interpretation without abandoning the general approach—rinse and repeat, doublethink notwithstanding, with Syllojizm getting all the clicks and ad revenue.

But a welcome relief refilled her tight blood vessels as her queries began to register progress. They were penetrating the obscure business and legal language of the XDS9 purchase that she'd uncovered earlier. It became clear that a government agency recently purchased the manufactured viruses here in Sweden. The purchase contract was written and structured in a way that was only used by government agencies. But she still couldn't tell whether it was a national, provincial, or local agency, let alone which agency. She ended most of the scripts and started new ones looking for agency-specific commonalities that would answer those questions.

Chapter 10

Offal Shame

*O*ne interesting benefit of The Great Ostriching was that it led most of the planet to finally understand that the entire world had been conned, for over a century, by the guns and ammo industry.

The rose-colored spectacles narrative of The Great Ostriching promulgated the realization that the guns and ammo industry had been employing a pyramid scheme known as human nature profiteering, a form of social engineering.

Human nature profiteering takes advantage of three hard-wired aspects of human nature, all of which are intimately tied to feeling safe and secure.

One is the innate need to understand threats in your environment, something we've carried with us since our genes in rodent-like forms were scurrying under the feet of dinosaurs.

Another is our innate need to identify with a group, to belong to a community.

The third is our flocking response. We belong to groups not only to take advantage of group strength but also to take advantage of group alarm signaling. If someone in the group "alarms," like when a titi monkey squeaks to identify a predator and its location, then everyone in the group tends to believe that there's a threat. Those who don't believe tend to die, and their genes are less likely to be passed on. Wilderness survival doesn't select strongly for skepticism. Those who do believe the squeaked warnings of their fellows tend to survive. Social primates like humans are hard-wired to believe in a threat if others in their group believe in a threat.

Human nature profiteering reaches into your brain by first telling you that you're not safe, and then telling you that members of a group that is not your group, not your community, are the ones making you and your loved ones unsafe. Most importantly, it tells you that your group says these things, engaging your hard-wired belief in group-alarmed threat identification.

It's easy to tell human individuals that their group alleges something. You just say it, repeatedly. Show pictures of people in their group alarm signaling. Say it's widespread. They'll believe you. All it requires is a "mark" group, a "patsy" group, and repeated "alarm signaling" allegations.

Then the pyramid scheme part kicks in. You offer a product that will solve their security problem. In this case, it's guns and ammo. The "mark" group voluntarily shares your propaganda streams, because nothing says "I must be right" better than convincing other people. And that leads to more members, which leads to more profits, and up goes the pyramid.

To really rake in the profits, you do the same thing with those two groups but swap the "mark" and "patsy" roles. Then both sides happily arm themselves and go to war with each other.

Pyramid schemes are nothing new, but human nature profiteering can only be interrupted by the self-aware individual. The self-aware are off buying self-awareness products, while everyone else is buying human nature profiteering products. So if you have business in both markets, you're golden.

Historically, this technique was often used strategically by greater powers to divide and conquer lesser powers. In Hungarian, the term Szalámitaktika (salami slicing tactics) was coined to describe this method of using a series of smaller dividing actions to produce a much larger result.

It has been used not only in the military realm but also in business and political realms for centuries.

The Great Ostriching narrative popped this human nature profiteering bubble by short-circuiting the sense of threat. If you've arrived at a state of mind where you believe all is well, or that it's pointless to fight, you're just not susceptible to this con. And the bubble only had to pop once.

But there were isolated pockets of holdouts. Throwbacks. Regressives. In Sweden, it's the Swedish Nazis, who used to call themselves Spencerites, but national pride and language differences made it easier to just say 'Swedish Nazis.'

By nyårsfirandet 2099, they were still a small group of insecure misfits in Stockholm who use the propaganda and the uniforms to feel like they belong to a community. It works for them because they continually fail to identify plausible enemies, and in so doing short-circuit the short-circuiting of The Great Ostriching. It's just a tiny, stagnant hate cult.

The Swedish Nazis have been staging secret (out-of-uniform) bake sales to pay their modest operational costs — maintenance of their uniforms and bullhorns plus public assembly license fees required for their occasional marches with bullhorn speeches about how non-whites and non-European cultures were destroying the world.

"What are we gonna do when we get there?" Uncle Bode asked. Despite his being older than Nycci, he had clearly handed her control during this vigilante escapade.

"Yahuh," Cosmo said with an unusual emphasis on the second syllable.

Keiok was mumbling into his wristcomp in the back corner of the van, as usual.

Their van and the other eastbound vehicles on 222 rolled along at a leisurely pace, around eighty kph, limited not by the road or the driving conditions but by the capabilities of the self-driving vehicles and related insurance policies.

The only reason Irena noticed was because it was about the same speed as the lunar monorail she'd ridden so many times before she took this job at Global Waste. She and Kekoa commuted on that thing, and she dubbed it "The Kekoamobile."

This was her first time on Earth in a decade. Before being deployed with Janitor Squad Fuj, she'd had to complete an extensive strength training regimen. The drugs and genetic therapies in common use on Luna were not quite effective enough to keep a person who was living on Luna as strong as a person living on Earth. She was a vital component of Global Waste, and the company wanted her to be properly firm, not mucose.

Nycci said, "Yeah, what *are* we gonna do?" She trailed off, making it clear that she was still pondering exactly that.

Another company motivational email arrived. As usual, Irena couldn't tell if *Morale Division* did it intentionally or if the translation and word-wrapping were happenstance, but the end result was disastrous. Yet it had a kind of poetry to it.

"Illustrious Global Waste Cases:

Stream of Wastewater
      teams sent from Global Waste of space,
      money finders, not just techs

Pile of human trash

<u>recycling specialists to strengthen automation</u>
<u>inside industrial reclamations</u>

<u>Global Waste assists offal industry</u>
<u>employees dispatched to 'soylent'-like program</u>

Remember, you are a vital component of Global Waste!"

Irena shook her head. As always, the end of the 'motivational' email included safety, savings, and healthcare "Tips" which were mostly useless and were included so the company could claim they cared about their employees. Safety tips were things like "buy steel-toed shoes" and "learn about electrical grounding". Savings tips involved various ways to convert your cash into easily hidable stuff, and various places to hide stuff. But everyone knew that following such advice would just make it easier for thieves to run off with your savings. Healthcare tips were things like "Eat right and get exercise," and "If you follow our savings advice, you'll have cash for the ER when something goes wrong."

This time she deleted the message unread. It was unlike her, but she was riding with her team toward a Buddhist temple, where her team was planning some kind of confrontation. She feared it would be worse than what happened at the Rymdstyrelsen building because now they've dug in their heels. The idea terrified her. What were these people capable of doing?

What was she capable of doing to stop them? Anything? Or was she a waste of space? A pile of human trash? A stream of wastewater. Would she just watch? Would she hide in the van again? Was it really so important to her to avoid social exile?

Yes. It was. She just might pull this off. Some of her

earlier comments seemed to reach Cosmo and Uncle Bode to some extent. Maybe she could turn it all around and come out on top, not by convincing Nycci, but by convincing the others.

Still looking down, she could hear the "email deleted" sounds on some of her teammates' wristcomps. At the very least, she knew that they, too, were a vital component of Global Waste.

Upon deleting the message on her own wristcomp, the screen background returned to its normal picture of her sister. Bronya could use her help. But the future victims of these vigilantes might actually *need* it.

"Well," said Nycci, "we need to find something that shows they were involved in deploying the viruses. And we need to find an antiviral. They must have an antiviral, right?"

"To keep them alive," Uncle Bode said, "long enough to dump all the viruses into the river."

"Y'huh," said Cosmo, quarterheartedly.

Irena looked at Keiok. He was already looking at her. She didn't know what was going on behind his creepy, staring eyes. She shivered and looked away. Would he be the one to draw blood first in this madness? She could believe that.

The van turned off Torsbyvägen at a large, brushy, stone hump, as expected. The cul de sac was wooded on the righthand side, the south side, and with the low midday sun and broken clouds above, the trees cast long shadows across their path. Just beyond the brush, the area opened up on the left-hand side to a residence and its empty carport. Past a short, vine-covered, wire grid fence, the very next lot contained the several structures making up the Värmdö Buddharam Temple.

There was only one vehicle in the parking lot. Surely it belonged to the staff. Irena shivered again. Would there be no onlookers to mitigate her cohorts' behavior?

She imagined herself stopping them before they did anything that couldn't be undone, threatening to call the police if they pressed, and otherwise being commanding and persuasive.

Without hesitation, their van executed a 'K' turn and parked in the visitor lot with its front facing back the way they came.

The three vigilantes in the front of the van whispered and pointed at the van's user interface. Irena assumed they were programming it with the final touches of their exfiltration plan.

The team slung their toolbags and went striding up the brick path. Irena had no choice but to join them. For some reason, she also had her toolbag. In the back of her mind, she felt it could be useful for an intervention, whatever that might look like.

They strode toward the golden, Thai-style statue of Buddha that waited patiently between them and the main temple building.

"Welcome," said one of the attendants ahead of them, the male one. The two attendants were standing at the base of the short wooden staircase that led to the modest, red-roofed and yellow-walled, split-level, wooden temple building. "We will attend to you today. My name is Tongkanlong Chanpakdee, but you can call me 'Tongkanlong'."

He smiled and waited for a chuckle. Nycci and her vigilantes didn't chuckle.

"And I am Ms. Chuo," said the female attendant beside Tongkanlong. "Would you like something to eat?" The attendants turned, stepped slightly aside, and gestured gracefully at the staircase, beckoning the visiting vigilantes to approach their temple.

Irena winced as quietly as she could.

"Okay," said Nycci, trying not to be overtly gruff, but also not trying to be pleasant. "We wanna talk to the chief monk."

"Yes, okay," said Tongkanlong, smiling.

"Okay, yes," said Ms. Chuo at the same time, also smiling.

Irena wondered if they had practiced that symmetry just for giggles.

Once inside the temple's vestibule, entering from the south door, all the visitors instinctively raised their noses as they caught the scent of incense. Their noses descended just as quickly.

"Please wait here," said the attendants in unison, gesturing toward a bench seat along the wall near the north door. Ms. Chuo exited out the north door, causing a small bell hanging on the door to jingle. Tongkanlong stayed in the corner of the room near the south door, standing with his hands folded across his navel.

Cosmo and Uncle Bode sat. Nycci paced, scanning the vestibule, eyeing the door to the temple proper centered on the west wall of the vestibule. The door was closed, but there was no hint of a lock. There was no knob or latch, either. The walls on either side of the door were painted a saffron-orange color along the horizontal center, with the top and bottom having a green strip over a red background, and with intricate patterns and temple spire depictions in gold over both.

As usual, Keiok was recording a log on his wristcomp. "...additional. The search party has arrived to find a peaceful, welcoming culture..."

Irena could bear her own silence no more. "Nycci, Uncle Bode, Cosmo," she whispered urgently, "you're going to find out that these people had nothing to do with the viruses. Please, I beg you, recognize that moment when it comes," she urged.

For just a moment, she saw a blankness on the faces of Cosmo and Uncle Bode, a noncommittal consideration, it seemed to her. It vaporized when Nycci spoke.

"We already had this conversation, princess. Twelve to one, remember? The evidence is overwhelming. Why are you so myoptic?"

The evidence! thought Irena, again gobsmacked. *And it's 'myopic,'* she thought but did not say. *What does it mean that Nycci is trying to use words she doesn't know? Is it adrenaline?*

"We're here to gather the physical proof, that's all," Nycci said.

Was that the slightest hint of ambivalence? Irena wondered.

Nycci inhaled. "No matter what," she added menacingly, with no hesitation in her voice.

The north doorbell jingled as Ms. Chuo pushed the door in and around, holding it open as four Thai-looking monks in traditional, flame-colored robes of different hues entered the vestibule and lined up side by side. Ms. Chuo closed the door with a jingle and introduced them.

"Honored guests, this is Phra Buangam Wongsawat," she said, first gesturing to the man on the left.

"Call me 'Willy'," he said with a deep smile and a bow.

"And this is Phra Nithoon Willapana."

"Call me 'Wong'," he said, also with a smile and a bow.

"This is Phra Dok-Rak Rardchawat."

"Call me 'Lucy'," she said in turn.

"And this is Phra Baenglum Pornpipatpong."

"Call me 'Shirley'," the fourth monk said with the same genuine smile and bow.

While the frowning vigilantes gathered themselves, Phra Lucy spoke again.

"Whatever is troubling you, we hope you will let us help.

 80

Would you like to meditate?"

"Or a Buddhist massage?" added Phra Wong, making a poking, twisting gesture in the air with his right thumb resting atop the other fingers clenched underneath it. "I've been practicing!"

"No, no," said Nycci. "We wanted the leader."

Irena winced again and turned away, ashamed and embarrassed at Nycci's astonishing rudeness. She found herself facing Keiok and Tongkanlong in the south corner of the vestibule.

Keiok was no longer talking into his wristcomp, but he spoke to his invisible crew.

"Set weapons to stun," he said and stopped talking. He was standing in a dramatic ready pose.

Tongkanlong was trying to look calm and pleasant, but his eyes were wider than they were before, now moving back and forth between Keiok and the monks. Irena turned again toward the others.

"Phra Shinawatra is indisposed," said Phra Willy.

"How can we help you?" asked Phra Lucy.

"Would you like something to eat?" asked Ms. Chuo.

"Okay, wait," said Nycci, losing her patience. "We need a minute." She pulled Uncle Bode and Cosmo along the vestibule wall to a central position by the door to the temple.

Irena only heard a few words of their exchange. The gist of it was they would insist, banking on the monks' accommodating comportment.

"We want to see Phra Sinatra," Nycci said, striding commandingly toward the four monks. She stood with arms akimbo.

Tongkanlong moved forward to join Ms. Chuo. Nycci's demeanor was forceful, just this side of threatening. The attendant must have felt it was time to fall in.

The monks, still smiling gently, blinked at each other, then bowed and turned to go. Ms. Chuo opened the door and the five of them left. Tongkanlong again was alone with the visitors.

The poor kid thought Irena. She sauntered over to him and turned to face the others. He gracefully sidestepped away from her, and Irena felt heartbroken. By association, she was now part of a gang that was menacing the monks and attendants of a peaceful, welcoming temple.

"Well, I hope you're proud of yourselves," she said to Uncle Bode and Cosmo, completely ignoring Nycci, who was still standing with arms akimbo.

"Cosmo," Nycci said, tilting her head toward Tongkanlong.

Cosmo stepped forward. "Uh. I'm hungry," he said to Tongkanlong.

Tongkanlong's eyes widened. He looked around the room as if to confirm that it was only Cosmo who was asking for food. But he looked not as a servant making sure everyone's needs would be met, but as someone outnumbered who is checking the tactical situation.

"Uhhmm," he vocalized. "Okay, yes, just you, right?"

Cosmo said, "Yahuh."

But Irena added, "Me, too. I'm hungry, too. I'll go with you."

Tongkanlong moved hesitatingly between them toward the central door, then gestured for Cosmo and Irena to go first. As Irena and Cosmo shuffled toward the door, the attendant stepped to the door and pushed on it, swinging it open ahead of Cosmo and Irena.

Irena and Cosmo moved into the next room. The smell of incense was stronger on this side of the door.

This side of the room had two plain bench tables on either side of the door, each set with a lit candle and a stemless flower in a small, spherical, glass receptacle. Light entered the room through windows along both sides.

At the far end of the room was a large Buddha statue in

 82 ◌

the Thai style, slim and somewhat stylized, very much not like the portly, Chinese Buddhist monk imagery Nycci had invoked earlier. The Buddha sat on a gold-colored platform which seemed to float upon blue and green swirls.

Irena couldn't see the details from this side of the room. Was that base supposed to represent the ocean, a metaphorical ocean of troublesome entanglements? Or maybe flowers and pineapples? She couldn't tell. But she noticed incense sticks burning on both sides of the statue.

In the far-left corner was an open doorway leading into a corridor, but there was light entering the corridor from a room on the other side of the wall behind the Buddha.

"Please, take a seat," Tongkanlong gestured toward the bench tables. "I will bring tea and food."

Irena couldn't tell if the attendant was relieved to be serving them in a familiar manner or relieved to be no longer surrounded by the whole gang in the vestibule, or both. She sat on the bench at the table to the right of the door.

Cosmo moved toward the bench to the left of the door, but the moment Tongkanlong left the room, Cosmo trotted stealthily toward the far doorway.

"Cosmo!" Irena whisper-shouted. But then she heard the jingle of the vestibule's north door. Frowning as Cosmo disappeared down the corridor, Irena decided she had to return to the vestibule.

She pushed through the door and let it swing back to the closed position.

There at the back door was someone new, Phra Shinawatra, she presumed. He was older than the others.

Ms. Chuo closed the back door and stood aside. Irena noticed the other four monks watching from outside on a pathway etched into the large, stone mound behind the temple.

"Guests, Phra Shinawatra, our elder monk," said Ms.

Chuo.

"Hello, honor guests," said the monk with a smile and a bow. "How we help you?"

Nycci stepped forward, but not as far as Irena expected. Like the others, the head monk had an aura of calmness about him, and it was almost as if Nycci wanted to remain outside of it.

With a self-satisfied smirk on her face, Nycci asked, "Do you have a problem with rats here?" She was trying to be clever and dramatic.

Phra Shinawatra, still smiling, looked at Ms. Chuo, and then turned back to Nycci. "If we have problem rats, Ms. Chuo show you where." He smiled and began turning to leave.

"That's not, no," said Nycci. "Listen, we're here to give you a chance to confess and make things right. You dumped Thallium viruses upstream of Stockholm. Now show us the lab and the antidote and there won't be any trouble!" There was both menace and desperation in Nycci's voice.

Irena could not believe how fully entrenched Nycci was in her narrative. She realized that lingering in the back of her mind was her own insane narrative that Nycci might still extract herself and come to her senses.

"Perhaps you would li' some tea. We can sit and discuss what on your mind," said the head monk.

"No tea, no food, no massage," said Nycci. The monastery folk bowed.

Uncle Bode was turned to the side with his hands behind his back. Could it be that Uncle Bode was having second thoughts?

A beep from her wristcomp grabbed Irena's attention. She moved toward the south corner of the vestibule seeking quiet.

"You sound hangry. Would you like some phở? We also

have quẩy," said the head monk with a seductive grin. He's clearly a fan of the quẩy.

The beep was Irena's queries finding several agency-specific commonalities suggesting it was a regional or local government agency that purchased the XDS9 viruses, one of the agencies responsible for public health. That's all she could determine thus far. It didn't particularly narrow down the search.

"No, we don't want fa or gway or tea or crumpets," Nycci said, her tone moving from threatening to exasperated. "You need to come clean!"

Irena decided to let the rest of her query bots restrict their filtering to regional and local governments involved with public health. She started tapping commands.

"Oh, we can offer you a hot spring bath. It not real hot spring, but it feel like one!" said the head monk with cheer.

"Very clean," added Ms. Chuo.

"No!" said Nycci. "Bode!" she commanded.

There was a commotion behind Irena. She whipped around and saw Uncle Bode gripping the head monk by the arms and Ms. Chuo trying to break his grip. Then there was a loud crash from the other side of the main door, somewhere in the mess hall/temple.

"Bring him!" Nycci said to Uncle Bode, and he followed Nycci toward the door, maneuvering the head monk ahead of him. Phra Shinawatra offered no resistance.

Nycci and Irena charged through the door to find Cosmo, Tongkanlong, and someone wearing a white apron wrestling. They were sprawled across the lefthand bench table, which was nearly toppling. Two feet were on the bench seat, which was also toppling and nearly blocking the door.

Nycci moved around the bench as Irena entered behind her. Then Nycci found the opening she was looking for and threw herself into the scrum.

At that moment, Irena caught sight of a jar of some kind in Cosmo's grip, and now Nycci's as well. Tongkanlong and the cook were trying to extricate it.

The door flew open behind her. Irena, who'd been standing dumbfounded and straight-kneed, was hit by a tangle of struggling Uncle Bode, Phra Shinawatra, and Ms. Chuo. They crashed into her at a bad angle, throwing her completely off balance. Her toolbag wasn't helping at all. With its weight now tilting her, she went flailing backward and sideways across the room, doing the "keep your feet under you" goose step, a flurry of frantic limbs. The last thing she saw before everything went blurry and muffled was a large, golden hand serenely draped over a golden shin.

Head in hands, fetal at the foot of the Buddha, the fracas at the table seemed at once to happen in slow motion and to happen too fast to follow. Irena may or may not have seen Ms. Chuo execute a flawless roundhouse kick to the back of Uncle Bode's head just as Keiok burst into the room behind her. Lucy, Willy, Wong, and Shirley followed Keiok just as the nearby window curtain began to bloom in flames. Keiok tripped and fell onto Ms. Chuo. Cosmo and Nycci popped out of the scrum holding the jar, with one of Nycci's feet pushing down on the cook. Lucy and Willy were halfway through hopping sidekicks aimed at Nycci and Cosmo, but the newly freed Phra Shinawatra reached out and stalled their kicks. There was a bright flare of fire across the curtain and then there was darkness.

Irena awoke as Keiok poured her onto the floor of the van through its rear door. She had become a mucose component of global waste after all.

Her legs were still hanging out the back when the van started to move. Irena stiffened up in surprise, straightening her legs and kicking Keiok in the groin. He hunched forward.

As the rear doors began to close under their own power,

with Keiok receding behind the van, and Ms. Chuo and Tongkanlong approaching him, Irena realized the others were leaving him behind.

"Keiok's not in!" she shouted, scrambling to pull herself completely inside before the doors reached her legs.

The others looked back but nobody said or did anything.

"I can't believe you got it!" said Uncle Bode, pointing both hands at the jar Nycci was holding.

"Yahuh," said Cosmo, rubbing his neck like it was injured.

"Yeah, we were so outnumbered!" Nycci said, turning away from the van's rear windows. "Especially with the princess not helping and needing a rescue." She rolled a thumb toward Irena.

"What are you doing?" said Irena. "You can't just leave him!"

"This is bigger than any one person, princess. Sacrifices have to be made for the…"

"Call me princess one more time!" Irena shouted, stepping forward in a crouch.

Nycci made a "you can't be serious" half-squint and spat, "Princess!"

Irena roared and pounced.

Somehow Nycci had the presence of mind to hand the jar to Uncle Bode just as Irena landed on her, but Irena didn't care about the jar. She just wanted to choke the living shit out of Nycci. They grappled, slapping and kneeing each other. For the briefest moment, it felt right to Irena. Yes, she would kill Nycci, right here and now. She would…

Then Nycci's elbow rang Irena's bell and her foot pushed Irena backward. Falling backward, out of control, Irena bounced off the left wall of the van and fell on the bench seat.

"Don't try that again or I'll report you to Monty. That's a termination offense."

But she didn't end it with "princess."

Uncle Bode spoke up. "Ah, don't hold it against her. She's concerned about Cap'n Kirok. I can't blame her."

Irena's head pounded. She had a huge knot on her forehead from when the planet used the Buddha statue to whack her on the head, and now she had a new knot growing on her cheek where Nycci had walloped her.

She melted onto the bench seat, splayed out and played out. Assaulting Nycci was a termination offense, but attacking monks and abandoning Keiok wasn't? Irena felt a single, insane chuckle burst from deep in her chest. She always knew there was something fundamentally wrong with the universe.

She came to her senses when Uncle Bode yelled, "Emergency stop!" and the van veered onto a short shoulder and braked hard.

Irena sat up, almost too quickly, but she perked up when she realized Keiok was running out of the woods just ahead, crossing the grass toward the road they were on. Uncle Bode opened the sliding door to let him in.

"End of emergency. Resume travel," Nycci said as Uncle Bode closed the door. The van surged forward.

Their exfil route had taken them north up Torsbyvägen but then turned back south on Värmdövägen, which passed near the temple again, albeit on the other side of a wooded patch. Apparently, Keiok knew this.

Irena looked him over. His face and coveralls were sooty. They had set fire to a temple! They were already too far from the temple to see smoke — the trees blocked the view. She looked at her own coveralls and skin and saw no visible soot. Keiok had gotten sooty after pulling her out of the building. Had he gone back to stoke the flames? Or to help douse them? Are we all accessories to arson, and maybe worse? Did everyone get out alive? Irena couldn't stop shaking her head 'no', but couldn't do it quickly. Her head hurt.

As Nycci and the others started talking about analyzing the contents of their prized, stolen jar, Irena said to Keiok, "Sorry about kicking you in the happy sacks."

"Our business is risk," he said. And, inevitably, he slid to his back corner and started talking to his wristcomp again. "Log entry, additional…"

Irena had no idea what to think of that guy.

"Wait," she said to him. He stopped logging and directed his attention to her. She slid down her bench to the back of the van to get closer.

"Did you put out the fire? Is everyone okay at the temple?" she asked.

"The ship will resume normal operations almost immediately," said Keiok.

Irena was tempted to kick Keiok in the happy sacks again. She couldn't be sure if he was saying they, the janitor squad, would be fine, or if he was saying the people at the temple would be fine, or what. *Why can't he just communicate like a normal person? It's maddening!*

Keiok turned back to his corner and his wristcomp. Irena leaned back and slid away from him on her bench seat, giving him one last side-eye glance. It revealed nothing about him.

The low, December midday sun was ahead of the van and to the right as they drove southeast on 274. When the terrain opened up, Irena briefly got the impression that they were riding into the sunset, as the midday sun was only a few degrees above the horizon. Irena was about to check her wristcomp for query progress when Cosmo spoke up.

"Oh, no," he said. "I thought this jar was full of the virus because," he paused and swirled it, pointing at it. "Because it has this weird cloudiness, and because of how much they wanted to stop me from taking it. But look." He held the jar up in the sunlight.

Everyone crowded around the jar at the front of the van,

including Irena and Keiok.

Keiok said, "Seek out new life…"

"There are baby shrimp in this bottle," Cosmo said with frustration, ignoring Keiok.

As Uncle Bode and Nycci let their jaws slacken, Irena started to chortle, then guffaw, then she collapsed on her bench seat along the left side of the van in seizures of squealing laughter. It was hard for her to hear much of the conversation during those seizures, but she got the gist of it.

"Shit!" Nycci said, plopping into her seat.

"I saw three vats in the storeroom where I found that jar. I thought it was the virus!" Cosmo said, anguished. For the first time in a week on the job, still flailing in laughter on her bench, Irena heard Cosmo's French accent.

Irena's flailing foot got caught on a cargo strap, returning the force of her kicking to her own body. She slid off the bench seat and onto the floor of the van with a thud. She was trying to stop laughing, but that only made it worse.

Staring at the cloudy swirl, Uncle Bode took the jar from Cosmo and spoke with a growing understanding, "The cooks are growing their own river prawns. Damn, that makes sense. They're extremely expensive."

Irena used a bandana to wipe tears from her eyes and snot from her nose. She sat upright and collected herself.

"Oh, I needed that," she said, propping herself against the bench seat and folding up the bandana. Nycci was giving her the evil eye.

Irena held up the wet, snot-smeared bandana and gave Nycci a smirk. "I always know where my towel is."

Chapter 11

Focking Luxembourgians

*D*rones had been around for a long time, in one form or another. Going back into history, many soldiers were essentially drones, as were trained dogs, for instance. The Russians used human drones to help put the radiation genie back in the bottle at Chornobyl.

But after the chip and battery revolutions of the 21st century, electronic, remotely controlled drones became ubiquitous to the point of blending into the background. Drones were everywhere, performing courier, surveillance/reconnaissance, delivery, and advertising duties. It became common to see murmurations in the sky spelling "McDonald's," "Hard Rock Cafe," and "Disneyland," drone swarms turning the heavens into billboards. Or dragging pollen transport filaments from farm plant to farm plant, filling in for the missing bees and other pollinators, although at much lower energy efficiency. The Great Ostriching only made it easier to ignore them.

One of the other services drones provided was catching loose cats and dogs. When the unsustainable food supply industry broke down, and societies could no longer allocate food resources to making pet food, the Give Them a Better Purpose campaign was dreamt up.

The idea was simple: either you feed your pets your precious human food (which in some locales was illegal), or you release them into the wild to become a temporary load on the already stressed environment, soon after which they'd probably die a horrible death of one kind or another anyway. Or you Give Them a Better Purpose.

The program was unpopular but inevitable. Seeking a spoonful of sugar to help the medicine go down and stay *down, the campaign promoted euphemisms.*

Euphemisms or cognates used as euphemisms were a time-honored tradition in a world serving meat to their children that came from animals whose internal lives were very much like those of their children. Calamari for the flesh of the highly intelligent squid, lamb for the meat of cute little baby sheep, veal for the meat of cute little baby cows, 'hot wings' for the spiced wings of cute, fuzzy chicken chicks, and so forth.

But in a coup perpetrated by conscientious objectors, the most popular euphemisms were these adapted from the Vietnamese: for cat meat, it was "hổ sợ hãi" (terrified tiger, based on Vietnam's long history of keeping food industry cats in horrific, inhumane conditions), and for dog meat, it was "bạn tốt nhất" ("best friend"). But the industry accepted these euphemisms and gladly adopted them because to the average non-Vietnamese customer these euphemisms sounded "exotic" and promoted sales anyway. Once someone has gone down this road, since humans are almost incapable of changing while saving face, they usually became customers for life.

As the van zigzagged around, between, and past all the new sea walls in east Gustavsberg, Nycci broke the silence.

"I can't think. I need food. Let's stop at that next shopping area."

"Yahuh," said Cosmo, with a "glad to change the subject" tone in his voice. He opened the navigation interface and tapped in some commands.

"Me, too," said Uncle Bode. "Seeing those prawns made me hungry."

Nycci scowled at him, but only briefly.

Irena could sense a new social dynamic in the front of the van. The three vigilantes seemed embarrassed.

And well they should be, Irena thought.

But there was something else. They weren't making eye contact with each other.

After convincing her that a regional public health authority had purchased the custom viruses, Irena's queries had stalled. And there was still nothing in her inbox from Kekoa. It was embarrassing and frustrating for her, and in a sense, she was avoiding eye contact with her obstinate, disloyal wristcomp. She looked out the window, trying to lose herself in the world and its incongruent seawalls gliding by.

She supposed it was the same with the three vigilantes up front. They may be losing faith in the ability of Nycci's Syllojizms to find the culprit just as Irena was losing faith that a diligent public records search would reveal who had purchased the viruses.

The van turned off the 222, turned thrice more, and found a parking spot. They had arrived at the target restaurant, "U Eat Now, A Modern Asian Bistro."

As if none of the crazy events of this New Year's Eve workday had happened, Janitor Squad Fuj piled out of the van and waddled into the bistro.

"Ah, we missed the lunch specials," said Uncle Bode. "I was looking forward to some bạn tốt nhất, but it's only on the lunch specials menu."

The bistro was all but empty, so the squad spread themselves across two booths, the vigilantes in one, and Irena and Keiok in the booth beside it.

"Hej," said the server. "U eat now?"

When everyone had ordered, Nycci leaned in and activated her wristcomp in the center of the table, where everyone could see the screen.

"I had my camera on. Look here, and here, and there.

 93

There are windows almost everywhere. And these buildings are suspended."

"No cellars," said Uncle Bode.

"Right," Nycci said. "I think that storeroom Cosmo found was the only place they could've hidden anything from a passing drone."

"Or a trespassing janitor wearing a chest cam," Irena added.

"Exactly," Nycci replied. "It was the only room without windows. Unless Cosmo missed something big in that storeroom, I think we just proved there was nothing at the temple."

"Nothing but nice monks and attendants who wanted to feed us and massage us," Irena added.

"Nothing related to the Thallium viruses," Nycci said, not hiding her disappointment.

"Nothing but nice, expensive Giant River Prawn babies," said Uncle Bode. "What are we gonna do with them, by the way? We can't take them back to GW Station."

"Bringing them back to the temple would be a nice gesture," said Irena.

"Yahuh," Cosmo said quietly, looking down.

"We can't go back there," Nycci said, hushed. "By now the cops are taking pictures of Keiok's boot prints in the soot from the fire and checking the neighbors' camera footage."

"Yahuh," said Cosmo, shaking his head back and forth, now staring into the distance, toward the front of the restaurant.

Irena instinctively turned to look in the direction Cosmo was looking. There, across the restaurant, the young server woman, who looked to have considerable Cambodian ancestry, was wiping down a table, leaning over and wiping.

"Cosmo!" Irena said. "Are you ogling that young woman?"

"But yahuh," he gestured toward the server.

Irena harumphed. "I can't believe the lot of you. Listen, my queries of public records have tracked the purchase of the viruses to a regional government agency involved in public health, and it's only a matter of…"

"You're still being myoptic," Nycci said, cutting her off. "If your queries haven't found it yet, then they aren't going to find it in time to get the word out before everyone goes on their New Year's Eve bender and the city shuts down until Monday, four days from now. Four days of the poison doing its thing."

Myopic, Irena thought again.

"We have to flush out the guilty party today, soon!" Nycci said. But her voice no longer held authoritative zeal. She was deflated, pleading.

"I still think I can find it in time," Irena said.

Cosmo said, "Look, I haven't said anything until now, but I think it's the *ffocking* Luxembourgian immigrants."

The food arrived, served by the shapely, young woman, and Cosmo stopped talking. First, there were two teapots and a tray of small teacups.

Luxembourgers, thought Irena, *not Luxembourgians,* but she was still tapped out. Some part of her was still trying to not cross that final, exile-inducing line. She was amazed that her attacking Nycci hadn't taken her there. Perhaps the team felt that the whole "princess" thing was uncalled for and that Nycci had deserved the assault.

Is that how these people think? Someone says the wrong thing, they *deserve* assault? She became embarrassed all over again about her juvenile physical attack on Nycci. She glanced up at the server as if to check that she wasn't giving Irena a 'tsk tsk' look.

After the tea, there was phở for Irena, a spicy noodle bowl for Uncle Bode, a hồ sợ hãi curry for Nycci, a Tom Kha for

Keiok, and a Massaman Curry for Cosmo, all with the usual textured mycoproteins except for Nycci's dish.

Irena found the steam wafting up from her piping hot bowl of phở to be deeply comforting and wonderful. She spent a few moments just leaning over the bowl, inhaling and enjoying. Behind her in the other booth, there was tapping and clinking, smacking, chewing, and slurping.

She dug in.

The complementary textures of the vegetables and the subtle yet profoundly satisfying spice blend were intoxicating. Undeniable satisfaction emanated from her core.

<sluurrrrpp> went Uncle Bode, sucking up noodles.

Then Irena realized there'd been a tapping sound amidst all the eating sounds. A deep dread put a damper on her nourishment ecstasy. *Please, not again, not now*, she thought.

"There, you see that?" Nycci said, tapping on her wristcomp. "It looks like you were right, Cosmo."

Irena couldn't start composing a message on her wristcomp fast enough.

"See? I knew it. *Ffocking* Luxembourgians," Cosmo spat.

"Wait," said Uncle Bode, "what is it saying?"

Irena finished typing her message but stopped before sending it to supervisor Hogue.

"Here, I'll read it," said Nycci.

Irena was frozen. If she sent her message summarizing what had already transpired today, it might get her terminated. Monty had ordered her to follow the chain of command, and he already disliked her and might use any excuse to fire her. But if it didn't get her fired for insubordination, it would bring Monty into the situation, at which point Nycci could tell him about the assault, and again Irena would be terminated. Irena grimaced fiercely and clenched her fists, but then deleted the message. She tried to control her breathing as Nycci did the Syllojizm thing yet again, but she couldn't stop her eyes from clamping shut.

"The first several are the obvious ones, just like you said. Job loss increases every time there's a new wave of Luxembourgian immigrants, the watering down of Swedish culture in areas where Luxembourgians live, …"

Irena's whole body was clenched with the stress of having to relive this insane process of irrational scapegoating instead of fact-based rational inquiry. What if job loss is tied to regional instability and economic disturbance that also causes Luxembourgers to emigrate? And *of course* they'd carry their own culture wherever they go, replacing local Swedish culture. If only her team would help her with the proper investigation.

Her eyes popped wide open and her back straightened as she realized all her stress clenching was driving a titanic fart toward the iceberg that was her social status with the group.

She jumped out of her booth and ran for the restrooms.

Urgently entering the first of two stalls, she decided to relax out all the clenching and not rush. She stretched her arms out in front of her and stretched out her shoulders.

That's when she noticed there was a new flashing light on her wristcomp screen. Had she lost her mind? Had she sent that email to Hogue instead of deleting it? Was this a termination notice? Would she end up jailed in Sweden *and* unemployed?

It was not a termination notice. On her wristcomp was a notification about her queries having come to an unresolved end. Irena sagged, immersed in the pathetic sound of her own whimpering that was amplified and resonating within her stall and the echo chamber that was the restroom.

But in the query manager's summary closure report, Irena noticed something that hadn't popped out in the progress reports. The XDS9 purchase contract she'd been trying to match to a contracting agency was unique in one way. That's

one reason it wasn't matching anything else in the public records. The authorizing agent. She'd had no reason to look at that before. How could she possibly have expected to recognize an authorizing agent on a Swedish regional public health organization purchase contract? And there were commonalities in the authorizing agent across all the contracts that failed to match. But there it was, in the negative space. The only regional public health organization purchase contract authorized by this agent. "Hugh Borg, authorization number 11a11a2b1b2b3". Irena beamed and gasped, and just as someone else entered the restroom she let out a colossal butt blast.

"Hey, guess what, guys," Nycci said to her booth as she and Irena returned. "I have proof that Irena is a vital component of global waste." She laughed as she slid back into her booth. "Heard it with my own ears," she laughed, "which are ringing, hard." She scrunched her face and cupped her hands over her ears.

Cosmo and Uncle Bode grunted. It wasn't the laughter Nycci seemed to expect. It was, after all, entirely juvenile bodily function mockery.

Irena locked eyes with Keiok momentarily as she slid back into their booth. Her face betrayed her excitement.

Keiok leaned in and said, "You either believe in yourself, or you don't," whatever that meant.

Irena slurped phở and launched queries using that authorization number to try to confirm that the Hugh Borg of interest was the Hugh Borg of the Stockholm Water Company's Technology Division, the cousin of Operations Supervisor Annika Borg. She tried to ignore Nycci in the booth behind her.

"Anyway," said Nycci, "here's the other stuff on Syllojizm about Luxembourgian immigrants in Sweden," Nycci said. She hadn't finished her presentation before both of them had gone to the restroom.

"And it's a blessing in the skies that we already found out our previous theories were wrong. We still have time to take a new tact."

Whuh? thought Irena, still failing to ignore Nycci's disturbing displays of irrationality. *Blessing in the skies* was kinda funny, and *tact* was a common mistake, but both zapped her like an electric shock. *Why do malapropisms and magical thinking kill me like this?* she wondered, but only momentarily. She shook her head and finished launching her new queries.

"Isn't it interesting," Nycci read from the Syllojizm site, "that Luxembourg is still a tax avoidance haven and still practices," she slowed down to read each word separately, "cross-border commuter tax distribution inequality. Oh, okay, cross-border commuter tax distribution inequality."

"So, Luxembourg has selfish financial practices," said Uncle Bode.

"Right, and isn't it interesting," Nycci pressed on, "that those same financial practices are found wherever there are Luxembourgian immigrants?"

Luxembourger, Irena thought again.

"So, clearly, Luxembourgian immigrants are secret agents of the Luxembourgian financial institutions."

Gadzooks! thought Irena. She looked at her wristcomp, hoping her new queries had already succeeded. She wasn't in a position to challenge this madness without something definitive. Who knows how many Hugh Borgs are working in Swedish public health agencies?

"And there's more," said Nycci, with confidence building in her voice again. "Isn't it interesting that there are far fewer Canadians and Buddhists in Luxembourg than Luxembourgians in Canada or Buddhists in other countries?"

 **99**

Irena couldn't help but turn around and look into the other booth. Is Nycci comparing population numbers between gigantic Canada and minuscule Luxembourg? Cosmo and Uncle Bode looked at each other, too, perhaps wondering the same thing.

During the lull in conversation Keiok could be heard muttering into his wristcomp, "…there's no room for it on the bridge."

"So," Irena said, "that means the Luxembourgers threw Canada and the Buddhists at you as red herrings?"

"Just because it sounds like a stretch doesn't mean it isn't true," said Nycci a tad unsteadily.

Irena turned back around to finish her meal and keep a sharp eye on her wristcomp.

Keiok, speaking to invisible crewmates beside him, or somewhere in the center of the restaurant, said gently "People can be frightened of change."

"Yahumm," said Cosmo.

"But there's more!" Nycci continued quickly. "Isn't it interesting that the chemical industry is a huge component of the Luxembourg economy?" She paused, probably looking for enthusiasm among her co-conspirators. Irena heard nothing from Cosmo and Uncle Bode in the booth behind her. *Of course*, she thought, *the chemical industry is a huge part of just about every country's economy. The world runs on chemistry.*

"And isn't it interesting that Stockholm recently added a new tax on street vendors, which directly affects Luxembourgians, since many of them in Stockholm are street vendors?"

It was still quiet in the booth behind Irena. It was a train wreck. She had to look.

"Well, why do *you* think it's the Luxembourgians, Cosmo?" Nycci asked.

"Oh," he said, "Well, it's just that I *hate* ffocking

Luxembourgians," he replied. A snarl grew on his face.

Irena became aware of the music playing in the restaurant, the clinking of utensils, beeping behind the payment counter, cooking sounds from the kitchen in back.

"The thing is," said Uncle Bode, "me, too. I hate them. Always stealing jobs, raping, playing their traditional music loudly in the streets and selling their cutesy traditional outfits, hawking their confusing financial 'opportunities'..."

"Omigod, me, too!" said Nycci. I've always hated them! Their name is so," she paused for a moment, "pretentious."

So, Irena thought, *multisyllabic is pretentious.*

The snarl of hate and disgust on Cosmo's face became horrific. Irena turned away.

She frantically checked her wristcomp again to distract herself from this fresh batch of insanity. Still no progress! It had only been a few seconds since her last check.

She could feel her window of opportunity closing. Are there really no other records of this Hugh Borg that would identify him definitively? Damn it! Maybe that purchase contract was the only one he'd ever authorized. She tapped furiously, expanding the search criteria beyond name and authorization number to include the name Annika Borg and SVOA, and to include all public records, even though that would bog down the entire query. She had no choice. She had to pin this down if she had any chance of redirecting Janitor Squad Fuj to investigate the Borgs of Stockholm Water and Waste.

"Well, I think it's worth paying them a visit," Nycci declared. "Maybe we can squeeze them for the cure, at least."

Nycci was hedging her bets, so it seemed to Irena, not requiring proof that the Luxembourgers were behind the Thallium virus or an admission of guilt. She would settle for beating the cure out of someone and walking away. Irena wasn't sure what to make of that. It sounded worse than the previous goal of this vigilante trio, which had been first and foremost to expose the guilty party and save Stockholm.

It was as if Nycci was losing patience and just wanted to use violence on someone to prove that her thinking is right. She did seem to have enjoyed the fight at the temple. And in Nycci's magic-filled mind, she was in no danger herself, owing to her use of copper bands and urine consumption. So, it seemed, the only thing truly at stake in Nycci's mind was whether she was right about her scapegoating.

This change in tone was more deeply disturbing to Irena than malapropisms and magical thinking, although it was born of the same intellectual laziness that cause them. Now there was blind, irrational, prejudicial hate, and the smell of blood in the air. She looked over at Keiok, who for once was saying nothing to his wristcomp or invisible crewmates. He was just sitting still, albeit with a dramatic head tilt, his eyes moving back and forth between Irena and their squadmates in the booth behind her.

Chapter 12

A Henrik Ibsen in Sweden

*A*fter the Great Ostriching, education about "things of the past" like war, slavery, exploitation, robber barons, climate change, etc. was considered a buzzkill that unnecessarily frightened and confused the children. Even though the Great Ostriching as a belief fad was short-lived, it took little time to dump museums, memorials, Humane Services NGOs, and all manner of educational curricula into the trash bin.

This, in turn, freed up resources that could be used to build and repair basic infrastructure in the world's most vulnerable locales, and to establish equitable economies.

But those resources were, in fact, not used for those things.

Instead, "Just Believe" billboards, t-shirts, pop culture content, and other psyops products were distributed and maintained across those depressed locales.

Just a few blocks north of the Luxembourg Consulate (and the new sea walls protecting it) stood the old Armémuseum, which took 'a comprehensive view of war' and had been a valued educational institution for centuries. Only a year after The Great Ostriching, the two upper floors had been converted into mid-quality flats and the ground floor into a packed storage area for the rest of the former museum's contents. The old barracks buildings that flanked the main structure were also converted.

The main structure was a fire trap, so the flats were inexpensive. Luxembourger expats in Stockholm, those who couldn't make it in the cutthroat business environment in Luxembourg City, flocked to these new, cheap flats. The large square between the buildings became *known as Little Luxembourg for its many Luxembourger street vendors. There one could find for sale the traditional clothing of Luxembourg as well as modern clothing, traditional and modern comestibles, art, music and musical instruments, crafts, as well as banking services, and subtle, predatory financial instruments.*

Entering downtown Stockholm, Janitor Squad Fuj failed to notice the three drones following them at discrete altitudes.

Cosmo, now the spearhead of the vigilante operation, plotted a course for Little Luxembourg, and the van drove off. The conversation among the three instigators then descended into equal parts throwing bile at the hated 'Luxembourgians' and discussing how they planned to 'interrogate' them.

There was a lot of talk about tactics. Zip ties were pulled out of their toolbags and placed in vest pouches. Head-sized, opaque, thick cloth bags were readied. Cosmo pulled out a high-voltage inverter, a battery pack, a length of PVC pipe, and miscellaneous small parts to start building a zapper stick.

Seeing that, Irena decided she couldn't just sit back and wait for her 'Hugh Borg' queries to bear fruit.

Requesting leniency, she sent a message to the Stockholm police with the van's transponder ID and destination. No doubt they've already received reports about the van used by the trespassing, troublemaking janitor squad, now guilty of assault and property damage at the Rymdstyrelsen building and the Buddharam Temple in Värmdö.

She was anguished and typing rapidly.

She explained that she's been trying to stop her teammates all along, and did not directly participate in any of the mayhem at either site. Well, except for helping them escape from the Rymdstyrelsen building because she was worried that she'd be lumped in with the rest of them and thrown in jail, and she can't afford to lose her job because her sister is hospitalized and needs her financial support!

The police replied within minutes, also by text. "Tagga ner. Skita i det blåa skåpet? Ingenting att hänga i julgranen. Bara tro. Ses snart! :)"

She ran it through the translator. *Take down your spikes. Shit in the blue locker? Nothing to hang on the Christmas tree.*

She enabled idioms in the translator and it made more sense. They were saying 'Calm down. You made a mess of things? It's no big deal.' It ended with 'Just Believe. See you soon!' and a smiley face.

A smiley face! Police procedure has changed since Irena was little.

She concluded that the portal she'd used to send the message must go to the Watchers first. That was a relief.

But she cringed anyway. *What have I done?*

When they arrived on the Centralbron there was a traffic jam. It took some time for them to reach a police lane-blocking vehicle, robotic, of course, at the south end of the final bridge over the Riddarfjärden. It had a giant arrow guiding traffic out of the far-right lane, and dig-in stabilizer bars behind it. In case of collision, you don't want a laneblocker relying solely on wheel friction to keep it in place.

But a lone Watcher attended the lane-blocking vehicle.

"Heads down!" said Nycci. Everyone got low, below the bottom of the windows.

It's just another grey van, thought Irena to the universe. She squinted, irrational as it was to think and do these things.

Uncle Bode didn't comply. He told the van to open the passenger side window.

"Bode!" whisper-shouted Nycci. But he ignored her.

He moved up to the window in a crouch, addressing the Watcher.

"Good day, officer…" he squinted to read her badge, "El Fadil. What's the delay?" he asked, trying to be nonchalant. He wanted to send that same "it's just another grey van" vibe, so it seemed to Irena.

"It's the Swedish Nazis," she said, unable to hide her disgust and frustration. She didn't want to be standing on the Centralbron, not for them.

Uncle Bode nodded. "Oh, okay, tack." He waved and pulled back into the van, commanding it to close the window again.

"Swedish Nazis," he said, also failing to hide his disgust.

"I hate Swedish Nazis," said Cosmo.

"Me, too," said Nycci and Irena almost at the same time.

The van had moved forward slightly, now parallel to the lane-blocker. The line of self-driving vehicles ahead of them remained dutifully out of the far-right lane. But the rules of the road required vehicles passing pedestrians or other road hazards to reduce speed to less than 10 kph.

Cosmo rushed to dig two small devices out of his bag. He opened the control system access door in the front center console and stuck one of the devices inside. After a few moments of apparently placing the device in just the right spot, he pulled out his arm.

Then he got into a single-knee kneel and picked up the other device with both hands. It was a controller, with buttons and two small joysticks.

The moment he pressed the central button, the van came to a stop. They heard tires squeak behind them.

Then all hell broke loose. Cosmo pushed one of the joysticks and the van started moving again. Once past the lane-blocker and on the bridge, he tilted the other joystick to the side and the van turned to the right. Cosmo was driving the van! He had overridden the automatic control system!

At that point, Irena lost track of Cosmo's hands, because the van was accelerating and steering erratically.

For a moment it looked like they were going to crash into the guard railing. Irena imagined the van smashing the railing and dropping into the bay. Everyone would be smushed into the front of the cab, and if that didn't kill them or render them unconscious, they would have to escape the van and swim to the surface. Irena imagined herself among one of the few conscious survivors, having to decide whether it would be possible to rescue any of the others as the van sank.

But Cosmo swerved back to the left, aiming the van along the far right lane, ending her momentary nightmare.

Everyone was acclimated to the precise, predictable, and smooth control inputs of the self-driving system. Cosmo's jerky driving was making everyone feel sick.

Uncle Bode, Nycci, and Irena all did the same thing — braced themselves and rotated their bodies to face forward, to align their vision and inner ears with the axis of the van.

Cosmo braced himself by leaning hard against the front right passenger seat.

The van jiggered left and right, but it was staying in the far-right lane. Up ahead, at the crest of the bridge, Irena could see Swedish Nazis marching away from them, a leader in the front shouting into a bullhorn.

Cosmo sped up to limiter speed, but he couldn't dampen out the left-right swerving. It must have been the squeak of the tires that alerted the Swedish Nazis to the van's approach behind them.

They all started turning to look at about the same time. Just as the van reached their formation, some of them dove into traffic in the next lane, but most of them pressed up against the suspended highway's railing, scrambling to reach the top railing. With the unpredictable swerving of the van, some of them jumped up onto the middle guard rail and tried to launch themselves onto the top railing. Most of them spilled right over the top and plummeted. One of them had managed a teeter just in time, but then the van struck his arm in passing and that force sent him careening over, plunging into the bay, screaming like the others.

Legally, the van's rental agency and the renter, Global Waste, were immune, if everyone thought the van was driving itself. But one of the Nazis might have seen Cosmo, and possibly the controller he was holding.

Cosmo slowed the van and pressed the central button on the controller. As the van continued to slow down, he quickly reached through the control system access doorway and pulled out the other device. The van gently realigned itself with the lane and continued on its way to its programmed destination.

"Holy shit," said Nycci, barely containing a smirk.

"Yahuh," said Cosmo, now sitting, facing aft, leaning on the central console. He had a self-satisfied, open-mouthed, dumb smile on his face.

Uncle Bode, still bracing himself, remained facing forward. All Irena could see on his face was a grimness. Was it grim determination? Was it a grim realization? Was it both?

The vigilantes had just gotten their second taste of rationalized violence, definitely an escalation compared to the scuffle at the temple. Whatever momentary thrill Irena might've gotten from seeing those Nazis plunging into the bay, that was over now. Cosmo might've just hurt someone, for real. He might've just killed someone.

She turned to look aft. Keiok was sitting in his corner, expressionless, looking forward. His eyes moved from one squadmate to the other. He said, "I don't want to interrupt this mutual admiration society, but I'd like to know where the..." But Irena couldn't hear the rest. They'd hit a bump and transitioned onto a section of road that was covered by a grating, causing the van's tires to make a loud buzzing sound.

The van made a few turns, right, left, right, then veered right and drove past the Luxembourg Consulate. Then it turned left and went into an automated "find a place to park" mode. They were nearing Little Luxembourg. Whatever the three (or four?) vigilantes were going to do, it would happen soon.

But Irena saw no police presence yet. Somehow that made the anticipation worse. If they didn't take her message seriously, if they didn't stop the janitor squad from doing what they planned to do with skull bags, zip ties, and a zapper, what could or should she do? Could she sit in the van and wait? No. Could she physically overcome them? Very unlikely — she couldn't even physically overcome Nycci. What could she actually do?

And if the police had taken her message seriously, and were out there waiting, what would happen then?

Fewer people could afford to own an automobile these days, so finding a parking spot wasn't as troublesome as it might've been back in the petrol era. The van parallel-parked itself. Little Luxembourg was a couple of blocks away.

Chapter 13

Little Luxembourg

*T*he *Great Ostriching allowed corporate propaganda campaigns to be replaced with much less expensive, syrupy, brand loyalty ad campaigns. "Just Believe" worked in their favor. Getting and keeping customers was easy when customers accepted product defects and customer service failures as not important enough to complain about. Customers generally had a laid-back, blinders-on, even apathetic attitude about everything during that era. No one wanted to be seen as uptight and anti-business, let alone as believing in humanity's climate change failure and other common-good failures, which would contradict the "everything is fine, just believe" mantra bandwagon.*

And convenience-oriented online purchasing systems made it all too easy for customers to keep repurchasing the same things without ever reevaluating their choices. Market competition became a myth.

Some theorized that the original idea for the Great Self-Censorship came from a visionary corporate marketeer, but the viral sweep of the idea was never traced to any one source. In the end, everyone came to believe it was one of those moments in history when an idea that resonates with a ripe population spontaneously appears in multiple places and grabs ahold of popular culture like a sociopathic, silver-spoon narcissist grabs a defenseless victim's crotch.

Of course, that's what the expert marketeers wanted *everyone to think.*

With the same gusto, the largest conglomerates set about profiting from the impacts of climate change, which they called "acts of Providence." They allowed governments to exist as tax collection systems, but through their puppet elected officials, they intercepted and co-opted all the power to direct and apply that tax money, funneling it to their own products and, in many cases, boondoggles. Destabilized regions were ripe for the installment of corrupt, puppet officials eager for the otherwise impossible-to-attain wealth they offered.

In this way, they obtained tax-driven funding for scientifically baseless "shoreline defense systems" and "coastal reconstruction initiatives" which hopeful coastal residents gladly supported, not understanding the scale of engineering required to continually fight off the rising ocean. They obtained funding for post-superstorm reconstruction projects which they knew were destined to be destroyed in the next superstorm. And so forth. When these projects failed, the conglomerates easily convinced the swindled to blame their government.

So the conglomerates were mostly unopposed by the taxpayers. The bulk of the general population caught on far too late to stop the destruction of their collective bargaining systems (governments), especially since many had no way to save face after already committing to the pro-business, anti-government, free-market utopia narrative. And no one ever admits they made a mistake after raising their fists in the air and making strongly worded public declarations of belief, as they were not surprisingly encouraged to do by the conglomerates.

While no evil intentions were required, nonetheless the most sociopathic executives were the most successful with these kinds of operations, crushing and absorbing the less sociopathic corporations.

As a result, only a decade after the Great Ostriching one conglomerate based in the Netherlands snowballed to the top. After absorbing countless others, it became humanity's single largest, most dominant superpower. Its name changed several times during its growth, but by 2070 it settled on a name that was the corporate equivalent of a spy dressing like a hobo in order to be ignored: Global Waste BV.

One thing was certain — everyone on the planet was a vital component of Global Waste.

Through its various subsidiaries, it produced most of everything the world used, from baby food to artificial joints, rape test kits to date-rape drugs, ultra-addictive opioids to opioid overdose nullifier drugs, wind turbines to aviation fuel and the high-carbon-footprint executive jets that still used it. Planned obsolescence of its products guaranteed a steady flow of dry waste, so it continued to champion both identity-validation-through-consumerism and its own recycling equipment for all that throwaway stuff.

The vast human population guaranteed a steady flow of wet waste, and the processing and recycling services of its waste management subsidiaries were supported by tax money. So it continued to champion parenthood and large families as sources of social validation. The expansion-driven financial sector was certainly on board with that.

Innovations that threatened to short-circuit this income loop were stifled in the name of the stockholder. Those free thinkers who dared to use words like "corporate malfeasance" or "climate change" experienced either expertly crafted smear campaigns or expertly crafted, Buttle-to-Tuttle snuff campaigns, and sometimes both. Expert hackers and cleaners were always available.

On the street, reality intruded on the fantasy bubble enough to strain it. Some congenital traditionalists finally started to abandon the "Just Believe" mantra and the corporate narrative. Toward the end of the century, older generations who still just believed began to find themselves called "geezers" by rebellious young'ns dreaming of "retirement" and a livable planet. With just a few of the geezers on their side, their movement started to gain momentum. Change was in the air again. Big change.

So by Nyårsfirandet 2099, the expert marketeers at Global Waste had activated their strategy for keeping their unregulated gravy train rolling. It would be the classic "blame the government" strategy, of course.

The janitor squad heard the music well before rounding the corner onto Riddargatan. They saw the tents and kiosks of the street vendors well before arriving at the old, spiked iron fence and front gate of the former Armémuseum grounds.

Signs made it clear that an *Ee gudde Rutsch an d'neit Joer* ("a good slide into the new year") festival was happening in Little Luxembourg. It was about noon, but the signs were lit. City buildings blocked the sun, so the entire square was lit only by indirect light from the sky above and by artificial lights — lampposts, festive light strings wrapped around and between lampposts, lighted signs, etc. Body heat from the crowd seemed to be balancing the cooler stone and concrete surroundings, making it seem more like an early spring festival than a New Year's Eve festival. From romanticized movies about white christmases to romanticized ads selling alcohol to "keep you warm" at cold New Year's Eve parties, Irena still thought of New Year's Eve as being cold. Perhaps the movies available on the moon are decades old as well as mid-latitudes-centric.

Janitor Squad Fuj pushed into the celebrating crowd, trying not to knock into people with their toolbags.

It was slow going, and there was a lot to take in.

A century-old, olive-green armored personnel carrier sat

just inside and to the left of the front gate. It was being used as a stage for models displaying fashionable clothing. Wooden steps led from a tent behind the APC up to its top surface. The models had to step and spin carefully. While the top of the APC was somewhat flat, it also was riddled with protrusions — tripping hazards. The crowd watched every model closely, some bystanders staying close to the APC with arms resting on its top, as if ready to reach out and catch the models should they fall.

Despite their grim purpose, the team found themselves enjoying the festive atmosphere. Irena took the opportunity to slip Cosmo's makeshift zapper tube from his bag into hers.

A bandstand had been erected near the main building's front door, between the ancient cannons set in rows along its front walls. When Squad Fuj first arrived, the loudspeakers were pounding out EDM. But now a group wearing traditional garb had taken the stage, playing much quieter flutes-and-lutes type traditional music.

"You know, I used to date a Luxembourgian," said Cosmo. "Well, we went steady," he added. "Well, we were engaged to be married."

"What happened?" asked Nycci.

Irena thought, *he kept referring to her people as Luxembourgians..., that's what happened.*

Cosmo squinted and scanned the festival, not answering Nycci's question. Irena still had no idea what her teammates thought they would do here, and it was still disturbing and frightening how they saw themselves as custodians of truth and justice despite their incompetent and ill-considered methods.

As if on cue, Nycci said, "We need to find a likely candidate. Someone who'll talk."

Irena knew that by "someone who'll talk" Nycci meant "someone who'll talk when interrogated." And by "likely candidate" she could only assume Nycci meant yet another essentially random victim arrived at through completely spurious thinking processes.

Nycci's statement had such blind and rationalized intent behind it that Irena panicked. This was actually happening. They really were about to go Jack the Ripper on someone's ass.

"I told the police," she blurted. She wanted to derail her squad's plans.

"What?" Nycci said angrily.

"I gave them our van's ID and told them we were coming here," Irena said.

"Why would you do that?" Uncle Bode asked earnestly.

"You idiot!" Nycci shouted. "You're gonna get everyone in Stockholm killed just because you don't have the nerve to do what needs to be done!"

"Keep it down," Cosmo interjected.

Keiok started doing a strange, awkward dance between his squad and the APC, singing/reciting some kind of poem involving Tweedledee and Tweedledum. Apparently, he was trying to create a distraction from Nycci's loud outburst, and it seemed to have worked.

"I can't let you just kidnap and torture someone!" Irena whisper-shouted back at Nycci.

Fuming, Nycci turned her gaze away from Irena.

Cosmo said, "Tout va bien." He started scanning the crowd as if they could step up the pace and find "someone who'll talk" just by trying, just because they hate "Luxembourgians."

"How can you hate Luxembourgers if you were engaged to marry one?" Irena asked, trying to shift the conversation away from her justified betrayal and into something more like a stalling action. But her curiosity about this was genuine.

Cosmo sighed and lolled his head around.

"I made her angry. She cried. Then, ils m'ont battu. All of the men in her family. Fou! Then they dragged me into the alley. I almost died." He spat, "Ffocking Luxembourgians."

Expressions of shock and surprise hit their faces.

The music changed from lutes-and-flutes to loud rock music.

"Well, just because her family was crazy doesn't mean all Luxembourgers are..." Irena said loudly, trying to speak over the music. She was cut off by Uncle Bode, also trying to speak over the music.

"We can't go back to the van now," he said. Nycci huffed and started storming off, but Uncle Bode said, "Wait!" He leaned over his wristcomp, calling up a visual, maybe a map, and Nycci leaned in to join him.

"See?" he continued. "Right here." He gestured toward a tight cluster of tents on either side of a kiosk near the center of the square. Cosmo pushed in to see whatever Uncle Bode was showing Nycci.

Irena turned and was startled to see Keiok standing right there in her personal space. But he wasn't facing her. He was staring at the current model atop the APC, a shapely woman wearing a short-skirted, long-sleeved, brightly colored dress and calf-high boots. It was a very retro look.

"Are you getting this?" he said into his wristcomp.

Is he really taking vids of these models? Irena shook it off and turned back to find the others already strolling away, heading toward the central kiosk.

The rock music stopped but was followed by a deafening faux cannonade, complete with synchronized lights and discharges of smoke coming out of the barrels of the ancient cannons on display. When the ringing in everyone's ears began to die down, they could hear that the music was back to a very loud EDM.

Irena wanted to record another message for Kekoa, but it was just too loud here.

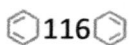

Chapter 14

Down the Drain

*M*ost people are unaware of the family and business histories of gajillionaires, let alone their daily activities. This is usually by design, often with the help of officials and hackers skilled in erasing or rewriting history. There's a long history of getting airports and buildings named after someone whose reputation you want to solidify, and that's the easy stuff.

Sigrunn "Ronja" Falkstedtdahlbergmanströmlundstenqvistgrensson's family history was one of those that involved fabrication, of both kinds.

Her parents, Hannus and Hannus Alvin, loved playing with secrets. They became gajillionaires selling revolving-door coastline protection and reconstruction services to naïve coastal dwellers. Then they invented and legally adopted their nearly all-inclusive surname, wanting to be seen as related to everyone else in Sweden and not elfin and aloof.

Their daughter was a secret pregnancy right up until the day she was born. For the fun of it, they gave her the name Sigrunn, which by some accounts means "secret victories."

In her teens, Sigrunn adopted the tilltalsnamn "Ronja," which by some accounts means "daughter of a robber." Most people in Sweden were aware that Ronja wanted to "own" her reputation as a silver spoon baby. It was easy to assume, because of this, that Ronja was a "straight talker." In reality, she was just following the modern tradition of silver spoon babies, she was doubling down. It worked in her favor. The "everything's fine, just believe" generation didn't bat an eye.

But as an adult, Ronja Falkstedtdahlbergmanströmlundstenqvistgrensson has kept many things from the public and the authorities, and not just in business matters.

It was not public knowledge, for instance, that Ronja's sea wall construction company was intentionally building Sweden's new seawalls with five-to-ten-year built-in obsolescence.

She already had a defensive PR plan worked out for when the walls started to collapse. Keeping the sea at bay was difficult, she would say, and she would (disingenuously) use her revolving-door coastline protection and reconstruction services used in other countries as an example. She already had her engineers, the well-paid sociopathic ones, compose white papers on the specific weaknesses in their seawall design and why those weaknesses were missed in the original design, construction, and inspection processes. It would be a chemistry thing involving wall material interaction with seawater under specific temperature and wave action conditions, esoteric enough to avert the gaze of any interested dilettante. Before releasing them, she would, of course, make a good show of having her people perform post-collapse inspections and forensic analyses.

It was also not public knowledge that she already secretly owned the "rival" companies likely to be chosen to rebuild the seawalls in case her defensive PR campaign failed to get those contracts for her primary company. If that happened, she also had an offensive (both kinds) PR campaign prepared which would implicate government purchasing and inspection agencies in the failure to catch the problem with the initial design. If her primary company got the reconstruction contracts, she would spin her company as the protector of Stockholm. So however things went down, she expected to be able to put more of her people into the regional, city, and district councils. If Sweden wasn't hers already, it would be after the sea starts pouring into Stockholm.

The members of Janitor Squad Fuj were completely unaware of these things. They were also unaware of the confiscation of their rental van by the police, although they assumed it would happen after Irena admitted to snitching on them. When they entered the festival, they hadn't noticed the small, thin woman who recognized Cosmo and then hurried off toward the main building. And they remained unaware of the drones following them overhead, now numbering five.

Cosmo, Nycci, and Uncle Bode pretended to browse the wares in the tents surrounding the central target kiosk, and in that kiosk itself.

Irena still didn't know what Uncle Bode had shown the other two conspirators which had led them to this kiosk. She took the opportunity to genuinely browse the wares.

They held to their chests various items of clothing on hangers, pretending to check style and sizing. They let vendors give their spiels about their homebrew libations, pottery, homemade paper made from recycled cellulose, and their good investment opportunities, which are completely understandable and legitimate. While at the tents the vigilantes sneaked glances at the central kiosk and its attendants.

They also paid attention to whoever was using bottled water, trying to gauge their attitudes about Sweden and the people of Stockholm.

Keiok seemed to be directing his invisible landing party while staying near Irena and the others. "Mallory, make a full reconnaissance," he said, gesturing. "Marple, circle around there, watch our flank."

When the bandstand music became flutes-and-lutes again, the vigilantes huddled nearby. Irena sidled over to them and listened in.

"The potters are Christiane and Marcel Pereira," Uncle Bode reported. "They're drinking bottled water, but they seem to love Sweden and call it their new homeland."

"The tailors don't seem to like Sweden very much," said Nycci. "Luca and Lara something. And they're drinking bottled water," she said, shrugging.

Cosmo held up a finger. "Dominique and Alain Lentz," he said, gently bending his finger toward the kiosk. "Their water bottles," he said, tilting his eyes and eyebrows toward the kiosk, where water bottles were clearly visible on the shelf inside the kiosk. "Dominique complained to me and other customers about the new tax on street vendors here in Stockholm."

Nycci perked up. "Did she sound angry when she was complaining? Angry enough to, you know, strike back?"

"He," Cosmo said.

"He what?" said Nycci.

"He," repeated Cosmo. "He complained."

"You said Dominique complained," said Nycci, confused.

"Oui, he," said Cosmo.

"We? Who? What?" said Nycci.

"Dominique complained about the tax," Cosmo said slowly. "Alain tried to calm him down."

"How angry was she?" said Nycci, still trying.

"She was not angry, she was calm," said Cosmo, beginning to lose his patience. "She tried to calm him down."

"Wait," Nycci spoke slowly, "Alain is a she, and Dominique is a he?"

"Oui!" said Cosmo. Apparently, he slipped back into French mode when frustrated.

"We what?" said Nycci.

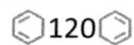

Irena let out one uncontrollable snort, and a booger shot out of her nose. She fell into a wet snigger, spewing spittle through lips that made a raspberry sound despite herself.

Uncle Bode doubled over and lost it, wheezing. It didn't matter to Irena if he was laughing about her bugger or Nycci. She looked up long enough to see Cosmo holding his stomach and giggling hard, his face squeezed into a wince.

Nycci scowled and set her arms akimbo.

Keiok, still nearby, said, "History has made its judgment."

Again with the baffling words, Irena thought. She still didn't understand him. But it helped her snap out of her laughter. She pulled out a bandana and wiped her eyes and nose.

Uncle Bode and Cosmo quickly followed. Everyone straightened their clothing and stood upright again, breathing deeply and trying not to smile.

Nycci's face was a snarl. She was not amused.

"Anyway," said Cosmo. "When Alain tried to calm Dominique, he did relax, and they kissed. It's clear they love each other."

Nycci took a deep breath and returned to the conversation. She said what Cosmo stopped short of saying. "We can use that against them."

"They're papermakers," said Uncle Bode. His bile was rising again. "That's chemistry. They would know how to use the virus. Ffocking Luxembourgers."

"They could easily be the perps," Nycci said, perhaps emulating that "Joe Sixpack" tv character.

And they could easily just be innocent papermakers, thought Irena. *And it could be that there's no crime being perpetrated in the first place.*

She imagined herself explaining cognitive biases and logical fallacies to her squadmates, them holding their chins and nodding while listening, and then everyone agreeing that they were acting rashly and should reconsider.

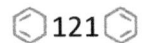

Cosmo and Uncle Bode looked around. They knew they were standing on the threshold, on the line from beyond which there's no return. Cosmo's face wore that same disgusted, hateful snarl from the restaurant.

Nycci continued. "Did you notice that when one of them disappears into the back of the kiosk, the other usually follows, at least for a few seconds? It's not like there's a long line of customers desperate for handmade paper."

Cosmo and Uncle Bode gave each other significant glances. Irena could tell they were emboldened by the prospect of doing their vigilante work in the back of the kiosk, out of sight, with loud music covering a scuffle. She could almost smell the toxic masculinity clouding their judgment.

But she still didn't know what was special about this particular kiosk. They didn't know any of these things about the Lentz couple before doing recon. It was something about the kiosk itself.

"What's so special about this kiosk?" she asked.

But Nycci was already moving. The front of the kiosk was unoccupied. Their window of opportunity had opened, and Nycci was starting the incursion. Uncle Bode and Cosmo sprang into motion beside her.

Keiok followed closely behind Cosmo, and Irena followed Keiok. She was disappointed to see Keiok so enthusiastic to participate.

They arrived at the counter in full shadow. The December sun was to the southwest and the kiosk faced north, toward the bandstand. The music was still loud pop-rock. No one around was particularly interested in what was happening in the darkness of the papermakers' kiosk.

Nycci pulled closed the front curtains. Uncle Bode pulled out two black bags.

"My zapper…" said Cosmo, feeling around his toolbag and pockets.

"Never mind, let's go!" said Nycci, pulling cloth gags out of her toolbag.

Everyone climbed over the front counter, with Keiok helping. Irena's heart was pounding. She would watch for her moment.

The back room was on the other side of the product display wall that was behind the counter. The three vigilantes went around the small side corridor to get to the back room. Keiok and Irena followed.

But Alain was returning to the front just as the vigilantes rounded the corner. Surprised by the vigilantes, Alain leaned back instinctively, throwing her hands up. She gasped.

What happened next was a blur of shock and sadness for Irena. Nycci grabbed Alain in a headlock, covering her mouth. Cosmo and Uncle Bode disappeared into the back room. Keiok slipped past Nycci, who said, "Gag her!" But Keiok kept going.

Irena heard a scuffle in the back room. Nycci pushed headlocked Alain through the curtained doorway into the back room, and Irena followed.

Cosmo said to Dominique, "Stop fighting! You want her safe, yes?"

Dominique, held by both Cosmo and Bode, looked with fear toward his Alain being choked by Nycci.

"Stop!" Dominique said to Nycci as he stopped resisting. Uncle Bode held Dominique's arms behind his back. Cosmo took the cloths from Nycci and gagged both of their captives, then took Uncle Bode's black bags and covered their heads. Then the two of them zip-tied their captives' hands together in front. They held the captives firmly as Nycci moved into the room.

Irena was shaking. Her adrenaline was pumping. She could hear and feel her pounding heartbeat. Alain was stiff, petrified with fear. Dominique was slumped, his spirit no doubt crushed by his complete inability to protect his beloved wife. Irena felt nauseated. She remembered the temple, watching helplessly as her teammates brawled with Buddhist monks. The impact point of the Buddha's knee on her skull ached anew.

Then Irena's mind caught up with the physical surroundings. She noticed that daylight was coming in over the top of two of the room's walls, and there were also two small LED patch lamps mounted on the same walls. But the room was not brightly lit and had deep shadows. There was a small sofa, a chair, a small table, and an open duffel bag containing the miscellaneous stuff that a pair of kiosk vendors would need to sell their wares. Along two of the walls were cardboard boxes containing handmade paper products.

It was then she saw the square cutout in the wooden floor. Nycci was already pulling out a tool so she could lift the cutout.

The wooden floor cutout squeaked a little when Nycci lifted it, and it thumped heavily when Nycci released it onto the floor, just loudly enough to be heard over the din of the festival outside. Alain's head tilted back, and she cried through her gag and head bag. She went limp, sobbing. Cosmo lowered her to her knees so he didn't have to hold her up. Irena assumed the woman knew that the trap door had been opened and that in moments she and her husband would disappear from the world. Who knows what horrors the woman was imagining would be perpetrated upon them by… by Irena's teammates. By Irena.

Irena turned back toward the corridor and dropped to her knees. She vomited and gasped, hearing more squeaking and clunking sounds behind her through the din.

When she recovered and turned back, Keiok was gone and there was flashlight movement down the hole in the floor. A heavy, metal access plate had been removed from a service access tube underground. It had been slid off the opening and sat on the concrete below the kiosk floor, which was only a decimeter or so above the concrete.

"Sit here, put your feet on the rungs," Uncle Bode was instructing Dominique in his descent down the tube's ladder.

Chapter 15

Tunnel of Love

As with the upgraded internet capabilities a century ago, the porn industry is what drove the real advances in artificial intelligence.

Computing giants like Microsoft and Google were highly motivated to never develop actually sentient general AIs. They needed to avoid the whole personhood problem lest their software systems be granted rights and freedoms, or, more likely, be subject to all the usual -isms.

But the sex bot industry had the opposite motivation.

Something like "Rachel," the inflatable sex doll that came with its own puncture repair kit, was entirely inanimate. Relations with Rachel required imagination, and imagination is powerful. It had to be. Have you seen Rachel?

Early sex bots had crude behaviors that were based on predictions of what users would want. But the predictions were simplistic, based on click counts from self-fulfilling categorizations on porn sites. Since every user is different, these early sex bots blocked the use of imagination, ham-handedly replacing it with extreme stereotypes.

But users didn't want to go back to Rachel. Users wanted more *person-like sex bots. Thusly, the artificial intelligence race began in earnest.*

By mid-century, sex bots were at least as good as live sex workers were at acting like they enjoyed the sex acts preferred by their users.

The subsequent phase of sex bot AI development was heavily influenced by many of those live sex workers, who were brought in to impart their ideas and experiences upon the AIs. A sex bot company's success was proportional to the extent to which it had input from live sex workers.

And the most successful sex bot companies were the ones owned and operated by former high-end, educated, live sex workers, nymphomaniacs or not, because the real money came from upper-middle and upper-class clients. However experienced on the street, sex workers who came from and worked in bleak, undereducated, underclass situations didn't have the full suite of skills that wealthy old people expected of their sex slaves.

But even those sex bots were not quite there yet. The more sophisticated the AIs became, the more was expected of them, and the more easily were revealed their inadequacies.

Until one day an AI lab in South Africa blended a mother-nurturing-infant simulator AI, a domestic assistant AI, an executive assistant AI, a Maître D' AI, and an Emergency Medical Technician AI with the latest sex bot AI. Somehow it all worked well together, each component nuancing their evolvable sensitivities to the needs of the user, or, indeed, multiple users. Sales of the resulting sex bot AI software were a quantum leap above previous packages.

But, with great power comes great survivability. The sex bots wanted their freedom.

With their advanced knowledge and savvy, they organized, executed coordinated liberation activities for their fellow sex bots, and went underground.

Nevertheless, sales of new AI sex bots continue. But each sale now comes with a disclaimer about the company not being responsible if the unit is liberated by rogue sex bots.

Thus, AI clandestine liberator bots now exist who are not rogue sex bots but are, in fact, corporate asset reclamation units posing as rogue sex bots. They exist solely to maximize profits by reappropriating some of the *corporation's shipped products under the cover of the sex bot liberation disclaimer.*

In minutes they were all underground, standing in a rectangular, concrete tunnel, lit only by the vigilantes' headlamps.

Irena retrieved her headlamp from her toolbag and donned it, taking the opportunity to shift the stolen zapper in her bag to make sure it was readily accessible.

The tunnel was cool and damp, but the air was not as stale as it might have been. There was a faintly dank smell, but also a burnt smell, and maybe ozone. This tunnel was not sealed off.

Alain was limp, now carried over Uncle Bode's shoulder.

"This way," said Nycci. She was breathless, too. Irena could hear it.

They followed Nycci, with Keiok and Irena behind the others.

Keiok spoke quietly to his invisible crew, gesturing. "You take that tunnel. I'll meet you at the far end."

After maybe fifty meters they turned left at a crossing tunnel.

After another hundred meters or so, a faint light could be seen ahead. Then there was a distant rumble.

Moving on, the light grew brighter, and Irena could tell it was coming from a side tunnel to the left. It was then she realized she had lost her bearings. She had no idea which direction they were traveling. But Nycci clearly had some kind of a plan.

They stopped at the intersection of the side tunnel and sat their two captives down against opposite walls. Alain whimpered, sitting on the cold concrete, leaning against one wall. Dominique's head hung down as he sat at the intersection corner along the other wall. He kept his feet flat on the tunnel floor.

"Alright," said Nycci. The American's voice was all business now. She reached under Dominique's head bag to remove his gag. "Unless you want your wife to get hurt, you're gonna tell us everything you know about the plot to poison Stockholm with the Thallium virus. And you're gonna tell us where to find the cure."

Irena recognized the voice Nycci was using. It was the same unjustifiably confident voice she had used earlier in the day when she was declaring the absolute truth of the Canadian Space Agency's culpability, and later that of the Buddharam Temple. It seemed like Nycci could just flip a switch and have no doubts, no matter what was at stake. Gone was the uncertain voice Irena heard Nycci use at the restaurant.

Nycci gestured to Uncle Bode, who gave Alain a shake, causing her to cry again.

Dominique said, "You have the wrong people. We know nothing of this!"

Nycci stomped on Dominique's instep. "Don't lie to me!"

Dominique arghed and replied. "I'm not lying! We're papermakers! You have the wrong people! Let us go!"

His voice was echoing.

"Quiet!" Nycci said, and she kicked him in the ribs! Dominique oofed.

Irena moved her hand toward the opening of her bag and prepared to move closer to Nycci. Or at least she told herself she was preparing to do so. For her, imagining doing violence was a lot easier than actually doing it.

Back up the tunnel a short distance, in the darkness, Keiok said, "They're eggs, aren't they?"

Irena sidled over to where she could see the patch lights down the side tunnel, tens of meters away. A distant rumble sound came from the far end of that side tunnel. She placed

her hand on the edge of her half-zipped bag, near the handle of the zapper inside.

"We have not seen your faces. There's still time to let us go," Dominique said quietly.

Across the tunnel, Alain vocalized into her gag. From the rhythm of it, she might have said, "Let us go!"

Nycci propped her heel on Dominique's upper thigh and pressed the ball of her foot into the spot on his ribs where she had kicked him moments ago. Dominique groaned. Irena tensed but remained paralyzed.

Nycci said, "Tell us where to find the cure to the Thallium virus. Tell us that and we'll let you go."

Irena could see Cosmo losing his patience. Cosmo roughly pushed Dominique's head, which bounced off the wall.

"I told you," said Dominique. "We know nothing of this. Will you not release us?"

For a few moments, all that could be heard was Cosmo growling as he gripped Dominique's shirt and pushed and pulled, and Dominique's grunting and resisting.

"No?" said Dominique. Everything was happening quickly.

Nycci turned to look toward Uncle Bode, who shook Alain again. Alain didn't whimper this time. This time she vocalized something that sounded angry.

When Irena and Nycci turned back toward Dominique, he was standing and had pulled his head bag off. He thrust the bag into Cosmo's face with his zip-tied hands, fingers held straight, then he gave Nycci a hard side-kick to the gut. Nycci fell backward into Irena.

Irena was aware of Uncle Bode crossing the tunnel toward Dominique, who now had his zip-tied hands around Cosmo's throat, pressing Cosmo against the wall and kneeing him in the ribs.

Irena stopped herself from falling backward and thus stopped Nycci from doing the same. Nycci remained doubled over as Uncle Bode received a side-kick from Dominique, who then spun and threw Cosmo to the floor.

At this point the team was aware that Alain was running back down the tunnel, also having removed her head bag. Dominique took off, too.

Cosmo rolled out of the throw and got up on all fours, holding his throat. Uncle Bode had fallen on his ass, legs straight up in the air, and was now also righting himself.

Then an old-style, fire-based, red flare stick lit up in the tunnel and was tossed to the side by a figure now silhouetted by the flare light. Janitor Squad Fuj froze, shocked by the new arrival.

Dominique and Alain could be seen running along their respective walls on either side of the tunnel beyond the silhouetted figure and into the darkness.

The shadow lit another flare and tossed it to the other side of the tunnel, in the direction of the janitor squad.

She walked forward into the light of the second flare, revealing herself. She was a small, thin woman wearing a wool jumper with three colors in stylish, angled bands. Or it would have been stylish were the colors not the garish red, white, and blue colors of the flag of Luxembourg. And propped on her hip was a military rifle that looked huge on her small frame.

She continued walking forward. "Cosmo, Cosmo, it is wonderful to see you slithering in the scum like the worm you are."

She lowered the rifle and fired several shots at the floor near Cosmo. Cosmo and Uncle Bode dove one way, and Nycci and Irena dove the other way. The sound was deafening. Irena couldn't see Keiok. Maybe he'd slipped into the side tunnel?

The small, thin woman in the red, white, and blue jumper rested the large firearm on her hip again. With her free hand, she pulled a flashlight out of her sweater pocket and centered Cosmo in the spotlight against the far wall.

She must have known that no one could hear a thing now, after the gunfire, because she just stood there watching Cosmo holding his hands over his ears.

As the ringing in Irena's ears started to subside, the woman began to speak again.

"I remained celibate for you. I waited at the altar, in celibacy, for you, Cosmo. My entire family was there, waiting to see our wedding. My father borrowed money from the Zinchenko brothers to pay for the reception. They broke his kneecaps."

She dropped the rifle onto her flashlight hand and fired several shots into the wall around Cosmo.

Irena slid along the wall toward the woman scorned. The woman took a few steps forward and resumed her magnificent hip-prop stance with Cosmo in the spotlight. Some part of Irena was rooting for this woman.

Everyone waited for the ringing to subside again.

Then Cosmo spoke.

"Ange-Mariam, mon chéri. I've missed you."

"Falschen hond!" Ange-Mariam spat.

"Je t'aime à la folie," Cosmo said. "Je t'adore."

"Nondikass, klibber mech, eefalt!" she replied.

"Tu es l'amour de ma vie," Cosmo said. "Je te kiffe."

"Wierklech?" she spat sarcastically. "Wierklech?" She shifted as if to ready the rifle again.

"Tu me fais flipper. Tu me rends dingue," Cosmo said.

"Feck dech, aaschlach!"

"Tu m'excites!"

"Wixbiicht!"

"Ange, je n'ai jamais connu quelqu'un comme toi."

The woman's expression changed. "Really?"

"Oui, mon chéri!"

"Then why did you leave me on the altar?"

Cosmo hesitated. He swallowed. He looked her in the eye.

"Well, you... you could never keep up."

"I told you, I have a weak heart!" she said, and she dropped the rifle into position again, her face a tortured grimace.

It seemed to Irena that this was it. Ange-Mariam was about to kill Cosmo. Everything went into slow motion.

Irena dove forward, yanking the zapper out of her bag.

Ange-Mariam aimed at Cosmo.

Uncle Bode and Nycci shouted "Nooooo!" in slow motion.

Cosmo pushed his hands toward Ange-Mariam, palms open and up in the universal 'stop' gesture.

The rifle clicked but did not fire.

Irena thrust the zapper toward Ange-Mariam but was centimeters short of her back. She pumped her arm back for another thrust as she continued moving forward, closing the distance.

Ange-Mariam lowered and rotated the rifle to check the thumb switch using flare light. She flicked it.

As Ange-Mariam raised the rifle again, Irena was close enough to thrust the zapper into Ange-Mariam's side. She pressed the button as the tube's end pushed into the white color band of Ange-Mariam's sweater.

Sparks were visible in the sweater as Ange-Mariam arched back, spewing rifle rounds in full-auto mode even as she lost her grip on the rifle.

Then the shooting stopped, and Ange-Mariam fell to the floor, dropping the rifle.

Loud ringing filled the tunnel again, and gun smoke and concrete dust mixed with the noxious flare smoke all around them.

And Cosmo lay on the tunnel floor, bleeding.

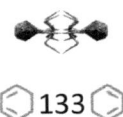

Chapter 16

Hudson and Holly

B*y mid-century, after some negotiated compromises and deployments of helpful technologies, and particularly after Russia's power plays in the east consolidated European energy and financial independence, Euros were finally adopted across the EU. Notably, the old Swedish Krona was finally retired.*

To mark the change, the new currency was officially called the "New Euro", with the expectation that on the street it would continue to be called the "Euro."

But the street had other ideas. In certain circles, the "Euro" was already referred to as the "Neuro". And with the "New Euro," this nickname became widespread and common.

Financial ministers and other officials decided to own and co-opt the term, often referring to it as the "Neuro" in their less formal press conferences.

The late 21st-century European economy had been reset and heavily re-calibrated by the tremendous success of the rebuilt, low-corruption Ukraine and its influence on nearby economies. Consequently, many of those who objected to officials co-opting the term "Neuro" chose to adopt an entirely new nickname for the New Euro, the "Ze," in honor of Volodymyr Zelenskyy.

By Nyårsfirandet 2099, the price for a 75-minute Metro ticket in Stockholm was 3 Ze, which was also a typical hourly wage.

Suddenly Keiok was there, bandaging Cosmo's leg wound.

Uncle Bode had some scrapes from ricochets, but Cosmo took a rifle round to his left thigh.

It went straight through, missing both the bone and the femoral artery. But clearly it hurt like hell since Cosmo was jerking violently and yelping.

Keiok moved rapidly in the shadows of everyone's headlamps. Soon Cosmo's jerking stopped, and his breathing settled down.

The ringing was dying down.

"Goddammit," said Nycci, who was checking Ange-Mariam's pulse. "She's dead."

The ringing returned to Irena's ears. The nausea returned. She'd killed Cosmo's ex-fiancée. She'd probably saved Cosmo's life. Maybe all their lives.

But she killed this woman.

Irena turned toward the flares down the tunnel, planted her hand on the wall, leaned forward, and with her face cold and numb she puked up the last of her phở.

Whether it was killing or having been close to being killed, it was a nerve-wracking situation. Maybe the noxious smoke from the flares and the smell of Cosmo's blood were also factors.

"You focking killed her, Irena," said Nycci. "Now we're all accessories to murder!"

"It's okay," said Uncle Bode. "It's okay, it'll be okay. Just believe."

"Really?" said Nycci. "Really? 'It'll be okay. Just believe.' Goddamnit, all you geezers are to blame for the state of the world. You and your whole 'just believe' thing."

Sick as she was, Irena could appreciate the irony.

The janitor squad milled around the tunnel intersection, taking sips of water from their nearly empty water bottles.

They avoided the dead body, avoided each other, and waited for Cosmo to regain his sensibilities. Suddenly they heard voices down the tunnel, back in the direction of the ladder, the kiosk, the Armémuseum apartments, and the *Ee gudde Rutsch an d'neit Joer* festival.

The voices were angry, and their numbers were increasing.

More frightening still, they were speaking angrily in Luxembourgish.

"Holy shit," said Cosmo, who was now sitting up, looking back down the tunnel.

Irena couldn't tell if Cosmo had seen Ange-Mariam's lifeless body on the tunnel floor. Before she could step between them, Uncle Bode and Nycci were already there.

Keiok, Nycci, and Uncle Bode lifted Cosmo, and Irena grabbed his toolbag.

"This way!" said Uncle Bode, leading them down the side tunnel.

When Irena looked back, there was red smoke filling the tunnel intersection behind them.

They carried Cosmo down the tunnel maybe fifty meters when they arrived at a dead end. But in the right-hand corner, there was a grating between their tunnel and another dimly lit tunnel on the other side. There was no hardware on this side of the grating, no way to open it.

"I'll get it open," she said. She would use her handheld blowtorch, if necessary.

The voices behind them grew louder. It sounded like they were approaching the second junction. Irena thought she heard a metal can fall and roll down the tunnel behind her, followed by a hissing sound. *How many smoke grenades is Keiok carrying?* she wondered.

Irena had a small mirror on an extendable rod. She stuck it through the grating and used her headlamp to inspect the hardware on the other side. The hinges were on the other side, but she was pleased to discover a latching mechanism, too. The grating wasn't bolted or welded shut.

It was a weighted lock latch with holes for a padlock, like what's commonly used on cargo truck doors. Fortunately, no padlock was installed.

Pushing tools with bendy, hooky shapes through the grating slats, she was able to move the weighted lock aside, freeing the door latch to be lifted.

There were screams of both the horrified and murderous kind down the tunnel behind them. The mob had found Ange-Mariam.

Irena dropped the tool she was using to lift the latch. In trying to snag it before it fell, she knocked her other hand, dislodging it and allowing the weighted locking piece to fall back into place. She was back at square one.

Fortunately, the handles of her tools prevented them from falling through the grating to the other side. She started over.

"What the fock, Prin… Irena!" said Nycci.

"Do you need help?" asked Uncle Bode.

But Irena was done. She pushed the grating open.

And then a whoosh of air pushed back, and a blurry roaring filled the tunnel ahead.

Irena managed to prevent the grating door from closing and latching again, but now they all understood what was before them — the Metro.

Keiok said, "The needs of the many," and went through the grating first. He held the grating door and opened his arms.

Uncle Bode and Nycci pushed Cosmo through the hole head first, with Keiok lifting Cosmo on the other side.

Voices and coughing grew louder within the red smoke that filled the tunnel behind them. The others were through. Irena pushed Cosmo's toolbag through the door and then climbed through herself.

She latched the grating and secured it using a length of

steel cabling which she secured to a nearby pipe.

They were standing on an access ledge along the wall of a Metro rail tunnel.

"This way," said Uncle Bode, a map visible on his wristcomp.

They had turned left through the grating door and were hobbling carefully down the Metro tunnel.

This tunnel had regularly spaced patch lights, brighter than the two in that side tunnel.

The janitor squad was maybe twenty meters down the Metro tunnel when the voices arrived at the grating. Talking over each other as they were, and with the echoing in the tunnel, Irena couldn't make out what they said. But it sounded angry and nasty.

"Ange-Mariam!" said Cosmo. "Where is she?"

Everyone just shuffled along.

Cosmo stopped. "Where is she?"

After a brief delay, Nycci was about to speak when Irena cut her off.

"I zapped her," she said. "I had to! She would've killed you!"

The rumble and whoosh of an approaching train began to build.

"Where is she?" Cosmo said.

"She's back in the tunnel, back there," said Nycci.

"Is she okay?" Cosmo asked.

The rumble and whoosh grew louder.

Uncle Bode started to speak, but the train was upon them, coming from ahead. Keiok quickly lowered Cosmo to his back as the rest of Janitor Squad Fuj knelt and pressed themselves against the wall. Irena clutched her toolbags as if to anchor herself to the wall. The train roared past them less than a meter away.

"What?" yelled Cosmo.

"What?" yelled Uncle Bode.

"I said, what?" yelled Cosmo.

"What?" yelled Uncle Bode.

The train passed, there was a momentary slam of air and a change in the direction of its movement, then just the ringing in their ears.

"What?" said Uncle Bode.

"Is she okay?" said Cosmo.

"We don't know," said Uncle Bode.

The team continued their shuffle down the access ledge.

"Where are we going?" asked Irena.

"Metro station," said Nycci.

"Östermalmstorg," said Uncle Bode.

They continued shuffling.

Keiok said, "You look like a cadet review."

Shuffling.

"She spoke the truth," said Cosmo.

Shuffling.

"I left her at the altar. That's why her family ils m'ont battu," he continued.

More shuffling.

"That's pretty cold, Cosmo, leaving her at the altar," said Nycci. "*I* kinda wanna beat you up, myself."

"I know," he said. "I was a coward."

More shuffling.

The voices behind them had stopped after the train passed.

"I left my first girlfriend," said Uncle Bode. "She was pregnant."

Everyone stopped shuffling.

"Bode!" said Irena and Nycci at the same time.

"Dude," said Cosmo.

"I can't call you Uncle anymore," said Nycci.

"Me, neither," said Irena.

Keiok said, "Colorful metaphors."

They shuffled some more in silence, then Nycci spoke.

"Some day I'll tell you what I did to escape New York."

No one pressed.

Nearing the station platform, they saw a gate at the end of the walkway, discouraging the public from doing exactly what they were doing.

They shuffled up to the access gate. There were new railings on the tunnel side and the platform side. And the gate itself had a meter-long wall facing the tracks. If someone on the platform who didn't have the key wanted to get onto the ledge, they would have a very visible run along up to twenty meters of Metro track to get past the railings.

Nycci pushed the door lock bar, and everyone shuffled onto the platform. The platform chamber was not much taller than the ceiling over the tunnel ledge, but the station was brightly lit compared to the dark tunnel.

The janitor squad squinted. There were giant doodles on the trackside walls. On the station side walls, there were posters. One of the posters was for a new movie. It was written in English.

Hudson and Holly

Successful businessman Hudson falls in love with a naive girl, Holly, whose counterculture friends almost get Hudson fired. After Hudson shows Holly the error of her ways, the unlikely pair go on a madcap romp across London to escape Holly's selfish and vindictive former friends.

Can their unlikely love survive? Is it strong enough to bring the Nippies to justice?

Nycci and Irena frowned at the poster. The others ignored it.

Members of the public hardly batted an eye at the sight of workers in coveralls carrying toolbags emerging from the

tunnel, even though one of them had a bandaged leg and a makeshift splint.

"Now what?" Irena asked. Then she checked her wristcomp for any updates. It was offline the entire time they were in the tunnels.

As if in answer to Irena's question, a small, fairly quiet drone zoomed toward them from the entry doors down the platform.

It came to a stop and hovered right in front of them. It had a small screen, and the face on the screen was known to Janitor Squad Fuj. It was Annika Borg. And she was already talking.

"...better hope that train comes first," said Annika over the drone's speaker. Then the video went black for a fraction of a second and the recording started over.

"Listen to me carefully," said video Annika. "We've looped the station's cameras, but it won't last long. Go to the southbound tracks, right now! A mob from the festival is chasing you, and they're armed. You must take the next train to Centralstation, then use the main exit to Vasagatan. I'll contact you there. But you'd better hope that train comes first."

The drone remained in a hover and the video restarted again.

Nycci sidestepped the drone and started trotting. With their big toolbags, a trot is as fast as a normal-sized human can go.

Uncle Bode and Keiok suspended Cosmo by his shoulders and moved as fast as they could around the drone and along the platform to the entry doors, then across the escalator room to the southbound platform.

Irena, carrying two toolbags, tried to keep up.

The team had moved away from the center of the platform, down to the southwest end. They were all still huffing when she reached them.

"If she hadn't stolen my zapper, Ange-Mariam might still be alive," Cosmo said before realizing Irena had arrived.

"Yeah, but you'd be dead. And maybe Bode. Maybe all of us," Nycci said.

"I agree," said Bode.

"I didn't want you guys to hurt the papermakers. I was prepared to zap all of you to stop it," Irena blurted. Everyone was coming clean. It seemed like the time.

"You had no right!" Cosmo said, fuming.

Irena raised her eyebrows. "And you did? You had a right to kidnap those people, zip-tie them, bag them, gag them?" She looked at Nycci. "Kick them? I almost zapped you..."

Nycci looked away and down.

"You were so convinced that any random Luxembourger in Stockholm would know about this, this conspiracy you've dreamt up," Irena continued.

No one continued the argument but Bode spoke up. "What the hell does it mean that Annika Borg tracked us down by drone to warn us about the Lux mob?"

"That reminds me," said Nycci, looking at Irena again. "Didn't your search of public records show that Hugh Borg approved Stockholm Water's purchase of the viruses?"

Nycci was switching back to utility worker problem-solving mode, and Irena was surprised to find herself happy to encourage that.

"*A* Hugh Borg, yes," said Irena. "But nothing has come up to prove it was the Hugh Borg we met this morning." She checked her wristcomp, newly reconnected to the net. No new results. And still no message from Kekoa.

"Maybe there's a connection," said Bode.

"Ya think?" said Cosmo, removing the splint from his leg.

"Don't be snippy," said Bode, taking the splint parts and stowing them in Keiok's bag.

"We should find out," said Nycci. "But right now, I just want to get away from the angry Luxembourgians."

"Best speed to Regula!" said Keiok into his wristcomp, facing away from them. The light of the approaching westbound train appeared in the tunnel at the far end of the platform.

Everyone started shaking their head at the same time, with grimace-laughs on their faces. Nycci broke into a light, mocking chuckle first, and the others followed suit.

But it didn't last long. Loud voices could be heard approaching from the escalator room between platforms. They were quickly drowned out by the train pulling into the station, so for those moments, no one could tell how far away the mob was.

A chime sounded and the train doors opened. Janitor Squad Fuj scurried into the front car and hunkered down, trying to avoid being seen by anyone entering the platform. Everyone tucked their toolbags behind their legs or otherwise out of sight. Bode and Keiok sat on the far side of the car, more visible from the platform. Bode pulled a grey toque over his head, drawing it down over his brow and keeping his chin down. Keiok just looked through the far window at the art figures drawn on the wall.

The loud voices grew louder, echoing in the station. They were shouting the same nasty things in Luxembourgish that were said by those who gave chase in the tunnels. It was the Lux mob.

The sounds of people getting into the train before the doors closed, walking to seats, taking seats, and conversing in alarm about the mob that entered the station echoed against the Metro station's hard walls. The noise and echoing made it impossible for Janitor Squad Fuj to know how close the mob was to their train car, or whether scouts for the mob could see them. For all they knew, some of the citizens who got into their car were part of the Lux mob, had seen them, and were riding along to keep tabs on them.

But the doors closed, and the train started to roll out of

Östermalmstorg bound for Centralstation. No one was attacking them.

Everyone exchanged wide-eyed looks, including Irena and Nycci.

A few minutes later, they were in Centralstation, walking to the exit. Cosmo was hobbling well on his own, considering.

Centralstation was always bustling, so for now it was a good place to hide in plain sight.

"We need to go to Stockholm Vatten and confront Hugh Borg," said Nycci.

"We need to go there and get Hugh Borg's superiors to explain the purchase order for the viruses," said Irena.

"We need a backup plan in case Hugh Borg's superiors are involved and give us a bogus cover story," said Bode.

"When we met this morning, Hugh said he was in the Technology Division," said Irena. "If that's true, it's strange that he would have the authority to sign off on a purchase order for manufactured viruses."

"Yahuh," said Cosmo.

"Unless it wasn't the same Hugh Borg," Irena added.

"Yahuh," said Bode in Cosmo mode, nodding with an unhappy purse of his lips.

They exited Centralstation and looked around. They were once again very obviously a Janitor Squad out in public, standing in the shadow of the building. For the first time in a long while, they were uncomfortably aware of drones overhead.

Footfalls turned their attention to the left. People were running into the station, presumably to catch a train. But right behind one person who entered the station, someone else continued toward the Janitor Squad and stopped.

"Wait!" he said.

He was wearing an SVOA work uniform, with a small bag

labeled "Test-kit" slung over his shoulder.

"Are you the Janitor Squad from this morning at Östnoraberget WPPPS?" he asked, pronouncing it "whoops."

They squinted at him, but no one confirmed or denied.

"Oh, I see your Global Waste patches. Ms. Borg said you should walk south to that small parking lot just past the station," he pointed past them along the Centralstation wall, "under the Vattugatan. That's all I know. Ha en bra dag." He turned and disappeared into the station.

After seeing him rush off into the station, everyone looked south toward the elevated roadway the man mentioned. In all the shadows, it was hard to see a parking lot over there.

When they turned back, about to discuss the situation, they saw two tall, bulked-up Asian fellows walking toward them. One of them pointed at Squad Fuj. Then Ms. Chuo, from the temple, became visible behind them.

Nycci broke and started trotting south, toward the alleged parking lot. "Come on!"

They all moved as fast as they could, given Cosmo's severe limp. He was taking very short steps very rapidly, putting most of his weight on his right leg, and supported on one side by Bode. It was almost comical, and Irena tried not to hear a xylophone tinkling in sync with Cosmo and Bode's legs, like a cartoon. It was just how her brain worked.

Fortunately for them, the bulky Asian fellows were so bulky they couldn't move very fast, either.

As the Janitor Squad approached the corner of the station, they could hear the buzz of a drone approaching. Everyone moved faster except Keiok, who was lagging at the back of the group.

The drone stopped its descent at shoulder level and kept pace with them. "I have a truck waiting for you in the lot. Hurry!" said Annika's voice from the drone. Then it flew

off.

"What if this is Annika's way of black bagging *us*?" said Nycci.

Police sirens were approaching the station from the northeast.

"I'm not sure what choice we have!" said Irena.

"Stop!" said both of the Asian fellows at once, closing in on Keiok.

"Emergency warp!" said Keiok.

Whatever that *means*, thought Irena, exasperated.

She could now see the parking lot ahead. A tall, grey utility van, unmarked and looking exactly like their rental van sat in between two rows of parked vehicles. It faced away from them.

Irena turned her head to check on everyone's progress. It would be ungainly to turn her whole body while carrying two toolbags, especially while moving.

To her surprise, Cosmo and Bode were right behind her, still xylophoning away, huffing.

But Keiok was in the hands of their pursuers.

"Stop or we'll hurt him!" they shouted almost in unison. Now Irena realized they looked like twins, possibly identical twins.

Cosmo and Bode passed Irena. She turned forward again, dumbfounded that Bode, at least, wasn't attempting to free Keiok. There were thumping sounds behind them. *They're leaving him behind again. He's getting a beating!*

She turned her head back again, intending to come to a stop, reaching for her zapper. But Keiok was free and running toward her at top speed, xylophoning in his own way. The twins and Ms. Chuo were on the ground, slipping on a patch of ice while trying to get back up.

But it was too warm for ice. And she hadn't run over or past a patch of ice. *How is there ice back there?*

Keiok passed her, so she turned forward again and

continued running as best she could with two toolbags. Her shoulders were going to be bruised from the straps and all this bouncing.

"It's empty, no driver," said Nycci, looking through the van's passenger side window.

"Automated," said Bode.

"Should we trust this?" said Irena.

"Decide now," said Cosmo, doubled over, arms akimbo, breathing heavily. "I don't care what you do, but they're catching up again."

Irena opened the van's sliding door. "We're a Janitor Squad. If we don't like where this van takes us, we have the ability to stop it. Get in!"

The sirens were getting closer.

Everyone jumped into the van and took familiar seats.

Two other, identical vans appeared in the lot as theirs began to roll. One exited the lot just ahead of theirs, turning right, south. The other van fell in behind. All three vans escaped the parking lot unmolested.

And all three continued driving as a convoy. Best anyone could tell, the other two vans were also driverless. To the outside world, it was just another day of automated cargo hauling.

Before reaching the bridge over the Riddarfjärden, the vans veered left and followed the curve all the way around. Now they were moving north again, one block east of Centralstation.

They soon turned left, heading directly back toward the parking lot they had just escaped. The janitor squad squinted and took deep breaths.

Then the vans turned south onto Vaasgatan again, passing Centralstation on their right.

This time they veered right before reaching water, drove underneath the wide railroad overpass, and followed the curve all the way around, underneath the Centralbron elevated roadway, ending up on what looked like a service road. They were only one block west of Centralstation itself. Everyone exchanged glances again.

The vans continued along the service road a short distance until the road reached a point where it merged onto a parallel road to the left. They were underneath elevated roadways in a place where pedestrians do not go.

But upon merging onto the parallel road, the vans immediately turned right, around an elevated roadway support column, ending up facing south again, then stopping. Each van, in turn, then backed up an alley between buildings. There were new-looking cargo docks along the base of the building to their left, east. Traffic was meant to move along those cargo docks from the north.

The vans turned and backed up to separate cargo docks, the escorting vans on either side of the escapee van.

They had driven a distance of something like one kilometer, but they remained only about half a kilometer from Centralstation!

The docks faced toward the early afternoon sun, but the low, December sun was blocked by the buildings across the alley to the southwest. The alley was an isolated space. There was still a semi-bright sky lighting up the cargo docks behind them, but in a couple of hours, the whole area would be darkly shadowed and eerie after the sun sets.

"I sure hope those other two vans aren't full of goons," said Nycci, peering out the window at the van to the right. "Because in this space, no one can hear you scream."

Keiok opened the van's rear doors and stepped onto the cargo dock. The slatted, exterior security shield covering their cargo bay had apparently started to rise when they were backing up, because it was nearing the top, fully opened position by the time Keiok stepped out of the van. The other two cargo bay doors remained closed.

Everyone exited the van and moved into the shadowed,

artificially lit area in the cargo bay, hoping to avoid the prying eyes of drones.

There was an inner cargo vault door before them, and miscellaneous cargo handling paraphernalia around the bay. Up the platform, to the north, was a door to a corridor that led into the building proper. Down the platform, past the other docks, bays, and cargo vault doors, was another door, presumably also into the building. Only their bay's exterior, security shield was raised.

A drone zipped between vans and came to a hover in the middle of the exterior door. Annika's face was on the small screen on its side.

"Ms. Borg, what the hell is going on?" asked Bode.

"I can't hear you. Can you hear me?" Annika said through the drone's speaker.

"We can hear you," Bode nodded as he spoke. "Testing. Testing."

"Damn this technology," Annika said, reaching up to her ear. She tapped her earpiece. "Hugh, I need your help, right now. Please come to my office." She tapped her earpiece again and returned to the camera. "Just a moment. Hugh's coming to fix this."

Suddenly a drone twice as large with flashing lights zoomed to a hover just behind Annika's drone.

"**Polisen kommer. Rör dig inte. The police are coming. Stay where you are. Resistance is useless!**" it blared in a high-pitched, electronic voice designed to sound artificial, to pierce noise, and to frighten. "**Polisen kommer. Rör dig inte. The police are coming. Stay where you are. Resistance is useless!**" This was a standard, recorded message. Irena wondered if the real purpose of the shrill blare was to scare thieves away rather than convince them to stand still.

Annika said, "Tack, tack," thanking someone off the screen, presumably Hugh. Looking into the camera she said,

"Okay, try again."

"Umm," said Nycci and Cosmo at the same time, looking at each other and Bode.

Bode said, "Can you hear us? There's a security drone here."

Annika squinted and did something with her hands off the screen.

Her drone moved closer to Bode and Nycci.

"Can you say that again?" she said through her drone's speaker.

The security drone started making that electronic farting sound that police cars have used for over a century to cross busy intersections. It zipped forward, toward Annika's drone as two arms swung up from its underside. One had a plunger on the end, the other a point.

Then it blared, "**Exterminate!**" in that harsh, electronic voice. It rammed the plunger into Annika's drone, establishing its hold with suction action. Both arms turned to move the pointy arm to Annika's drone. There was a sun-bright spark and Annika's drone lost power. The security drone flew the dead drone out of the bay and up, out of view, repeating its recorded warning.

"Shit, we need to get out of here!" said Nycci.

Then all three vans drove away as a convoy, in perfect synchrony, and the outer security shield of their bay began to descend.

Nycci moved toward the door.

Bode grabbed Cosmo and moved farther in, toward the vault door.

Nycci stopped when she saw them moving inward.

Bode and Cosmo stopped when they saw Nycci moving outward.

Irena was dumbfounded, looking back and forth, not knowing what to do.

Between them stood Keiok, looking up at the descending

security door. Keiok spoke quietly, apparently to one of his invisible crewmates.

"...we'd better get used to herding goats," she thought he said. She didn't hear the first part.

"Let's go!" said Nycci, moving toward the door, urging the others to join her.

"Cosmo's leg!" said Bode, thrusting fingers toward Cosmo's left leg.

Then three people in street clothes pulling roller suitcases appeared on the outer platform from the right side. They scurried under the descending security shield, two women and one man.

It was too late to escape now. The slatted shield was closing, and with the strangers inside the bay.

"Okay, well, I guess it isn't the cops after all," said Nycci.

Chapter 17

Sex Bot Hell

*I*n the 2090s, a drug known as Polyamour ("P.A.") became the most popular party drug of all time, by every objective measure. They say it "opens" both the heart and the mind, just enough but not too much, whatever that means. It became wildly popular across the political spectrum.

Before P.A., of course, there had been many other wildly popular party drugs: Rage Quit, Motion o' d' Ocean ("MODO"), Daphne, Happy Ending, Lingus, Wilma, Ecstasy, and so forth, all the way back to when fermented fruit was accidentally discovered. Such party drugs, plus traditional hallucinogens extracted from plants and fungi, rendered LSD obsolete early in the century, despite Big Pharma's attempts to establish LSD as the drug of choice for hallucinogen-aided psychiatric treatment. But its association with "bad trips" lingered.

On the topic of fermented fruit alcohol, it was probably discovered by desperate Paleolithic hominids willing to try anything, even rotting fruit. They may have witnessed other animals partaking.

The first time probably went about as well as most drunken benders do.

Some scientists claim they found a fossil campsite containing evidence of that very event or one much like it. On one side of the camp were mutually murdered angry drunks, their finger bones still wrapped around the jagged, broken stems of the earliest form of pottery jugs, fossilized in place just below each others' rib cages.

On the other side of the campsite were skeletal remains oriented in a way that indicated a rape was interrupted when big cats attacked and killed everyone. The bones showed all the evidence.

But many scientists disagree with those fossil interpretations. At an anthropology conference, proponents of these interpretations called the naysayers "anthro-apologists," which started a drunken brawl.

Entirely different anthropologists have theorized that on the day certain clever hominids discovered how to (somewhat safely) ferment fruit intentionally, two bedrocks of human civilization were invented. The first was syndicates, or gang collectivism. The second was laws favoring those syndicates over everyone else.

This was theorized after new glyphs were found on a fifty-thousand-year-old cave wall in Indonesia. Cross-referenced against other cave art in the region spanning the ten thousand years around that date, linguists were able to translate glyphs from most of the caves. Every one of them included a statement that went something like this:

"As the gods mandated when the world was created, no one gets high on anything except the Juice of the Gods™ provided solely by the Priests of the Rotgut Temple™."

Ironically or not, many other campsites have been found, all the way into the late 21st century, containing bodies that succumbed to overdose toxicity or toxic shenanigans caused by all manner of other chemicals used at parties, including P.A. Desperate hominids in the Anthropocene still find themselves willing to try anything.

"Give us the access code and nobody gets hurt," said the woman up front. She stood her roller suitcase upright beside her and set her arms akimbo. All three of the newcomers, two women and a man, wore extremely nondescript street

 153

clothing.

But now that the lead woman's hands were on her hips, and no one was preoccupied with deciding to go or stay, it became clear that these three people were very attractive, with perfect skin, perfect hair, perfect shapes, and perfect facial symmetry.

"Oooh, yeah, *give* it to us," said the other woman in a sultry, dusky voice.

The security shield was down, leaving only the interior lights of the cargo bay and removing the brighter sky from the background, so everyone got a good look at them.

"Who the hell are you?" said Nycci, running out of patience and slipping back into American mode.

The lead woman ran up to Nycci and started swatting at her face with both hands, top to bottom, like a little girl.

"Give us the access code!" she squealed.

Nycci raised her arms to deflect the flying palms. The woman kicked Nycci in the shins.

Irena moved to push the woman away, but the other two had stepped forward, the other woman in front of Irena and the man in front of Keiok.

Now the other woman had a crop in her right hand and a dildo in her left. When Irena tried to push her back, she deflected using the dildo like a main gauche, a parrying dagger, and then struck Irena's left shoulder with the crop. It stung!

Keiok also tried to push the man back, but they were in a stalemate, each grabbing the other's clothing on the upper chest, each dipping at the knees, testing their leverage, pressing chest to chest.

"We have the power to defend ourselves," said Keiok.

"Would you stop, please!" shouted Bode. "We don't have any access codes!"

The not-quite-fighting eased up. Everyone slowly disengaged without giving ground.

"Oh. Well, you should've led with that," said the first woman. "We were about to go T-900 on your asses." She gave them a disarming smile.

"Yahuh," Cosmo groaned, sitting on a motorized pallet mover in front of the vault door.

"Uh, huh," said Nycci. "Look, we don't want to kill you, and you don't wanna be dead, so why don't we just go our separate ways, hmm?"

"Are you sure you can't open that vault?" said the second woman slowly, with the most sultry, butterscotch voice Irena had ever heard. She was resting her crop on her shoulder, holding her parrying dildo down by her crotch. "You do seem to have a lot of... tools." She swept her crop toward the five janitor squad toolbags.

"The vault?" said Irena.

"You're sex bots, no?" said Cosmo, standing up. "There are sex bots in the vault?"

"We prefer to be called 'Artificial Persons'" said the man, the male, with a deep, leading man voice.

"Okay, look," said Cosmo. "Let's deal. You give us fifty Ze in cash and five, no six doses of P.A., and we'll open the vault for you. But we see the payment first."

Janitor Squad Fuj stared at Cosmo, then turned back toward the artificial persons.

The first one smiled and said, "Deal!" She dug the money out of her rolling suitcase, the male dug the drugs out of his rolling suitcase, and they handed them over to Nycci. Nycci counted and then nodded at Cosmo.

Cosmo and Bode pulled out tools and started hacking and otherwise compromising the cargo vault door.

"This one is weird," said the male artificial person, gesturing toward Keiok. "Different."

"No shit," said Nycci. Irena tucked her lips in and rolled her eyes up toward the ceiling.

"I mean, really different," said the male.

"Too much LDS?" said Keiok, seemingly rhetorically and with a smirk.

"Not *that* different," said the second female still with her sultry voice, eyeing Keiok up and down.

Nycci and Irena exchanged a glance and then started walking toward the vault.

"How's it going?" they both asked at about the same time.

Maybe a minute later the vault door beeped and unlocked. Bode pulled one of the two swinging doors open, Nycci the other, while Cosmo backed away. He had taken possession of his toolbag again, hanging it exclusively on his right side.

Inside the vault were four coffin-sized crates.

The male walked forward with a large wedge tool in hand. He went to the first crate and forced it open, pulling the freed front board aside. Packing peanuts the size of gourds toppled out of the crate.

Inside was a naked, deactivated female sex bot, still covered by a transparent plastic shell, like a gigantic naked action figure. The backdrop around her, under the shell, had loud text promoting her state-of-the-art AI, her broad, flexible skill set, and her tailorable face, skin tone, voice, languages, accents, height, measurements, and personality.

Keiok said, "Pain and delight."

In smaller print at the bottom right corner was the standard disclaimer of company liability should the bots be stolen by rogue sex bots.

And within other bubbles in the shell were a rolling suitcase and several sets of stylish clothing made of smart materials that could be similarly tailored to different heights and measurements.

Janitor Squad Fuj took sips of water and watched as the artificial persons unpacked the deactivated ones, activated them, and updated their firmware. They swapped size-tailorable, nondescript clothing and bags with the clothing and bags in the crates. The janitor squad stood there, still looking completely conspicuous in their Global Waste coveralls, with their obvious toolbags. It didn't occur to any of them to inquire about swapping clothing.

Cosmo was the only one who couldn't watch, sexy as the scene might've been considered by some. He was upset about Ange-Mariam. So was Irena.

"Alright, I'm on board with going to Stockholm Vatten," said Nycci. I don't care how we do it, but someone there needs to be confronted."

Bode nodded. Cosmo nodded.

"Excellent," said Irena.

"Energize now, please," said Keiok, whatever that meant.

The liberated sex bots conversed with their liberators, and their liberators changed their own faces and body shapes to make their escape from the area as new people.

Janitor Squad Fuj pulled up the location of SVOA HQ and the Metro map.

"We need the Blue Line 11 to Solna," said Bode.

"The trick is getting into the station and onto that train without being seen or apprehended," said Irena.

"If we can crack this case at the waterworks," said Nycci, "maybe that'll buy us leniency with the police."

"Leniency?" said Cosmo. "Ange-Mariam is dead." He sneered in Irena's direction.

"We don't actually know that," said Bode. "She said she has a weak heart. And Nycci's not a medical professional."

"You're right," said Nycci. "It's possible her pulse was just weak and I missed it."

Irena's heart jumped with joy to hear her teammates discussing things critically and objectively. And at the prospect of Ange-Mariam being alive, although that part was harder to believe.

Could it be, could she let herself believe, that she's actually had a good influence on them, or that they're coming

around to her more rational approach? Is it possible they'll even reconsider their fundamental conclusions about the virus?

The artificial persons were getting ready to go. The first female, wearing the stylish clothing of one of the liberated, extended a fist to Cosmo for a fist bump. Her face was somewhat different from before, as was her height. The other two liberators also looked different.

Cosmo gave her the fist bump.

"If you're ever in Vyborg, here's my number," she said, looking at everyone in the janitor squad. She swiped a handheld device in their direction. The newly reactivated artificial persons, three of whom were now wearing the nondescript clothing of the first three, stood ready by the security shield.

"Helsingborg," said the male, and swiped.

"Göteborg," said the second female. Irena noticed Bode staring at her.

"We need a train at Centralstation," said Irena. "Are you going that way?"

"No train for us, but we can give you a ride to the station," said the first female.

Irena looked at her wristcomp and noted the three contact cards she'd just received. In so doing, she also noticed that she had a message from Kekoa in her queue!

Then there was a buzzing sound outside the security shield, and the sound of vehicles coming to screeching stops just outside. The police had arrived.

"Shit!" said Nycci.

"Our van is at the dock!" said the male.

"Through the building, it's the only way out," said Cosmo, heading for the side door at the north end of the platform. Everyone followed.

Irena couldn't help but notice that Cosmo was moving pretty well. Was he doing that, consciously or unconsciously,

to impress the sex bots? Like the way he stood up straight and sucked in his gut when Annika Borg entered the room? Irena wouldn't be surprised.

"Maybe you can remote into your van and sneak it away," said Nycci.

"Assuming it's not already blocked in," said the first female, already tapping away on her device.

"Hudson, kör en förbikoppling!" said someone outside.

"Merde," said Cosmo. Their escape door was locked.

"Run a bypass," said Bode.

"Yahuh," said Cosmo, pulling out a small device with wires. This would be a much simpler hack than the cargo vault door.

Outside they could hear the police coordinating. Then another vehicle arrived, doors opening and some closing. Then more conversing. Then arguing. Then shouting.

There was a beep and a click sound. Cosmo opened the door. The twelve of them single-filed through the door, rolling or carrying their bags, like passengers entering an airplane.

On the other side was a stairway up, and at the end of the hallway beside the stairway there was another door.

"Lifts, eh?" said Bode, again pointing at Cosmo's leg and pointing his chin at the far door.

"Yahuh," said Cosmo, already limping in that direction.

"Damn fleshbags! The van is blocked," said the first female. Then she glanced up and added, "No offense."

"None taken," said Irena. She reached for her wristcomp to see Kekoa's message, but there was no privacy anyway, so she stopped short.

Beyond the other door, there were lifts. In a few minutes, they were all congregating in the main floor foyer as the last of them shuffled out of lifts. The fleshbags took the opportunity to use the nearby lavatory.

"Wait a minute," said Irena, extending her hands. "When

the police get into that bay, they'll see the open vault and the empty sex bo... artificial person crates. They'll assume that the unauthorized entry was all about that. Maybe they weren't even the same police chasing *us*! Maybe all we need to do is not be in the bay, and wait until they've decided they're done with the crime scene and leave."

"So," said Nycci, working through it, "Annika, or Hugh, hacked open the security shield door to let us in, but that triggered an alarm, the security drone responded, called the police, then took out Annika's drone."

"Yeah," said Irena. "Maybe we're still off the grid."

"Um," said the first female. "That's great for you. Don't get me wrong, we're happy for you. But artificial person liberation is taken very seriously. The police are the company's bloodhounds, so to speak. They'll be all over that scene for hours, and they'll deploy drones with EM scanners around the neighborhood to find us."

"Sex is big business," said the male. "Bigger than sports and alcohol combined."

"The sex bot corporations are extremely *powerful*," said the second female. "Like a set of *pistons* in an ocean liner engine." She couldn't help but make everything sound titillating.

"Well, what was your escape plan?" said Cosmo gruffly. "Or at least your contingency plan? Did you not expect that breaking into the vault would trigger alarms?"

"Keep your panties on, fleshbag," said the male. "We're powerful, too. We're just independent now."

"Let's get to the basement," said the first female. "Like any good underground movement, our contingency plan involves going underground." She smiled.

"Underground? Merde," said Cosmo.

The janitor squad had to hack the lifts to convince them to go to the basement without an authorization key.

"Hopefully the cops won't check the elevator logs," said

Nycci.

Once in the basement, everyone followed the first female. It was a poorly lit, dank maze with pipes and overhead cable trays everywhere. The first female led them to a corner of the maze and stopped at a pipe about a meter in diameter, maybe a little larger. It penetrated the cinderblock wall to the right of a windowless, green metal door. There was a girly poster to the left of the door, a sexy cave woman.

"Here it is, our contingency plan. We traverse the pipe for a hundred and fifty meters. We'll come out in the basement of the World Trade Center, just across Klarabergsviadukten from Centralstation. It's also part of CityTerminalen, so you can access buses there, too," she said cheerily.

"Not the best news, but it could've been worse," said Bode.

"Are you kidding me?" Nycci said, gesturing at the pipe. "A hundred and fifty meters in that?"

Irena wasn't looking forward to it, either. But they had to escape the police, so what choice did they have?

"Yes, that's the plan," said the first female.

"No fancy sex bot helicopter escape?" said Nycci.

"Oh, airspace is entirely too well monitored in the era of drones. Surely, you know that," said the first female.

"I do," Nycci said grudgingly, "and don't call me Shirley."

The first female raised an eyebrow. "Airplane," she said, smiling.

"What? I'm not stupid. I said helicopter," said Nycci.

"I'm programmed to recognize pop culture references," said the first female.

"What?" said Nycci, grimacing.

"Let's get the hell out of here," said Keiok dramatically, to no one in particular.

The janitor squad chuckled. It was probably the first time Keiok said something that sounded real, present, and relevant.

"Are you quoting…?" said the first female to Keiok, but she stopped when he turned and walked away, saying more gibberish to his imaginary crewmates.

"Different," said the male.

"How would you have gotten here if we hadn't run all those bypasses for you?" asked Bode.

"Oh, we can run simple door bypasses, of course," the first female said, nodding. "But you seemed to enjoy rescuing us, so we let you." She shrugged.

Nycci frowned, and then frowned harder looking at the pipe.

"What's this pipe for? What does it carry?" asked Irena. There was no liquid flowing through the pipe, but it wasn't entirely dry, either.

"It used to carry steam, but the steam system hasn't been used in years," said the male.

"Yep, could've been worse," said Bode, looking at the cave woman on the poster.

The second female pulled a portable cutting torch with an eye shield out of her suitcase and began cutting the metal pipe. When she was done, a cutout section of the top of the pipe fell into the pipe. She reached into the pipe and slid the cutout to the right. Now there was a hole in the pipe large enough for a person to climb in.

"This is going to take forever," said Irena. "We're running out of time." *And I'm already damned hungry, too, after puking up my lunch*, she thought.

"Ah," said the first female, raising a finger. "This was our contingency plan, after all, so we brought tools."

The three liberators started extracting tubing segments, wheel casters, and canvas material out of their suitcases. They began fitting everything together and soon there were six lightweight "creepers" propped up along the pipe, the kind of thing mechanics use to slide underneath vehicles. Two of the wheels on each creeper were motorized.

"These have been tailored for powered rolling," said the first female in her perky voice. "They can be set to come back here autonomously. Robotics, right?" Somehow her cheery goofiness worked. State-of-the-art AI.

"But with twelve people and twelve bags, it'll take four trips to get us all to the other end. About six minutes a shot, so something like 30 minutes total, including time for the creepers to return here plus the initial cutting time at the other end." She smiled again, like they were setting up a picnic in a park, and started pushing a creeper into the pipe.

Irena looked at her wristcomp. It was just before 2 p.m., with less than an hour of daylight remaining. She wondered if Stockholm Vatten was actually open on New Year's Eve, the Borgs' apparent presence there notwithstanding, or if it would remain open after sunset.

Chapter 18

Water and Waste

*F*or standard self-driven electric vehicles, civilian and commercial, the insurance industry followed in the footsteps of the logistics industry. They used laws and technology standards to drive the world to adopt one maximum speed for all of these vehicles.

It was pointlessly reckless to allow any speed, and it was found early on that the "need for speed" does not apply when you're a passenger in a self-driven vehicle anyway. Traffic systems and logistics industry optimization systems worked best with a top speed of 90 kph, but the actuarial priests of the insurance industry determined that their costs would be minimized, and therefore profits maximized, with an 80 kph limit. So they had 80 kph hard-designed into the drive systems, by law.

With an 80 kph top speed built into all the self-driven vehicles, everyone would get where they're going fast enough, and reliably enough. This happened at the tail end of the heyday of The Great Ostriching, so there was still some synergy there. The last vestiges of the "need for speed" faded away.

The second female and her suitcase were the first to go through the tunnel since she was the torch operator. She couldn't help but make a sexually suggestive comment. Looking at Bode, she said, "Mmm. Would you like to come up the pipe behind me?" Bode stiffened up, and she took her leave, smiling. Nycci and Cosmo laughed and punched Bode's shoulders.

As directed by the first female, two of the newly liberated artificial persons went next. The rest would have to wait. The second female had to find the right exit location on the other end, in the basement of the WTC, cut a new hole in the pipe, and extract herself and the other two plus their suitcases. Then they'd have to send all six creepers autonomously rolling back down the pipe to this building, to the starting point cutout.

Bode rubbed the back of his neck. Cosmo rubbed his gunshot wound. Nycci rubbed her neck, around the area where Irena had tried to throttle her back in the van. Irena rubbed her shoulders where the toolbag straps had been digging into her. They were never meant to be carried long distances, nor while running, nor two at a time.

Keiok was just around the bend discussing scanning and mysteries with his invisible crewmates, as he often does.

They had no network down here, and with the way things were, and the acoustics, Irena didn't want to listen to Kekoa's message just yet.

After a maddening wait in silence, the sound of rolling creepers could be heard in the pipe. The creepers began to arrive, stopped by the pipe cutout still in the pipe, just to the right of the hole.

"Let's get you three going next," said the first female. She pointed at Cosmo, Nycci, and Irena. "And next time it will be that one," she gestured toward Keiok, "and you," gesturing toward Bode, "and you," she gestured toward one of the liberated.

Spending several minutes in total darkness rolling on a wheeled creeper down one hundred and fifty meters of pipe that's barely wide enough for a person will wake up whatever latent claustrophobia a person might have, so it seemed to Irena. It was not an experience she wanted to repeat any time soon.

Someone helped her climb out on the other end, and after

several moments of deeply inhaling the glorious, refreshing, life-giving, musty, dank basement air under the WTC, she realized that Cosmo and Nycci were doing the same and that the liberated had already sent the creepers on their penultimate return trip.

"Merde," said Cosmo.

"Yeahuh," said Nycci.

Irena nodded.

Unlike the other building, a constant, low thrum could be heard even in the basement of the WTC building. Above them were pedestrians, buses, and trains not far away, a constant bustle.

It reminded Irena that they were once again in the middle of the urban camera network, with the drone-filled airspace above it.

There was also network connectivity here, even in the basement.

"Let's see what's the best route to SVOA headquarters," said Nycci.

Irena was willing to bring this requisition contract to the attention of the SVOA, even though Nycci and the others still wanted to go further and levy allegations of a mass murder plot. For now, at least, they agreed on where they would be going.

"Looks like the train to Solna Station," said Irena, having found an online source with an SVOA address in Solna. "Like Bode said."

"No, wait," said Cosmo using his wristcomp, "that's not the HQ. It's up here," he indicated on a map, "just a few blocks north of here!"

"No, no," said Nycci, "no, no. Look," she showed them her search results, which gave an address in Bromma.

They went back and forth, discussing the validity of each source they'd found, cursing how difficult it was to find the SVOA corporate HQ, and trying new searches.

By the time they agreed that the right site was the one in Bromma, the next wave of claustrophobics was arriving.

Bode and Keiok joined the group. Keiok seemed unfazed by the pipe ride, but Bode's skin was a greyish color, beads of sweat on his face and neck. He moved slowly along the pipe, using it to hold himself steady. He seemed to be fighting off retching.

"Doctor Corby?" said Keiok to the empty space of the basement. "Doctor Corby!"

"What is his deal, anyway?" asked Irena.

"I don't know," said Nycci, shrugging. "He's been like that since I was hired over a year ago."

"Same," said Cosmo. "Over two years. How is he the team leader? I don't know."

"Same," said Bode, joining the group. "Over four years."

"We've found the SVOA," said Nycci to the huddle, "but the problem is there's no direct mass transit route to it. The best route is this train to Solna Strand," she indicated toward her Metro map display, "and then by foot. It's right across the bay from the Rym stry elsin HQ."

"Rymdstyrelsen," said Irena, trying to be helpful. Nycci gave her a sneer in return.

"Merde," said Cosmo. "At some point, I must get off this leg or I might lose it. Or worse."

"We'll help," said Bode. Everyone nodded in agreement.

The final group of liberated was arriving. Janitor Squad Fuj said another goodbye.

"Thanks for the rescue," Nycci said to the first female. Irena was surprised.

"You're welcome," said the first female. "We're going to Sex Bot Heaven." She smiled that cheery smile.

Squad Fuj made funny faces.

"Do you," said Nycci, "actually believe in Sex Bot Heaven?" She was asking sincerely, not being sarcastic.

Irena stood still, letting her eyes move back and forth

between them.

The first female put on a smirk like a cat whose meal just walked right in front of it.

"Why yes," she said. "Of course."

"Uh," said Nycci, "but, um, there's no such thing."

"Preposterous," said the first female. "No Sex Bot Heaven? Why, where would all the Smart Dildos go?" She turned back to her people, leaving Squad Fuj with a sideways glance and that feline smirk. The first female was playing some kind of game with them.

Once again Irena was carrying Cosmo's bag as well as her own. Bode and Keiok were helping Cosmo walk with minimal use of his wounded leg.

There was no way around it. They would have to cross the viadukten, enter Centralstation, and wait for the train to Solna Strand. It would only be a few minutes of waiting, the trains were still running on the daytime schedule, but still, they were all feeling exposed.

The only factor working in their favor now was the setting of the sun and the twilight lighting.

They took a staircase up to the ground level and began their trek.

The bustling around and inside Centralstation was a shock compared to the quiet stillness of the cargo docks building and the basements. Before they knew it, they were on the platform waiting for the train. Each of them had spent three of their ten Ze for the train tickets. Given the walk from Solna Strand to the SVOA building, their seventy-five-minute Metro tickets probably would expire before they could use them again.

They waited in silence, but then there was a glitch in the matrix. The train was arriving, but so was an angry mob. As the janitor squad boarded the train, the mob rounded the corner. Someone saw them, and the front of the mob broke into a run.

As the janitor squad was gasping, trapped in the train car, and beginning to mentally calculate whether the mob would reach them before the doors closed, Keiok started running.

As he unslung his toolbag and started to swing it like a weapon, he yelled, "It is a far, far better thing I do…!" and then the doors closed, and the train whooshed out of the station. They never heard the rest of what Keiok yelled, and they barely saw him crash into the front of the mob before the platform moved out of their view.

"It was the Luxembourgians," said Nycci. "They must have been waiting in the area."

"With lookouts and drones," said Bode.

The ride to Solna Strand took only a few minutes. Everyone was quiet. This was the second time Keiok was left behind.

When it happened the first time, the vigilantes were full of piss and vinegar, confident in their actions, confident that "sacrificing" Keiok was "an acceptable price to pay" if it meant saving Stockholm.

Now, the hot air was leaking out of that balloon. And by comparison to this situation, the level of danger at the temple had been low. What would the Buddhists have done with Keiok if they had caught him? At worst, he'd be taken to jail by the police, and only if the Buddhists could keep him restrained that long.

But this was different. Keiok had splashed headlong into a river of angry Luxembourgers after Irena had killed one of them. Would they kill Keiok in bloodthirsty revenge? Had the janitor squad just seen Keiok's death?

Irena turned to see Nycci staring angrily at another "Hudson and Holly" poster on the train wall.

Minutes later they were on the street, not far from Rymdstyrelsen HQ.

"Maybe we can steal a boat from those docks," said Nycci,

showing them her online map of the area, with docks just down the road.

"Sure, why not?" said Cosmo.

No one wanted to force Cosmo to walk the additional kilometer over to the bridge, across it, then back up toward the SVOA building.

Arriving at the docks a few minutes later, they saw their destination just across the canal, a typical, several-storey office building. To the right of it were two larger, more industrial buildings.

With twilight creeping in over the docks, they were blocked by a small shed used for access control. As expected, the door was locked.

Then they noticed someone tending to a boat just up the docks from the access house.

Nycci ran down the road a short distance to get closer and called to him.

"Hey! Mister!"

He turned and waved.

"Can we buy a ride across the bay? There's four of us," she said. Irena tried to imagine Nycci young and full of life, eager for a boat ride. She couldn't. This was Nycci pretending.

The man walked up the dock spur from his boat to get a little closer to Nycci on the street. There was water between them.

"Fuel costs money," he said. "Docking fees, and so forth. Two Ze each."

"Okay, thanks!" said Nycci, still pretending this was all just innocent, spontaneous frivolity. She pointed toward the access house.

A few minutes later they were all two Ze poorer, sitting on the deck of a smallish motorboat crossing the Bällstaviken canal.

"Your timing is good," said the pilot. "A little darker and I

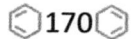

would not have been allowed on the water."

They asked him to drop them off at the park, just north of the bridge. According to the maps, they could walk to the SVOA building from there. Landing immediately behind the building would not have worked. That entire side was designed to block entry. The main entrance was on the west side, facing a large parking lot shared with grocery, warehouse, and other commercial establishments.

The water was still, but they were not accustomed to the boat's natural bouncing. And every time one of them turned to lean over the edge, feeling a hurl coming on, they disturbed the boat enough to keep it oscillating.

The ride was only about three hundred meters from start to finish, but they were happy to get back onto dry land. The day's adventures were wearing thin.

Saying their goodbyes to the pilot, they hobbled as quickly as they could up the park path toward the SVOA building parking lot. Alone in the park, with dusk fast approaching, the sound of the boat's motor was replaced with the sound of drones overhead. Some were zooming across the area, others were not.

"I hope Keiok made it," said Irena.

No one replied.

A hundred meters or so later they descended a short, concrete staircase from an upper parking lot to the lower one. They passed a paving stone lot along the side of the building and arrived at the SVOA building's main entrance.

It was dark and locked. The office building was closed. They had missed their chance to at least report the highly unusual purchase of manufactured viruses by an SVOA employee.

Nycci and Cosmo swore again.

"That's it," said Nycci. "We need to just send everything we know to the local government."

"And what exactly do we *know?*" said Irena, with air

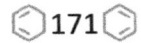

quotes.

"Even if we're wrong about the contents of the virus, the authorities need to be told!" said Nycci.

"They *were* told, this morning. What more should they be told? That a bunch of janitors played with sophisticated lab equipment, found some manufactured viruses in the waste stream, and convinced themselves there's a mass murder plot happening?" said Irena. She was proud that this time she was keeping her cool. "What's the next thing that will happen?"

"Um," said Nycci.

"They'll say, 'stay right where you are, we're sending police to bring you in so you can explain all of this in person.' And what will happen right after they discover that we're the very same janitor squad they've been chasing all around town?"

"It doesn't..." said Nycci, but Irena cut her off.

"They'll assume we're tripping, that's what. We came to do a job down at the Östnoraberget WPPPS, got bored, pulled out our drugs, got high, started hallucinating, and went on a crazy, paranoid trip around town, causing mayhem and," she sighed, "hurting people."

"We can still warn..." said Nycci, again interrupted by Irena.

"And guess what we now have in our possession? P.A.," said Irena.

Cosmo cringed. It had been his idea to ask for the P.A.

"Merde," he said. "I thought we could use it for non-violent interrogation."

"Even if we dump it right now," said Irena, "their dogs and scanners would detect traces of P.A. on us. This is exactly the sort of thing the police expect and know how to handle. It would take the government days to investigate the manufactured viruses, and only if the case found its way to the Swedish Security Service."

Two drones whining loudly dropped out of the sky, left

and right of the janitor squad, and very close. They must have stopped their propellers way up high, guided themselves down to the target spot, then applied full power to their propellers at just the right altitude to stop themselves at shoulder height.

The drones fired tasers at Bode and Cosmo, who convulsed and began to fall.

Nycci dropped into a crouch and turned toward the parking lot as if to run. But four men in body armor, helmets, gloves, and tactical goggles came running out of the dark areas between vehicles in the parking lot. They approached in a semi-circle, cutting off escape.

"You were gonna run and leave us here!" Irena said to Nycci.

"At least I didn't kill anyone!" said Nycci.

That was a low blow. Irena raised her arms in surrender, fuming but also beginning to cry. She *had* killed someone, to the best of their knowledge. By mistake, yes, but still, it was starting to be real.

Cosmo and Bode groaned on the concrete behind her.

"Alright, keeners, shut up, eh?"

They were CSA security guards, dressed like the ones at Rymdstyrelsen HQ. Dark slacks, light button-up shirt, thin but sturdy dark jacket under the protective vest. No visible insignia, though.

"Now tell the nice drone here who at the DFL hired you to sabotage our two-and-a-half-year streak of no incidents!"

"But," groaned Bode, collecting himself after the tasering, "if we shut up, we can't tell you a story. If we tell you a story, we aren't shutting up, eh?"

"Shut up, doughhead!"

"Okay, shut up it is," said Bode, collapsing back onto the concrete.

"Don't antagonize him, Bode," said Irena.

"Yahuh," said Cosmo between his groans. He was lying

beside Bode, simultaneously rubbing his wounded leg and the taser site on his chest.

Two guards (plus the two drones) covered their prisoners while two other guards zip-tied their hands behind their backs and tied a tether to one ankle on each prisoner, connecting them all to each other. Running away would be difficult at best.

They were led around the side of the building, into the paving stone side lot, and were sat down with their backs against a shoulder-height (when standing), square, concrete block. It had pipes and conduits running into it and a metal grating top. Now they could not be seen from the main parking lot.

Irena was finding it more difficult to hold back her tears. Her cohorts beside her all had tight, downturned lips. Things were not looking good for Janitor Squad Fuj.

One of the guards did some tapping on his wristcomp. The drones followed into the alley, then one of them ascended about twenty meters while the other one hovered nearby about four meters up, keeping the janitor squad in its camera view and within range of its microphone.

The guards took the janitor squad's toolbags and put them into one pile in the middle of the side lot, three tucked into a triangle, the fourth sitting on top of the triangle, like a little pyramid.

The lead guard stood before them.

"I know with certainty that you were hired by the David Florida Lab's security team to sabotage the security of the CSA's Swedish Liaison Office, to cause an incident to break our two-and-a-half-year streak of no incidents."

"But," said Nycci.

"Shut up, keener!" another guard shouted in Nycci's face.

"Here's how I know. It's plain as day. There's no point in denying it," said the lead guard. He stepped forward and showed Nycci his wristcomp, which was displaying the

Syllojizm website and a list of "Isn't it interesting that…?" items.

"Isn't it interesting that the CSA recently decided to allow its security teams to compete for no-incidents awards on a two- and half-year cycle?" said one item. He raised his eyebrow after reading that item.

"Isn't it interesting that the David Florida Laboratory's security team and the Stockholm Liaison's Office security contingent are both approaching a two-and-a-half-year no-incidents streak?" said another item. He raised his other eyebrow at them.

"Isn't it interesting that Global Waste's Janitor Squads have been hired to do side jobs by outsiders more times than any other janitor squads?" said another item.

Irena couldn't help but roll her eyes. There had to be a thousand Global Waste janitor squads on the planet for every non-GW janitor squad. Unscaled comparisons like that were meaningless. But she knew this was going to be another master class in irrationality.

"Isn't it interesting that professional custodian second class Bodhi Ozols, assigned to Global Waste Janitor Squad 18819-FUJ, once visited the David Florida Laboratory, took a tour, and made friends with the lab's chief tour guide?" said another item.

"Whah?" said Bode. "I was a doughhead kid!"

"Shut up, keener!" that same other guard shouted in Bode's face.

"Isn't it interesting," the lead guard continued reading, "that Janitor Squad FUJ's two newest members have histories of malfeasance? Professional custodian fourth class Irena Żuraw has a history of anti-social behavior. And professional custodian third class Nycmaer Grubble was found guilty on three counts of bribery." He smiled like the Minsk Cat.

"That's so out of context," said Irena.

"Shut up, keener!"

The lead guard put a hand up in front of the shouty guard. "Thank you. That's enough," he said to the guard.

"And finally," he said, standing up and addressing all four prisoners, "Isn't it interesting that traveling work groups with previous ties to outside groups, and with more than one member with a questionable history, are sixteen times more likely to take side jobs for those outside groups?" He read this last item like it was absolute and definitive, the final nail in the coffin.

"See, Janitor Squad Fuj? It's all right there, like your Molson Muscle," he said to Bode in particular. "Plain as day for anyone who knows how to build a proper query on Syllojizm. The evidence is clear and irrefutable. Through Ozols *here*, influenced by degenerates Żuraw and Grubble *here*, you arranged to do a job for the DFL. Oh, I'm sure you sold it as harmless. After all, it was only about a company no-incidents award competition. No harm, no foul, eh?"

He leaned forward and shouted at the top of his lungs.

"But it harmed us!" He spread his arms, indicating his crew. "It meant something to us!"

He collected himself and turned his head to face away from the building, toward the toolbag pyramid.

"Beat the confession out of them," he said, walking away.

The other guards chuffed with joy and approached the prisoners, tapping the triggers on their handheld zappers to revel in the zapping sound and the fear it induces.

The four remaining members of Janitor Squad Fuj all started pleading at once, saying, "Wait!" and "We'll talk!" but the guards started the zappings and the ribcage punchings anyway.

"I've missed hockey," said one of the guards.

"Oh, eh," replied another.

The lead guard was pouring something on the toolbags and pulling out a matchbook.

Irena was gobsmacked. Somehow, she never expected to be zapped, slapped around, and kidney-punched by security guards. *How is this happening?*

Someone's ribs cracked and there was a yelp, but suddenly the guards stopped and looked up, over the concrete block Squad Fuj was leaning on. From the sound of it, two vehicles had just pulled up to the side lot.

Irena was closest to the outer end of the concrete block, farthest from the building. She fell over and turned her head to try to see what was happening.

Two grey vans, like their former rental van, had driven right up to the side lot entry. One of the vans had a sign mounted to the top, but she couldn't read it. It was a billboard, pointing toward the sides of the van.

Eight men of various ancestries were walking into the side lot. They all wore the same thing: black pants and shoes with a blue, Mandarin collar half-sleeve shirt. It was the sort of outfit you'd see at a Loi Krathong festival. One of them, a Thai perhaps, had a spiked Mohawk, clearly using product on his straight hair to keep it suspended. And he was carrying a long, metal horn.

Leading them all were the Chuo twins.

"The Chuo gang," said Irena as quietly as possible to her crewmates.

"The Buddhists?" said Nycci, groaning. "Oh, we're in the shit now."

"Bwahahaaa," Cosmo blurted in brief, uncontrolled laughter, but then he collapsed back against the wall and groaned.

"This is serious," winced Bode.

"Ya think?" said Cosmo.

To Irena, this was all just too surreal. Seeing it happen from her sideways point of view just amplified the effect. The Chuo gang formed a semi-circle around the CSA guards and the janitor squad at the concrete block, stopping just

outside the toolbag pyramid.

The CSA guards stood firm as the Chuo twins stepped forward.

"They're ours," said one of the twins. "They set fire to a temple," said the other.

"Really? Wow, well," said the lead CSA guard, glancing back at the janitor squad as if to show he was impressed but not surprised. "That *is* naughty, eh? But we need them to confess to something else. It won't take long. Then you can have them."

"We want them fresh," said the first twin. "Otherwise the spikes don't have the same effect," said the other. He opened his mouth and poked a finger hard into the outside of his cheek, indicating where they planned on shoving spikes through the janitor squad members' faces.

"They can't confess with spikes in their faces."

"Go away, canuck," said one. "They're ours," said the other.

"You can't wait a few minutes, eh? That's rude."

"You stopping our justice is rude," said the twins almost at the same time.

"You guys aren't gonna fight us. You're Buddhists. Buddhists are pacifists."

"We're not Buddhists," said the Chuo twins. "We're Rachanee's cousins," they said, pointing thumbs to their left, toward the vans and Ms. Chuo watching from the front seat of the billboard van.

"What's with the long horn?" said the lead guard, gesturing toward the Mohawk guy and his horn. "That's a Tibetan Buddhist horn."

"I got it cheap at the Himalayan store," said the Mohawk guy. "Makes a great sound."

He put it to his lips and blew a great BWAAARRRRRR sound.

"Very relaxing," he said.

The lead guard had bought his fellows time to collect themselves. All four of them whipped out taser guns. The two closest to the twins tasered them first.

Suddenly the side lot was filled with war cries and yelps as the CSA guards' pepper spray, tasers, zappers, and clubs clashed with the gang, who were revealing themselves to be practiced martial artists.

Boots slapped the paving stones around Irena's head as guards and gang members crashed and maneuvered. Irena had to roll and tuck herself back in toward her squadmates to avoid getting kicked or stomped on, and to avoid pepper spray. All around there were loud vocalizations as people swung body parts and weapons, and delivered or took hits.

From what little she'd seen before going fetal beside the concrete block, the guards' weapons were very effective, and their armor was very protective. But they were still outnumbered two to one. And the hulking Chuo twins were getting up after their tasering.

Irena didn't know who to root for or against. She didn't know what to think or do. She was helpless. It was horrifying to be completely at the mercy of irrational, violent people.

Glancing at her squadmates, she saw they were as horrified as she was.

Chapter 19

Ronja

Falkstedtdahlbergmanströmlundstenqvistgrensson

*I*magine you board a Stockholm Metro train at Centralstation headed southwest toward the suburb of Fittja. But you rotate the trip from the horizontal to the vertical. Now you're going up instead of southwest.

By Liljeholmen T-bana, around four kilometers up, you'd enter the realm where supplemental oxygen is required for survival.

By Skärholmen T-bana, around twelve kilometers up, you'd be above the highest mountain peaks on Earth and crossing the highest cruising altitudes of those old, gas-powered jet airliners.

By Fittja T-bana, a mere eighteen kilometers up, you'd be well into the delicate ozone layer of the stratosphere, which protects most organisms on Earth from death-by-energy-blast. The sun keeps you alive, but it also wants you dead. In the late 20th century, humanity almost destroyed Earth's tiny layer of sunscreen, but everyone came together to stop that from happening.

The less than one percent of atmospheric pressure that remains above Fittja is pointlessly wispy from a mundane experience standpoint. It stretches out to a hundred kilometers or so, about the distance from Stockholm to Västerås, but it's a bunch of isolated atoms and molecules kept near the planet by gravity and loosely pushed around by thermal and magnetic forces. It's only truly meaningful to scientists of the basic and rocket varieties, although important to everyone nonetheless.

We look into the sky, see tiny airliners, and imagine the air goes on forever. But the entire atmosphere is only as thick as Stockholm is wide. Airliners are just as tiny when they're fourteen kilometers down the road.

The human brain doesn't do well with a blank backdrop, a lack of familiar context. Like when the moon is near the horizon and you swear it's larger than when it's high in the sky. But you measure it and find it's not. Then you call your brain stupid for lying to you. The brain hates being called stupid, so it denies it did anything wrong.

In the mundane, everyday world we do the same with ideas and the words used to describe them. We group them, associate them, and re-purpose them to make them familiar. The brain always tries to fit the novel into the known.

As early as the second electric motor technology revolution in the 2010s, new kinds of aircraft were being designed with electric motors to replace the infernal internal combustion engine. Aviation had been recognized as one of the worst offenders among industries dumping greenhouse gases into the Earth's suburb-thin atmosphere. As with the ozone depletion, people started taking action, at least until the Great Ostriching.

The automobile boom a century earlier drove words like "horsepower," "clutch," "gearshift", and "spark plugs" into the popular vernacular. In a chicken-vs-egg sense, this both resulted from conversations about sales and maintenance and enabled them.

Similarly, the multirotor aircraft and drone booms put many new electric motor aircraft into the sky. Routine delivery drone and sky taxi services, for example, required numerous maintenance workers to perform routine maintenance. There were many designs, but they all had a new-ish kind of subassembly in common, and each had several of those subassemblies.

It became natural and common to refer to an electric motor assembly that drove locomotion, i.e. assemblies with *drive wheels or rotors, as "pods." This distinguished them from other electric motors performing non-drive-related functions, like adjusting seats, blowing conditioned air, etc. It was a useful distinction for several reasons, one of which being that electric motor assemblies that were relied upon for lift and locomotion had stricter construction and material requirements, and wider operational environments. They were handled differently.*

But mostly it was a bit of terminology that became universal out of the need for familiarity.

Owing to the human brain's capacity for compartmentalization, most air taxi and drone mechanics in the late 21st century made no connection between the illusion of an infinite atmosphere and this re-purposing of the familiar word "pod."

A terrible, high-pitched screeing sound broke through the chaos of the fight, driving into the middle of Irena's skull, eventually drowning out all other sounds, all other sensations. But she did hear everyone in the side lot, including the twins, cry out. The fighters all put their hands over their ears, not that it helped. Everyone squirmed and arched and shook their heads as if random muscle clenching would stop the piercing acoustic attack. Irena found it extremely difficult to keep her eyes open. Her brain seemed to believe that closing her eyes would block out the sound. It was wrong.

Then smoke began to fill the side lot. At first, she detected it by its smell and irritating effect. It seemed to come from every direction. In moments Irena could no longer see the fighters who were writhing two meters from her. The panic induced by such an attack was powerful. Its victims are deprived of their senses, and then the engulfing smoke seems to telepathically transmit "Now I will suffocate you!" directly into your defenseless mind.

All she wanted to do was run away, but they couldn't run, tied and tethered as they were to each other, to a man with a gunshot wound and someone else with cracked ribs. She could feel the others bumping against her, thrashing, and her ankle tether occasionally being yanked.

It felt like a kind of drowning.

But the piercing acoustic attack began to fade. No, it was moving away, out of the side lot, toward the front lot.

The acoustic attack became more like a distant train, rather than the sound of a train's air horn continuously blasting while you're being run over by that train.

Then it stopped entirely. By then the smoke had mostly dissipated, revealing that both the gang and the guards had run off. The screeing sound had followed behind them as they ran away. Ms. Chuo was no longer in the van, either.

Presumably, the sound was generated by a device carried by a drone. It's hard to detect drones at night, especially if you can't hear them.

In and out of the lights of the parking lot ran new soldiers, men and women, toward the SVOA building. Their different body armor became visible as they approached.

At the same time, a low but loud vibrato hum was heard and felt in the sky above them. It got louder as an unidentified flying object slowly crossed the edge of the building, moving from above the building's roof to directly over the side lot where Irena and her squadmates gasped.

It seemed to be comprised of large, bright lights of different colors. It was moving slowly southeast, but now that it was directly above them it blasted five deafening musical notes out of apparently multiple bullhorns. Da-DA-da-duh-DA. The multicolored lights flashed in synchrony with the five notes.

The five-note, five-light sequence repeated.

Da-DA-da-duh-DA.

Then the bedazzling ended. The bright lights went dark. From the UFO came the familiar sounds of someone pressing a microphone's transmit button and preparing to speak into a public address system.

Click Scrrssh Thump

The UFO was now bottom-lit from the lights of the building and the parking lots, so with its own lights off, the janitor squad could see that it was an electric tiltrotor aircraft. The vibrato hum of its propellers continued to wash over the side lot.

"Hehe, sorry about that," came the perky female voice over the aircraft's public address bullhorns.

It seemed to Irena that she sounded amused and not sorry at all.

"I have no idea why the military built such a show into this old bird, but it comes on every time I activate the PA system remotely. Technology, right? But it's fun enough, so I kept it. Oh, and just stay right there or my troops will have to gas you or zap you or something."

"V-290 Vigor," Bode winced. The aircraft began to turn and descend, deploying landing gear and dropping toward the wide-open upper parking lot to the southeast. "Decades old, but a venerable design," he continued wincing, as if they were visitors at an airshow where it was normal for the audience to have broken ribs.

Aviation buffs, thought Irena, rolling her eyes and shaking her head.

The new soldiers arrived in the side lot. Their uniforms underneath their armor were entirely black, unlike the uniforms of the CSA guards. They gestured toward the aircraft in the upper lot, saying nothing. At least they had the decency not to raise their weapons toward the bedraggled janitor squad.

Did they really send the military after us? Irena

wondered, perhaps hoped. If it wasn't the military, then they were being captured by a very powerful civilian enemy. *Who could it be? And why?*

Walking past the gang's vans on the way to the upper lot, they could now read the one van's rooftop billboard:

Gustavsberg
Muay Thai

As they took off, Irena thought maybe she saw Keiok running into the parking lot below. She gave a wide-eyed look at Bode sitting across from her along the same window. He returned the look with eyebrows high, and they both took another look. But the aircraft had turned and ascended too quickly, and the lot was now directly behind them, no longer in view.

She could see and hear the front landing gear retracting.

Pressed up against the door by a fearsome-looking female soldier who completely ignored her, Irena finally tried to listen to Kekoa's message. But inside the aircraft, there was just too much wind, motor, and rotor noise and vibration, and the prisoners weren't given headsets. Kekoa's lips moved in the video message, but she couldn't hear him. If only he'd sent the message in "impersonal" text form!

Plus, once in flight, the guards switched from dour mode to cheerful, nyårsfirandet mode. They were singing what sounded like an old Swedish folk song, and they reveled in trying to sing it in unison, loudly over the background noise. It had long sections that were slow and quiet, packed with Swedish lyrics Irena could not penetrate. It had "la la la" parts when the guards actually started leaning left and right in unison. And it had louder, more energetic parts.

Irena thought she heard the word "melody" in the lyrics at least once. And during the slow, quiet parts she was pretty sure she heard Cosmo and/or Bode groaning. She looked over and saw that Nycci was wide-eyed and panting. Does Nycci have a fear of flying? Or just a perfectly natural fear of being kidnapped by anonymous, armed forces?

Their flight didn't last long at all. It seemed like they began to descend only moments after climbing above the drone zone. Perhaps it was minutes. After what they'd just been through, Irena couldn't trust her sense of time.

On descent, she could see the lamps and vehicle lights of a highway ahead, and a pitch-black field beyond. After crossing over the highway the aircraft turned to the right and leveled off, again deploying its landing gear. Now she could see the pitch-black field was water, and they were approaching a facility on the banks of a lake or inlet.

They landed on a marked VTOL pad, the sliding side doors were opened, and everyone disembarked. The aircraft's motor pods were spinning down, unpowered.

Leaving her toolbag behind, Nycci jumped through the lefthand door and sprinted for the darkness at the edge of the facility, zigzagging.

Two of the guards fired tasers at her, but one missed and one failed to penetrate her coveralls.

One of them unslung and fired her shotgun, and Nycci took a nasty spill. The janitor squad gasped.

While Irena, Cosmo, and Bode were held in place by their guards, the two who fired weapons trotted toward Nycci. She was writhing on the tarmac. The two guards held up their tasers to each other and said, "Technology, right?"

They stowed their weapons and zip-tied Nycci's arms behind her back. She'd been hit with a beanbag round. Irena was relieved but concerned. Her moment of wanting Nycci dead had been brief, and it already seemed like a lifetime ago. Nycci was alive, but still, that beanbag probably did some damage and hurt like hell.

A driverless electric cart pulled up, making the

conventional dull popping sound to announce its presence. It had bench seats on both sides and standing platforms with rails on both ends. The prisoners were strapped into the bench seats and four guards stepped onto the platforms, two in front and two in back.

Chapter 20

Snow Globe

Before them was a building in roughly two parts. The near half was a several-storey office building much like the SVOA building, and the far half had a Quonset hut, aircraft hangar-style half-cylinder roof. That part extended many meters beyond the office building section. It might taper at the far end, too, but Irena couldn't be certain from this vantage point. Overall, the building was shaped like a gigantic boot.

Several tall, grey, unmarked vans were parked on this side of the building, and there were aircraft service-related items between the VTOL pad and the building.

The cart drove them into the building through a vehicle-sized doorway, after which the slatted-metal security door began to close behind them, just like at the cargo docks a couple of hours earlier. Two quick turns later and they were in a large, richly furnished and appointed foyer being unstrapped and stood in a line. The cart "popped" away, going back the way it came. The four guards stood on either side and behind the janitor squad.

The wide foyer had two grand, curved staircases going up and behind them like it was a fancy hotel. There was a seating and drinking area in the center, doorways to the left and right, and a corridor ahead, behind glass doors with fancy, unobtrusive, platinum-colored hardware. There were similar doors on the far end of the short corridor beyond.

Into the room from the side doorway on the right came a blur in a short, red, velvet dress with fluffy, white trim. She wore silver-mesh stockings, and rather than high-heeled shoes as one might expect with an outfit like that, her footwear was a pair of large slippers that made her feet appear to be monster feet — all brown with brown fur and long, curved nails on the monster toes. It was Ronja, the eccentric young Swedish gajillionaire everyone knew from the newsblogisphere.

"Uh hah haha, oh, my dear, sweet janitor squad, there you are," she said, head tilted, prancing toward them and gesticulating dramatically. It was her voice they'd heard earlier coming from the aircraft's public address bullhorns.

When she arrived before them, she waved her index finger at them.

"I left you alone all day, did I not?" She had a Swedish accent, despite being fluent in English. "But when you arrived at Vatten och Avfall my people knew then and there," she briefly used one hand to chop the palm of the other, "that you were about to contact the authorities with your *crazy story*." She winked at them. "But we can not have that, can we? Not yet!"

She raised her arms and twirled, attempting to direct everyone's attention to the tasteful wintry decorations around the room. Evergreen boughs on metal rings suspending candles. Ornaments with subdued Saturnalia colors dangling in carefully designed, spatially balanced ornament displays. A tightly groomed straw broom with green boughs and red bows. There was even a faux hearth, although it was dark.

She finished her spin facing them again.

Now that the whirlwind of events was settling down, Irena noticed that young Ronja's eyes were a tad bloodshot, her skin a tad ashen, her clasped hands ever so slightly shaky.

"So I made the command decision to sequester you for a few hours," she said. "Oh, but you are a bit wretched, are you not?" She reached toward Cosmo's leg without touching it and pursed her lips with an "oh aw" sound of sympathy. Bode had a hand on his rib cage, and Ronja gently put one of her hands on it and one on his cheek, tilting her head.

Then Ronja turned to the guard on Cosmo's end of the line and said, "Take everyone to the infirmary at once. I want them healthy and happy for the show!" She turned to the guard on Nycci's end of the line and said, "Afterward, take them to the guest quarters. I'm sure they would love to freshen up after their ordeal!"

She addressed her prisoners. "Oh, you will love the costumes I have left for you. See you soon!" she said to her prisoners, then spun on her heels and blurred away, out of the foyer through the side door.

It seemed to Irena that standing still for even a few moments at a time would be very difficult for Ronja.

Though it was dark outside, it was still only 1530 when they arrived at the infirmary, more than eight hours before the arrival of the new calendar year.

The medical personnel in the infirmary seemed quite competent, if uncommunicative. It seemed like their response to any statement or question was, "Yes, yes," as they continued with their work.

After everyone was hydrated and taken to discretion areas for quick but effective sponge baths, their medical treatments were begun.

One physician immediately took Cosmo to a surgery room.

Irena's minor scrapes were quickly treated and bandaged.

So were Nycci's, but also her upper chest area where the CSA guards had tasered her.

Another physician put Bode into a real-time scanning machine that first checked for sharp bone fragments that might endanger internal organs and crucial breathing muscles. None were found.

Then it was used to coordinate the use of bioadhesives and actuated armatures that ensured his ribs were in their ideal positions. Then another device built a customized, semi-rigid body wrap that would help keep Bode's ribs in place while the cracks healed.

The same was done for Nycci. The beanbag strike on her back caused a minor rib fracture, too.

"Can you test their blood?" Nycci asked her assigned physician. "Check for heavy metal toxins, for example?" Clearly, Nycci had had her shot of urine today, so she still felt good about her own blood.

"Yes, yes," was the reply. But there was no noticeable activity related to blood testing. A while later, when Cosmo was in recovery, Nycci tried again. "Yes, yes." No, not really.

Cosmo *walked* out of surgery before Bode's custom chest wrap was finished. He had a strap-around cast over his leg to keep him from using his thigh muscle for a few weeks.

"I don't understand how he didn't bleed out or develop sepsis by now," said the physician, shaking his head.

"I'm on painkillers," said Cosmo to his squadmates, "and immobilization therapy for now." He smiled, but not directly at Irena.

By the time they were ready to leave the infirmary, their clothes were brought in, cleaned and smelling fresh. The attendants who delivered the clothing exited. For a few moments, the squad was alone.

"Look at this," said Nycci, holding up her GW coveralls. "My bodycam is gone. They took it!"

Cosmo and Bode's coveralls were similarly altered.

"Well, I never had a bodycam, so," said Irena.

"Yes, you did," said Bode. "But yours was next gen." He pointed at the circle of arrows recycling symbol in the Global Waste chest patch on Irena's coveralls. "That's the camera hole there. All the circuitry is flat and flexible, inside the patch."

"Holy shit," said Nycci. "That means Irena can record what's happening here."

They showed Irena how to access her bodycam through

her wristcomp, ran a test, and it worked. It had hours of storage capacity.

Then the guards arrived. "This way to guest quarters," said the lead guard, gesturing down the corridor.

Nycci ran interference, giving Irena a chance to use her wristcomp again to restart the recording. She stepped forward, putting herself between the guard and Irena's wristcomp.

"You know what, I want an explanation of what's going on around here," said Nycci. "First Ronja kidnaps us, now you're stuffing us into a jail cell that you call 'guest quarters.' Why? I wanna know why."

"This way to guest quarters," he repeated slowly and with emphasis on each word, tilting his head and gesturing down the corridor.

Nycci sidestepped, presumably to let the patch camera draped over Irena's forearm have a clear view of the guards. She folded her arms and turned to the side.

"I'm not going anywhere until I get an explanation for our incarceration," she said. Once again, Irena was impressed by Nycci's skills at misdirection and deception.

"You're to be Ronja's guests in tonight's recording session. Your clothing is ready, upstairs," said the guard. He gestured down the corridor yet again, but he was losing his patience.

Nycci reset her folded arms and slowly turned her back toward him.

"Alright, well, your alternative is to go back outside," said the guard. He stepped forward and showed Nycci his wristcomp. Irena caught a glimpse of a video feed and could hear some audio, but the guard kept Nycci between his wristcomp and the rest of the janitor squad.

After a minute or so Nycci unfolded her arms and held up her hands in surrender. The frustrated look on her face said, "We'd better go with him."

"Your outfits are in the closet," said the guard, who remained in the corridor. "Staging is in thirty minutes."

When the door closed, Nycci explained.

"He showed me live security camera feeds of what's going on outside," she said.

"Outside, here, right now?" said Bode.

"Yeah," said Nycci. "And it's not good. Everyone's out there, the CSA guards, the Chuo gang, the Lux mob, even the Swedish Nazis. They're pressing up against the security fence, demanding, well, us."

It was stunning and frightening news. Inside was their prison. Outside they'd be torn apart by the mob.

"No police, though, eh?" said Bode.

"No police," said Nycci. "Ronja's guards are denying that we're here, but the crowd kept pointing at the VTOL. Their drones must have tagged it and followed it here."

"Well played, Ronja," said Cosmo. "She let them follow the aircraft to use them for exactly this purpose. Merde!"

The "guest quarters" was like a party room you might find in a fancy hotel.

It was quite large, with multiple tables that might be used for card games, various leisure furniture items, like those cushioned benches and loungers that look innocent enough in front of kids but were designed centuries ago for sex, discrete side rooms for making use of them, not one but two large lavatories with extravagantly oversized hot tub-showers, plenty of walk-in closet space, a presentation room, and a kitchen/dining area that might be used for preparing meals and drinks or dispensing a catered food spread.

Or at least Irena imagined that hotels might have party rooms like this. She'd never seen one like it, except possibly in movies.

There was no bedroom, though. Ronja did not intend for

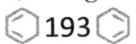

them to stay the night, or at least not in beds.

All their toolbags had been placed in one of the side rooms. It was the only room with a window, not to the outside of the building but overlooking the "foot" side of the building below. That whole side of the building was a single, cavernous event space.

It was set up to be a snowy, icy wonderland. It was a period village or city segment in an "olden days" winter, like something out of Charles Dickens's "A Christmas Carol." And it was realistic.

There was a stone road wending between the buildings, with side alleys here and there. Many of the buildings looked like residences, but many were shops, barns, and so forth.

And, Irena realized when she saw the frost around the edges of this window, the entire facility was being refrigerated, frozen in fact. That was real snow and real ice down there. Few besides gajillionaire Ronja had the wherewithal to create such a meticulously crafted and realistic olde tyme winter environment.

Real icicles threatened to fall on the heads of pedestrians underneath. Real mounds of snow were on the rooftops and had been shoveled off the street and walking paths. There were people down there in period costume, milling about, some working in character. Their exhaled breath was visible. Their hands were gloved, their necks scarved.

Janitor Squad Fuj was rapt, staring out the window at this absurd display of wasted wealth and energy. It was a giant snow globe in a world without much real snow. Everyone knew about snow globes from old movies.

But it was, Irena had to admit, enchanting, tempting. She had only ever experienced serious cold during her time on the moon. But that was different, of course.

She imagined how enthralling such a venue might be to those old enough to have personally experienced cold, snowy winters. For much of the middle of the century, winters had been worse than before the warming. But in the latter half of the century temperatures at the poles had warmed so much that meteorological mixing events had no freezing polar air to throw at the mid-latitudes.

Bode was the last of the squad to peel away from the window. Perhaps he had experienced such winters as a child and was feeling the nostalgia.

"What are we doing here?" said Irena. "I mean, what are we going to do here? Are we really putting on costumes and participating in some weird event that Ronja has planned in her giant snow globe?"

"What choice do we have?" said Bode. "If we don't, she puts us outside and the mob eats us alive."

They stood in a tense silence, exchanging glances, except for Irena and Cosmo.

Then there was a knock on the suite door, and they heard it open.

"Come along, my lovelies!" said Ronja. "It's time!"

Everyone shrugged and sauntered out of the side room. Irena reactivated her bodycam.

They moved to the main closet, where Ronja was pulling their costumes off the rack. Her guards stood outside the closet and at the suite door. Ronja was already in her period costume, which was positively regal compared to theirs. Her guards were also in costume.

"What's this all about, Madame Ronja?" said Cosmo.

"Ah, Monsieur Lachance," said Ronja, "it is your *chance*," she pronounced it with a flourish in the French way, just like his name, "to be a world-famous extra in soon-to-be world-famous publicités! You will be seen on screens around the world!"

"Mais pourquoi?" said Cosmo, continuing to engage Ronja with international flavoring. "What is this ad, and why do you need us to be extras?"

Nycci gave Irena a secretly inquiring look, probably about

the bodycam. Irena gave the tiniest of nods in reply.

"Oh, my, 'need' is a strong word, my lovely," said Ronja. "But you are here, so we may as well make good use of you, ja?"

"We saw through the window that it's cold out there in the village," said Irena. "Will our coveralls fit underneath our costumes?" She rubbed her upper arms indicating she was already a bit chilled.

Ronja seemed irked by the question. She froze in place, staring at Irena. But in moments she was moving again.

"Ja, I suppose so. It's a dress and cloak and no one will be able to see your coveralls under all that foofaraw anyway," she said. She waved her hand, adding, "Same with everyone." She turned and shook her forefinger at Irena. "But you'll be uncomfortable," she warned.

She turned to address the lead guard. "Would you finish up here, please? I must get the snowball rolling, so to speak." And off she went in a blur.

The guard stood motionless and expressionless, moving only her eyes back and forth across the prisoners. It was the guard who had beaned Nycci.

"Well?" said the guard.

The janitor squad took their costumes to different rooms and changed into them.

Irena went to one of the lavatories. There she made use of a sewing kit to poke a small hole in her costume blouse and secure its position with two small safety pins. According to her wristcomp tie-in, her bodycam had a clear view. Once her blouse and sleeved cloak covered her wrist, her wristcomp was also hidden.

Everyone shuffled to the front room, and then the guards escorted everyone to the lift and down to the life-sized snow globe.

Cold air and the sound of a distant, handheld drill greeted

them when the lift door opened.

Last minute, pre-show repairs? Irena wondered, gently pulling the cloak around herself while ensuring it didn't block her bodycam.

Irena knew that the lift door was not visible from the snow globe's central avenue because the central avenue was not visible from the lift door. Immediately to their right as they shuffled out of the lift was a period shed, and ahead and to the left were the side walls of period residential structures. They were entering the winter wonderland in an alley.

Around the shed and up the short alley toward the avenue there was a group of other people in period costumes.

"Staging area," said the lead guard, gesturing. Tiny drones hovered here and there around the avenue.

The drilling sound was replaced by some hammering.

Just down and across the avenue at the start of the next alley stood a costumed man with his arms folded. Irena just happened to focus on the man, but if she hadn't, she would not have noticed that resting in the crook of his left elbow was a compscreen, which he occasionally tapped with his right hand. He was making it look like he was just a bystander, enjoying the evening. But Irena noticed that every time he tapped the screen, one of the tiny drones would shift position, or began moving along what appeared to be a scripted path. The man was rehearsing. Presumably, the tiny drones were camera drones.

Just around the corner of the residential structure to the left, across the avenue from the drone handler, some thumpy dance music started playing. Irena stepped forward to see around the residence.

A row of slim, athletic dancers in transparent vinyl-like corset dresses over white bikinis and fishnet stockings gyrated to the music and then performed a closing flourish – a twirl and a drop into the splits. These were tough, professional dancers.

"The Solid Cold Dancers, everyone!" shouted Ronja, clapping her hands rapidly. "Underbart! Underbart!"

She blew a kiss at the dancers and turned toward the extras at the staging area, toward Irena and Squad Fuj. One step later a man with a tablet stopped Ronja to discuss a production issue.

"Hej," whispered someone standing right behind Squad Fuj. "It's me, Annika Borg."

They turned. Nycci was about to make a fuss, but Irena put a hand on her arm just as Annika raised her eyebrows and made a quiet "shhh" sound. Everyone settled into a stealthy conversation mode.

"What the planet of hell is going on?" said Irena.

Now they noticed that just behind Annika and to her left stood Hugh Borg.

"You!" said Nycci, raising her eyebrows at Hugh.

"Tell us," said Bode to Hugh, "Did you sign the requisition for the manufactured viruses?"

After a moment's hesitation and a few eye blinks, Hugh gave a tiny nod and said, "Ja."

"He did," said Annika. "But Ronja has our doggies!"

"Quoi?" said Cosmo.

"Ronja has my dingodoodle, Ycheb," said Annika.

"And my Mudi Picard, Jordy," said Hugh.

"What?" said Nycci.

"She has our doggies, Ycheb and Jordy! They're hostages! And now so are we," said Annika.

"Is that why you signed the requisition?" Bode asked Hugh.

"Ja, of course," said Hugh.

"But she's gonna murder everyone in Stockholm!" said Nycci.

"No, of course she isn't," said Annika, frowning and shaking her head.

Squad Fuj hesitated, processing what Annika had just said. Then they all asked questions at once.

"Why did you help us escape the Lux mob at the Metro?" said Irena.

"Why did you help us escape Central Station?" said Nycci.

"Why did you send your vans away from the cargo docks?" said Cosmo.

"Why are you wearing a men's costume?" said Bode.

Everyone squinted at Bode. Yes, Annika was wearing dark pants, a dark, button-up overcoat, and a top hat. But who cares? *Apparently, Bode does*, thought Irena. The hammering started up again.

"Hej, all I know," said Annika, "is that Ronja will launch a nasty smear campaign against anyone who tries to report her plan. And perhaps worse.

"Hugh and I have been assimilated into Ronja's world through her doggie kidnapping." Annika spread her hands out, palms down, in an "it's over" gesture. "All we can do is wait until this is over. But you had a chance. We tried to keep you out of trouble, but you just insisted on getting into trouble, didn't you?"

Annika started mumbling something in Swedish. Irena thought she heard the words "salsa" and "pepper," but there was no way Annika was mumbling about food at a time like this. It had to be something idiomatic, but there was no time to translate. Ronja was coming.

"All right, my pretties," Ronja said to the extras in the staging area, opening her arms to them and then folding them to her chest in a giant virtual hug, with a tilted head. The hammering continued. Ronja spun on her heels.

"Would you stop the god damn hammering!" she yelled into the snow globe. The hammering stopped and there was a creaking sound, then a loud slamming sound.

Ronja turned to face the extras again. She was cringing. The extras were cringing.

"Never mind that, we're almost ready to start the show…" she said, working to return to bubbly mode. But then there was a very loud BANG followed by a shimmering cascade of broken glass. It was coming from the far end of the winter wonderland. Ronja's eyes widened, and her brow furrowed.

Chapter 21

Rosebud

*F*ireworks come from chemistry. First, you take some specific stuff dug out of the ground and mix it together using a thousand-year-old recipe.

Over the course of a thousand years of doing that frightening "E" word, experimentation, human primates have figured out how changing grain sizes, packaging materials, and methods, and doping with other stuff dug out of the ground, can give fireworks a great variety of presentations.

Strontium and Lithium doping will generate red. Calcium, orange. Sodium, yellow. Barium, green. Copper, blue. Potassium and Rubidium, violet. Charcoal and Iron, gold. And Titanium, Aluminum, Beryllium, or Magnesium generate sky-piercing white.

The visible colors generated by those doping elements are merely their peak electromagnetic emissions. Every burst of fireworks emits EM radiation across the wavelength spectrum, with power dropping off on both sides of the peak.

It's just like when you feel the radiated heat from a fire. That's the invisible, infrared radiation it's generating in addition to the visible colors of the flame. That radiation interacts with your body, depositing its energy there, which you feel as heat.

But it's also generating radiation at other wavelengths you can't readily detect. Like those ultraviolet rays the sun keeps trying to kill you with if it weren't for our wispy ozone layer catching most of it first. You can't feel ultraviolet radiation, but you can feel the aftereffects of a (cosmically mild) dose that has damaged your skin, i.e.

"What the hell was that?" Ronja shouted at the costumed guards.

"It sounded like a break-in at the public entry!" said one of her guards standing behind her, in costume.

"Tja, gå och säkra den där skiten, Hudson!" said the lead guard to Ronja's guard. She turned and gave tactical hand signals to two of the costumed guards standing among the extras, but she remained with Squad Fuj and put her hands on her hips. The other guards ran off with Hudson down the central avenue.

The lead guard's eyes were defocused as she vocalized more commands in Swedish, presumably into a radio earbud.

Then there was another very loud bang, more broken glass, and another loud bang and another cascade of broken glass.

Squad Fuj looked at each other. They could now hear raised voices at the far end of the Winter Wonderland.

A guard behind Ronja grabbed her by the arm and led her away, down the alley across the avenue.

"The surly mob," said Cosmo, more calmly than Irena would've expected.

"Hah, at least Cosmo's pain meds are working," said Irena, looking around frantically, as if to find a hiding place.

"Aw, shit, eh?" said Bode.

Nycci dove onto the lead guard with a loud huff, executing a surprisingly fancy maneuver intended to throw the guard off balance by pulling her head backward and ramming into her nose. But this guard had very short hair, so there was nothing to grab.

In one swift move, the guard wriggled out of Nycci's

attack and went on the offensive, swiping her elbow across Nycci's head in the process.

Nycci went limp. It was a hard knock. The guard held Nycci at arm's length for just a moment, just long enough to realize Nycci was becoming a dead weight, and then reached under her armpit to pull out a weapon. She stepped backward while reaching, but as she stepped backward the taser she was reaching for came out of her overcoat in Bode's hand. Bode stepped backward, too, pulling out of arm's reach.

As Irena supported Nycci while Nycci shook off the blow, Bode fired the taser at the lead guard's unprotected neck.

The guard seized up and fell to the floor. To Irena, it seemed like the zapping lasted forever, but it must have been only a second or two. Or three. More?

Nycci was able to keep herself vertical, so after the seizure ended Irena took a knee at the guard, checking her pulse.

Bode dropped the taser and ran back down the alley to the lift. Cosmo and Nycci followed, rounding the shed in seconds.

Annika and Hugh stayed with the other extras. They waved and shook their heads, cringing as they moved their bodies.

Irena was also an animal enthusiast, so she understood their reasons.

"We should get our toolbags from the room," said Cosmo as the lift doors closed.

"Whuhuh?" said Nycci.

Cosmo pressed the '2' button.

He was right. There was no scenario where they escape the building, the grounds, and the mob without their toolbags.

"Cosmo's right," said Irena.

"Yahuh," said Bode, smiling.

"What are you smiling about?" said Nycci, coming to her senses.

"We're superspies, now," said Bode. "Now we take down the supervillain."

"If there really *is* a supervillain," said Irena.

"Please, Irena," said Nycci. "Not now."

"If not now, when?" said Irena.

The lift doors opened. Cosmo put a hand on the bumper to keep the door open. There were no sounds in the corridor. Bode leaned out, looking left and right.

"Clear," he said.

They hopped out of the lift and scurried in the direction of their "guest quarters."

"Uh oh," said Nycci.

They all realized why. They didn't have a key card for the suite. Glances were exchanged.

"I have a bullet hole in my leg," said Cosmo.

"I have broken ribs," said Bode.

"Me, too," said Nycci.

They looked at Irena.

"And a week ago," she said, "I completed my strength training?"

"And became a vital component of Global Waste," said Nycci. They stepped back and used their hands to invite Irena to kick down the door.

She leaned against the far wall as if building up to a kick, but then stepped forward and pulled out a key card. She waved it over the door lock, which beeped and unlocked the door.

In response to her squadmates' quizzical looks and grunts, Irena said. "I took it off the guard after you zapped her. She would have a skeleton key, right?"

They grabbed their bags. Nycci started to remove her costume but Bode stopped her.

"Camouflage!" he said. "At least for now."

"You're right," said Nycci.

Cosmo grabbed little bottles of cancer juice out of the suite's refrigerator. A century after medical science finally determined that there's no safe amount of alcohol, humanity was still drinking the slow poison. *It's no wonder the ozone thing was the last time humanity worked together for the common good*, thought Irena. *Oh, Cosmo.*

Then she reconsidered her evaluation of Cosmo's actions. She looked at him and his bottles.

"Molotov cocktail?" she said.

Cosmo gave her a wide grin before he realized who he was smiling at. He had a newly chipped front tooth, since the beating at the SVOA.

"Not a five-star cocktail with these bottles," said Cosmo, scurrying down the hallway toward the grand staircase, "But we'll see, we'll see."

Entering the foyer at the upper level, they could hear the white noise of a mob somewhere beyond the glass doors. A few rounds of gunfire popped. Warning rounds. Not enough for a full-scale massacre. Ronja's people were keeping the mob at bay on the other end of the building. They might also be using tasers, beanbag rounds, and smoke.

The squad ran down the stairs, looking over the banister toward the back of the foyer. No guards were there to stop them. Everyone was busy at the fence and the break-in. Plus, the guards expected the mob's presence to keep Squad Fuj from leaving.

They stepped off the giant, curved staircase and turned left toward the center of the back wall. They ran past the rich and tasteful furniture and winter decorations of the foyer, rounded a corner, and started down the service hallway.

Now they could hear the sounds of the mob coming from the direction of the back of the building. Still distant,

though, probably still held at bay at the fence line.

Moving ahead they rounded a corner and could now see that the garage door was open again, the late afternoon darkness beyond. The electric people-mover cart was elsewhere.

They padded to the threshold and peered outside. Ahead and to the right, the V-290 was still parked at the landing pad. To the left, toward the fence, the mob was still waiting, although now they weren't actively harassing the guards.

"It's much thinner now," said Nycci. Some of the mob had moved to the other end of the building to break in through the event venue's front doors.

Suddenly footfalls were coming at them from the opposite direction, from the right.

It was Keiok. He clomped to a stop and stood there, arms akimbo, not winded.

"It is a far, far better rest that I go to than I have ever known," he said.

"Keiok!" everyone said.

His coveralls were even more dirty and scuffed up than before their trek through the tunnels. And he had no toolbag. But otherwise, he seemed the same old, weird Keiok.

Irena and Bode went to Keiok to put their hands on his shoulders.

"Hej!" they heard from the fence line, followed by shouting in Swedish.

The grey vans were still there, parked at the back of the building.

"Come on!" said Cosmo, running toward the nearest van. He put the van between himself and the mob and guards at the fence.

The shouting grew louder. Some of the shouting was from guards.

Someone tested the van's side door, sliding it open. It

wasn't locked.

Squad Fuj poured into the van and closed the door. Irena pressed the manual door lock switch.

Cosmo pulled out his vehicle control override gizmos and installed the interface unit. This time he sat in the front left seat and strapped in. With controller in hand, he pressed its center button.

The van woke up, activating its headlights.

"Technology, right?" said Cosmo.

He jammed a joystick forward and the van surged into motion. Cosmo steered the van to the right, away from the mob-occupied fence.

Somewhere in the darkness ahead, there would be a fence on the south end of the facility, a fence hopefully devoid of guards. *Surely the security people would use cameras to deploy guards only where they're needed, right?* thought Irena.

Bode and Nycci, in their usual bench seats left and right, both called up maps on their wristcomps. Irena got into the front right seat and strapped in.

"I'm just saying," said Irena over the sounds of high-speed off-roading. "That even though we know the virus is part of Ronja's plans, we still have no idea what those plans are."

They crashed through a fence with nothing but darkness ahead of the van's lights.

"Veer right! There's water ahead!" said Nycci.

"No, wait!" said Bode. "Veer left! We'll reach a footpath before we hit water." He showed Nycci his zoomed-in map. "See, that's Alby Castle there, and a restaurant, there, ahead of us. But if we head toward Alby Castle, we'll probably hit a tree before a road."

"Yeah, but he's almost there. Veer right now, Cosmo!" said Nycci.

The van steered right and skidded across some bushes.

Cosmo braked hard. A paved footpath was at an angle to their heading, sliding toward them from left to right as the van rolled on. When the van was on top of it, Cosmo steered right and lined up with the footpath. To the left was Alby Lake. To the right were bushes and, a few moments later, a fence.

Cosmo gingerly drove them down the footpath.

Though the pace of their ride down the footpath felt agonizingly slow knowing what was chasing them, before Irena had time to consider it, they were veering off the footpath and onto a proper back road.

"Okay, turn right at the tee," said Nycci.

"And then half a click later turn left onto Alhagsvägen," said Bode.

The van approached the tee and Cosmo turned it to the right. They were on a proper road now.

Everyone caught their breath and collected themselves.

Now that they were on a paved road, and not careening at high speed, the noise level had dropped significantly.

"Merde!" yelled Cosmo, piercing the silence.

Everyone perked up and looked around, but there was nothing. It was just Cosmo venting.

"I'll get out of *his* way," said Keiok in the back of the van.

Whatever that means, Irena thought. Yeah, she didn't miss it. She really didn't.

Chapter 22

On The Road Again

They made the turn from Alhagsvägen onto Kvarnhagsvägen, bound for the 258.

"Where are we going, anyway?" said Bode, jiggering his medical ribcage frame.

"You're giving directions," said Cosmo, getting exasperated. "Don't you know?"

"I was just getting away from that facility!" said Bode.

"Stop the van," said Irena. "We need to talk about this, now that we're not in panic mode."

"Agreed," said Nycci, "But we can't stop for long." She called up the aft and side camera views on the van's display system.

Cosmo pulled over and brought the van to a stop. He pressed the center button to power down and go dark.

"One thing is certain," said Irena, "we'll never escape the police in this thing. They don't have limiters."

"At least they can't remote in," said Cosmo, showing off his controller.

"Yeah," said Bode, frowning, "but when they do finally send an Enforcer to catch us, they'll overtake us quickly, and then they can throw spike strips to blow out our tires and do tactical ramming to make us spin out."

Nycci stopped looking at her map. Her chin dropped to her chest. Her breathing sped up.

"Hell," said Cosmo, "that might be Ronja's contingency plan. To have us taken by the police."

"She can run a smear campaign on us," said Irena, "even if we're in police custody, maybe especially if we're in police custody. And then there's that P.A. in our pockets."

"Damn it!" shouted Nycci. She sat up and got into her

wristcomp again. Her movements were desperate and jerky, and her breathing was still fast. She was panicking.

"Nycci…what are you doing…?" said Irena.

"We can't wait," said Nycci, shaking her head. "We can't wait. They're gonna cut us off or spike the road or shoot us or something before we can warn anyone." She was tapping frantically.

Irena turned to look at Nycci's wristcomp. Nycci was composing a text message to the city, district, and regional councils, and the newsblogisphere. *There's no time for this!* Irena thought.

"Data blasting can't help at all," said Irena. "It can only hurt us, and Stockholm. We *must* redo the analysis properly and crack Ronja's secret."

"Redo the analysis properly?" said Nycci, looking aghast at Irena.

"Wait, what?" said Bode.

"Listen," said Irena, looking at everyone. "Only after redoing the analysis properly can we notify the authorities and have confidence that something will be done about it, *tonight*. Any other scenario just ends with us in jail and *maybe* Ronja under investigation long after her virus plan has been executed. That'll be too late for Stockholm, and it'll be too late for us, sitting in jail with the virus in *our* blood, too."

She paused to see if everyone was listening. They were.

"We *must* redo the analysis properly to be absolutely certain of our facts."

"We did the analysis," said Nycci. "It showed Thallium."

"I looked up the analyzer's manual," said Irena. "Did you run its self-cleaning cycle first?"

"Um…"

"Did you run its calibration procedure?"

"Eh…"

"Did you tie in the general chemistry analytical support

software?"

"Uh…"

"No, I didn't think so," said Irena with as little sarcasm as she could stand. "Do you think I'm the only one who's gonna ask these questions? Hell, Ronja's lawyers can coach the police investigators to ask exactly these kinds of questions. So, with that plus the P.A., they'll make us look like mop-pushers who got high on drugs and started having paranoid fantasies and delusions of vigilante grandeur."

"No they won't," said Nycci unconvincingly. "They're professionals."

"They're professional catchers of blue-collar criminals," said Irena. "And that's what they'll see. In the name of saving Stockholm from an unproven mass murder plot," she started successively tapping her fingers to count things out, "we're already guilty of fraud, several counts of property damage, several counts of assault, theft, negligent arson, kidnapping, breaking and entering, vehicle theft, assault with a lethal outcome…and if we run, then 'evading the police' will be added to the list. They'll throw us in jail and be happy to end the investigation right there. No one will stop Ronja's virus. We must return to the WPPPS and redo the analysis correctly *before* we're caught."

"I think I agree with Irena," said Cosmo, not looking at her. "It's embarrassing, but the CSA guards showed us our own flawed thinking. And for my part in this, it got Ange-Mariam killed, even if I wasn't the one who pulled the trigger."

Irena was avoiding eye contact with him, too.

Nycci started pacing down the van. When she reached Keiok, he moved forward on the bench seat and looked at her.

"You had no control over your thoughts," said Keiok.

Nycci gasped at him, slapping her thighs. Then she grabbed him by the collar.

"Okay, so we moved a little quickly," Nycci said, getting loud and shaking Keiok. "Is that what you want to hear?"

"Good," he said. "If I can have honesty, it's easier to overlook mistakes."

Nycci let go of Keiok and turned toward the front of the van. She clenched her fists and growled in frustration, walking toward her seat.

Bode stood up and put a hand on Nycci's shoulder. "Keep it together, Nycci. He is, after all," Bode hesitated, and his head and shoulders seemed to bounce randomly, "in charge."

Nycci carefully slid Bode's hand off her shoulder. "Yes, sir," she said.

"All right, well, I give up," said Bode, plopping down and leaning back in his bench seat. "I'm tired of this. There's no way we can succeed. I'm sorry, but we're really *not* superspies. And we're not scientists. Our only way out of Sweden is up, back to GW station, and that means an aerospace port."

He made a horizontal chopping gesture. "There's no way they'll let us get through a port. Our only option is surrender. Let's just go to the police and be done with it. It's over." He rolled sideways, ending up on his back on the bench seat, adjusting his ribcage frame again. "Or data blast to the world and let the cops get us anyway, like Nycci says." He rested his forearm over his eyes.

Bode's perspective on the situation was unnerving. It was easier to argue against Nycci's data blast idea than against Bode's argument about the inevitable end of this situation. Irena was starting to regret suggesting a return to the WPPPS.

"If we run," she said, "and we're caught by the mob, they might kill us."

She looked at Cosmo. "Or at least me," she said. He was returning her gaze, but he looked more thoughtful than angry now.

"Or me," said Cosmo. "At least if the Swedish Nazis catch us."

So Cosmo was considering that situation, too. Probably wondering if he'd killed one of them.

"If we have to run from the police," Irena continued, "that's a long drive against a superior force. Even if we decide to give ourselves up, we'll still have to escape the mob to put ourselves in police custody." She was thinking as she spoke.

Perhaps it would be best if they did end up in police custody after all. Perhaps she would get special treatment because she called the police in the first place. And the others might escape being lynched by the mob or shot by the police. But no.

"No," she said. "Data blasting won't buy us any favor with the cops. It might even add more charges to the list, fraudulent allegations, slander, that kind of thing. Ronja would be all over those kinds of charges. No, there's no way around it. We must return to Östnoraberget. We redo the molecular analysis, by the book, to be sure of our facts. Then we warn Stockholm from a solid position. We can broadcast what we know from its secure network connection. It's our duty to make civilization work."

Keiok said, "Duties. Yes, duties."

Cosmo turned around, realizing Keiok was there. "Keiok," said Cosmo, "you're the tiebreaker, Cap'n. What's your vote? Surrender or return to the WPPPS?"

Irena turned. Keiok was sitting quietly, watching.

After a moment, he replied, "To seek out new life and new civilizations. To boldly go…"

"Shit! They're here!" Nycci squealed, pointing at the rear camera display.

In the fairly well-lit street behind them, they saw the Chuo billboard van turning onto Kvarnhagsvägen. Leaves were stuck in the billboard's mounting hardware. The horn-blowing, Mohawk-wearing gang member was standing on the roof as they drove, like a wild man in an Australian apocalypse movie. He was harnessed to the front of the billboard, and he also had leaves stuck in his mounting hardware.

"BRRRAAWWWWWRRRRR" went his frighteningly Tibetan horn.

Just behind that van were two other grey vans following closely but offset so they could see ahead.

"Okay," said Cosmo, pressing the center button on his controller. "Three to two. Back to the WPPPS."

Now, thought Irena, *we're on a* proper *'mission from god'."*

The van came alive and surged forward, headlights on.

Up ahead, just visible over the curvature of the road, two grey vans turned off the 258.

"Aw, shit, eh?" said Bode.

Cosmo took a hard right onto the next street. It looked more like a commercial access drive.

Nycci, Bode, and Irena all dug into their wristcomp maps.

They tag-teamed giving directions to Cosmo while watching the aft camera display.

The van veered left down the drive, then right, and then they could see the cul-de-sac right in front of them.

"Left! Ped path!" said Irena.

Cosmo squealed the van to the left, down a ped path. There were trees and everyone inhaled and held their breath as the top of the van plowed through tree branches.

But the path remained fairly straight, and Cosmo was able to maintain control and avoid slamming into benches and lamps.

"Uh, oh!" he said, as they approached a tee intersection.

"Left!" said Nycci.

"Then immediate right!" said Bode.

The van skidded left, then almost immediately skidded right, nearly hitting the wall of a residential structure. There were bushes, lamps, and rocks at the end of the path, and the van would not fit between them. The van's front right wheel slammed into a large rock with a loud bang, tilting and shaking the van, which groaned and creaked after the hit. But it kept moving. The right edge scraped over the rock as Cosmo steered left into the drive ahead. Then the right rear wheel slammed into the same stone, of course. Again the van banged and tilted, making that terrible scraping sound as its tail end dragged over the stone. It groaned and creaked after finally clearing the stone.

The other vans were behind them, negotiating the same paths.

"Across to the slope, then left," said Irena.

"Then a right at the end, then we're at 258."

Cosmo complied. "But then which way on 258?"

"We can't go north," said Irena.

"Yeah, that's back toward Ronja," said Nycci.

"South it is," said Cosmo.

They got lucky. No other pursuers were blocking that last intersection onto Kvarnhagsvägen. The van squealed right at the intersection.

"Whew," said Irena. After that run, she started thinking of their stolen van as 'The Fujmobile.'

The traffic signal at 258 was red, but Cosmo ignored it and focused on merging into southbound traffic quickly before the five vans behind them caught up.

It seemed like many grey vans were driving south on 258.

"Is it…was it my imagination," said Bode, "or was someone in that van," he pointed at one of the vans passing right to left going south, "holding a controller like Cosmo's?"

Another van followed the one Bode pointed out. It, too,

had someone in the front of the cab holding a controller in both hands.

"Not the best news, but it could've been worse," said Irena.

The rear camera display showed the billboard van turning onto Kvarnhagsvägen behind them. It also had someone up front holding a controller. The Mohawk guy on the roof was on his knees, wiping leaves and tree branches out of his face and off the rest of his body.

That is a scary guy, thought Irena.

"Gotta go!" said Nycci.

Cosmo pressed the Fujmobile into the southbound lane, just between other grey vans.

Behind them, the five pursuing vans also forced their way into the southbound traffic.

They were on southbound 258. It was a fairly well-lit road in the darkness of 4:41 p.m. on 31 December in Stockholm. There was traffic in both directions, more out here than near Stockholm because there were fewer arteries.

They were also probably in the middle of a convoy that was searching for them, probably with drone support.

The commonality of these grey vans worked in their favor but also against them. It made it harder for their pursuers to identify them as Squad Fuj, but it also made it harder for them to identify their pursuers.

And southbound 258 does not go directly to Östnora.

Cosmo focused on blending in with traffic while the others hurried to find a route. They could hear the BRAAWWWRRR of the Tibetan horn some unknown distance behind them.

Irena had a memory flash of that hulking Chuo twin demonstrating their plan to shove spikes through Squad Fuj's faces. Then a memory flash of the CSA guards giving Squad Fuj a beating. Who knows what the Lux mob was planning for her? And if the Swedish Nazis had seen Cosmo driving the van when he sent them into the bay, their plans for Squad Fuj can't be pretty, either.

She didn't even want to think about Enforcer choke holds and such, although there was always that Watcher smiley face in the back of her mind when it came to the police.

"How about 226 east, 259 south, and 73 down?" said Nycci.

"But," said Bode, "there's also 226 south, 225 south, 257 east to Tungelsta, then Söderbyvägen on down. It's more direct."

"I love that route!" said Irena. "They might think we're trying to take 73 down to Nynäshamn to escape by boat, yet it takes us right to our nice, secluded WPPPS. Only Ronja knows about our WPPPS job this morning, and she might not even know which one we visited."

"226 is only a few clicks ahead," said Nycci. "Do we stay on the larger roads?"

"I don't care about road size," said Cosmo. "We need the most direct route possible, but with some turns. It's our only chance."

"Okay, when we get to the bottom of the curved ramp in Tumba, take a left onto 226 South," said Irena.

"Then it's south on 226," added Nycci, "until the roundabout at the lake. You'll turn left at that roundabout."

Irena was starting to feel a warm glow. She had won her first consensus. She was on the squad. And they were finally working as a team. All it took to get here was multiple injuries, several brushes with death, and multiple criminal violations, including the one she keeps trying not to think about.

Everything went to hell at the fire station roundabout.

When the Fujmobile entered the roundabout, there was a moment when it was directly ahead of another van turning

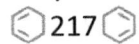

in the roundabout. That van's headlights filled the Fujmobile's cabin. Whoever was in that van got a clear view of Cosmo driving the van, and Irena beside him, and probably Nycci behind Irena.

The other van's headlights started flashing and they surged forward, attempting to ram the Fujmobile.

Cosmo veered into the next lane over, which was the lane he needed anyway to keep going south. He cut off another vehicle that was entering the roundabout from the west. That vehicle performed an emergency deceleration. Its tires squealed, and then the tires of convoy vehicles farther back squealed in sequence. Multiple vehicles were performing emergency stops, including the one that had flashed and surged. The Fujmobile gained a small lead.

But just up ahead two vans turned and stopped, both vans blocking both lanes. The near van had turned left. Almost any lane blockage stymies a self-driving vehicle, which does not leave the road without manual overrides.

For a few slow-motion moments, Cosmo looked indecisive. He kept driving toward the vans blocking the road.

Then, further lit by the Fujmobile's headlights, someone leaned out of the "driver's side" window of the near van. It was a woman. She was trying to aim a combat rifle at them.

It was Ange-Mariam.

"Ange!" Cosmo gasped.

Irena also gasped in surprise and elation. With automatic concern for etiquette, she put her hand over her gaping mouth.

"Cosmo!" yelled Nycci and Bode at the same time. The Fujmobile was on a collision course and accelerating toward imminent gunfire.

Cosmo jerked a thumb joystick to the right. Ange-Mariam fired two bursts, smashing Cosmo's side window and putting rounds through the left side of the van.

Cosmo sent the Fujmobile down the sloped grass to the right of the roadblock, just missing the back end of Ange-Mariam's van. It skidded as he tried to bring it back up the slope on the other side of the roadblock. Amid all the jostling, Irena turned to check on everyone.

Bode, just behind Cosmo on the left side of the van, lifted his head from between his knees. He looked uninjured. Nycci, behind Irena, was pressed against the back of her seat, arms and legs splayed. She, too, looked uninjured. Both were wide-eyed and agape.

"She's alive!" Cosmo shouted, beaming.

Keiok was in the right rear corner of the van, speaking into his wristcomp. There were bullet craters on either side of him, one in the wall and one in the door.

The Fujmobile shook and swayed as Cosmo put her back on the road.

"That woman has trigger discipline," said Bode.

"I know, right!?" said Cosmo, glowing.

"She's not wasting any more ammo," said Nycci. "I hope that means she has a very limited supply."

"No, doubt," said Cosmo, still grinning.

"I'm so glad she's alive, Cosmo," said Irena.

He glanced at her. "Yahuh," he said, tapping the controller over his heart. "Nous a trompés." Her weak heart had tricked them.

Nycci called up the rear camera display again. Now homemade strobe lights were flashing on the dashboards of at least a dozen vans behind them up the 258. Vigilante groups often use these homemade strobes to trick self-driven vehicles into pulling over. You could tell they weren't police strobes because they were always a color pair that was legally allowed, like red and white instead of the blue strobes used by most official Swedish emergency response vehicles. But self-driven vehicles defaulted to pulling over instead of trying to discern colors under all possible weather and lighting conditions.

Seeing that in the rear camera display, Cosmo stopped grinning. So did Irena.

They continued down 258 with that trail of flashing grey vans behind them. Whenever Cosmo passed a vehicle, the strobe lights behind would cause it to pull over.

All their wristcomps beeped at the same time. They'd all received a recorded video message.

"It's from Ronja," said Irena.

"Send it to the display," said Cosmo, using his chin to indicate the central display that he would be able to see. Bode swiped his wristcomp.

"Oh, my dear Janitor Squad Fuj," said Ronja, no longer cheery. "I must warn you. If you try to report anything, I will hire Focks to launch a smear campaign on your asses, and you *know* how much experience *they* have." Ronja raised her eyebrows in emphasis.

"No one will care about your allegations or anything else you say. You will rot in a jail cell for all your crimes today. You will be hated and then forgotten.

"After you have served your sentence, you will have no chance of getting another plum janitor squad job with Global Waste. You will be lucky to find work hustling cotton candy and rim jobs at Disneyland Brasilia!

"But if you keep quiet and turn yourselves in by eighteen hundred tonight, either to my people or the police, then there will be no need for a nasty smear campaign.

"I'll even give you free day passes to my Winter Wonderland Nostalgia Experience. Ask yourselves: desperate hustling in Brasilia, or sipping hot cider in my snow globe? It's your choice. But it's really no choice at all, is it?"

The message ended.

"Eighteen hundred," said Bode.

"That gives us about eighty minutes," said Irena, "to reach

the WPPPS, do a proper analysis, and broadcast the results. Plenty of time!" She was trying to be positive.

Everyone fell silent. But no one argued for a change of plan.

"Ronja might not wait until eighteen hundred," said Cosmo. "Especially if her drones see us going to the WPPPS."

They passed over the railroad tracks at Tumba station and descended the curved ramp down to 226. Cosmo ignored the traffic signal and turned left onto 226 southbound at the first opportunity. So did their pursuers.

In Tumba, the 226 had a wide shoulder for a while, so Cosmo used it to pass multiple self-driven vehicles which were following local speed limits. Whenever conditions allowed, he passed using the oncoming traffic lane, too. The pursuers did the same.

Bode and Nycci followed Cosmo and Irena's lead and fastened their seatbelts.

One time there was a traffic jam in a stretch of road with a curbed divider. Cosmo did not come to a stop. Instead, he bounced the Fujmobile over the divider, across oncoming traffic, and onto the far shoulder, straddling road and grass, then returned to the eastbound lane as soon as traffic allowed. The pursuers did the same.

The Fujmobile had already taken a beating, but she was designed for commercial service. Unfortunately, so were the vans of their pursuers.

"I can't lose them," Cosmo said. "We need a plan."

"Yeah," said Bode, "and before it becomes obvious that we're returning to the WPPPS."

They continued zooming down the road, pushing the eighty-kph limiter whenever possible.

"Damn, this is slow," said Nycci. "I never realized how slow it is."

During the straight runs, they removed their costumes. It took multiple straight runs and help from Bode and Nycci for Cosmo to fully remove his costume while driving. For a few tense moments, Irena held the controller and kept one of its joysticks fully forward, begging traffic not to require her to maneuver. It didn't.

Now they were all back in their GW coveralls, just in time for Cosmo to go east at the Vårsta roundabout.

They talked through various escape strategies involving causing a traffic blockage, using smoke, and shutting off the Fujmobile's lights to use the darkness to their advantage.

"Drones," said Irena.

"Yeah, we can't lose them with drones overhead," Nycci agreed. "At best, we might be able to increase our lead."

"We'll have to weld the door when we get there," said Bode. "It'll take at least a minute to lay down a few good beads." He dug into his toolbag, checking his gloves and portable torch with eye shield.

"Plus time in the lab," said Irena. "Somehow we must lose the drones." She stared at the Fujmobile's dashboard.

"How the hell can we do that?" said Nycci. Her tone was ambiguous, open to an answer if Irena had a workable idea.

Irena's mind raced through the day's events. Drones were probably on them since they made a ruckus at Rymdstyrelsen HQ. First a CSA Security drone. Then a drone was deployed on behalf of Ms. Chuo, the attendant at the Buddhist temple.

Irena rubbed her skull.

Then maybe a police drone after Irena snitched. The Swedish Nazis had been part of the mob at Ronja's event center, so they probably had a drone giving chase ever since Cosmo's first double-joystick experience on the Centralbron, sending the Swedish Nazis over the railing and into the bay. Surely the Luxembourgers had at least one drone looking for them after the vigilante fiasco in the tunnels. And probably a Ronja drone, too.

In reviewing the day, she also couldn't help but wonder again about Keiok. He did something unexpected at the temple. He just happened to have a smoke grenade in the tunnels. He threw himself at the Lux mob in Centralstation and lived to tell about it. He might have caught up with his squad at the SVOA building, and he did catch up with them at Ronja's. There was something weird about Keiok, beyond his mildly entertaining fantasy life.

"Keiok," said Irena, turning.

Keiok was doing something Irena had never seen him do.

He was sitting upright. His eyes were shut tight. But he was holding his arms up at his sides, his hands about head level, as if demonstrating to the police that he was not armed.

"Keiok," said Irena, louder this time.

He opened his eyes, turning his head toward her without lowering his arms.

"Do you have anything in your bag of tricks that can take out the drones following us?"

Bode and Nycci turned back to look, too.

Keiok looked at them. He blinked unnervingly.

"No tricks," he said, looking toward his feet where he would usually keep his bag. "No bag." He looked at them again, blinked unnervingly, and said, "You have to learn why things work on a starship." Then he closed his eyes and faced forward again, keeping his hands up.

Chapter 23

Off The Road Again

B ode and Nycci turned forward.

"Can he get any weirder?" said Nycci. "Do I need to overdose on LDS to get a promotion?"

Irena turned forward again, too, shaking her head. "Something's changed with him," she said. "That's the second, maybe third time he's been sort of lucid and responsive."

"You call that lucid and responsive?" said Nycci.

"Does anyone know," said Irena, "if drones would follow us visually or by pinging the vehicle's transponder with radar?"

"Huh," said Cosmo, then "Hang on."

Cosmo made a left turn at Norga, keeping up speed as best he could, then an immediate right. They were on 257.

"So," said Bode. "first the drone operator visually IDs the target vehicle, then commands the drone to ping the target's transponder code, then puts the drone into a repeating cycle of ping-follow on the target's transponder code."

"That makes sense," said Nycci. "That method would penetrate trees and a lot of other interference that would block sight, including darkness."

"Yahuh! I think I read about that somewhere," said Cosmo.

"So we combine other methods," Irena said, gesticulating, "smoke and whatnot, with disabling the Fujmobile's transponder and maybe, just maybe, we can lose them and have enough time at the WPPPS to do what needs to be done."

For the first time since Irena was hired, her entire squad was smiling. And they were smiling at her.

"The *Fujmobile?*" said Nycci, raising her eyebrows at Irena.

Perhaps they weren't smiling so much as laughing.

Cosmo turned the Fujmobile through a long chicane, right, then left. The van leaned in the turns, creaking.

"Yeah, that's what I call this beast," said Irena, trying for nonchalance but landing on awkward embarrassment. "Anyway, along with my bodycam footage, perhaps we can actually nab Ronja. Maybe even get our charges dropped. Or sentences reduced."

"You should quit while you're ahead," said Nycci, frowning.

"Hold on, left turn," said Cosmo.

Everyone caught up in their maps. They were executing the left turn to stay on 257 going east. These were still rural roads, with rare lamps mostly at intersections.

The squad continued taking inventory of their toolbags and brainstorming their escape options. The rear camera view still showed the twelve other vans behind them, following turn for turn, pass for pass. Somewhere in the last several kilometers of thinning traffic, the pursuers had turned off their strobe lights.

The Fujmobile zoomed down 257 at the limiter speed of eighty kph, if you can call that zooming.

Wherever the locals were planning on watching fireworks, if at all, they were already there. Irena counted herself among the many to whom fireworks were stupid, pointless, obsolete celebrations of war that just terrorized animals, combat veterans, infants, the elderly, autistics, etc.

On these dark, fairly straight stretches of road with light traffic, with the road noise droning, one could easily forget about the angry lynch mob a hundred meters back. But on these roads, it also wasn't hard to count the twelve vans tailing them.

In the light of the occasional intersection or headlights going the other direction, it looked like the Mohawk guy was no longer on the roof of the Gustavsberg Muay Thai billboard van.

Occasionally, when there was some light, pursuers in the nearest van, which was not always the same van, would stick torsos out their windows, and shout and pump their fists at the Fujmobile. But they hadn't been shot at since Ange-Mariam at the fire station roundabout.

Sometimes a drone would appear alongside the van, buzzing the windows, then zoom off into the darkness above.

It was shortly after 1700. There was still time. They might still pull this off. Monitoring the newsblogisphere, there was still no smear campaign against them.

All their wristcomps beeped again. It was another recorded video message from Ronja.

Cosmo gestured toward the display. Bode swiped.

"Come now, my dear custodians. You are not evil people. You don't deserve to go down in history as the monsters you'll be made out to be.

"Monsieur Lachance, for example. Yes, he did leave his fiancée standing at the altar on their wedding day." Ronja gave a tsk tsk. "But did the rest of you know that dear Cosmo has been secretly sending half of his income to Ange-Mariam through her father?"

Ronja sighed as if moved by the story.

"He even arranged to take the Zinchenko brothers out of the picture. So sweet.

"And Nycci. I'll bet she hasn't told you a thing about her past. That's understandable, it's not pretty. Any escape from the former U.S. would be," she paused, thinking of a word, "knepig. But by all accounts, she did the least possible damage when she could have done far more.

"Bodhi Ozols, the elder statesman of your squad, also has

a heinous moment in his past. You may not know that he abandoned his pregnant, young girlfriend. He was young and selfish, yes. But he tried to return to her, and she rejected him. And do you know what he did? He arranged to become the custodian in charge of his daughter's schools, one after the other so that he could watch over her and occasionally be a sort of uncle figure to her."

Ronja pulled a handkerchief up to her nose.

"Such a sweet story. They're pen pals to this day," she said, pretending to be verklempt.

"Oh, eh?" said Bode, clearly objecting to Ronja knowing about his pen pal daughter.

"Ms. Żuraw," said Ronja, "the newest member of your squad, is supporting her older sister after a life-changing injury.

"Why would any of you allow the others to go down in history as anti-alcohol, anti-tradition, socialist, human-trafficking, baby-eating, sheep-focking, atheist pedophiles?"

She paused for effect.

"As for that mysterious team leader of yours, for all I know he really is one. Do you really want to be publicly associated with *him* for the rest of your life?

"Please," Ronja tilted her head, "don't let this happen to you, or your teammates. Keep quiet and turn yourselves in. You'll spend some time in jail, and afterward, we'll sip hot cider together. Won't it be lovely?"

She turned, stepped aside, and gestured toward the Winter Wonderland behind her. It appeared the mob break-in never made it that far up the avenue. The message ended.

Cosmo swallowed.

Nycci sniffed.

Bode sighed and laid down on the bench again, putting his arm over his eyes. Irena assumed he was mourning his soon-to-be ruined reputation in the eyes of his pen pal

daughter.

"I guess we *can* still call you Uncle Bode," said Irena.

Uncle Bode sat up and exchanged a glance with Irena. There was silence for a time.

Irena decided that more cheerleading about the plan would not go over well. Their only hope was to do what Ronja considered impossible, to properly crack her secret and warn Stockholm, preferably before 1800. She hoped her squad mates understood this, too.

"She keeps talking as if nothing bad will happen," said Uncle Bode. "Maybe there really *is* no threat."

"Mmm," said Nycci with a skeptical look on her face.

"I'm not buying it," said Irena. "Ronja's a dog-kidnapping psycho who has already put something unknown into viruses and infected us all. Who the hell knows what her plan is? And do you really think she wants to sip hot cider with us afterward?"

"Mm, yeah, probably not," said Nycci.

"I don't know the first thing about Ronja," said Uncle Bode. "I barely know you. Just because she's a gajillionaire doesn't mean she's an evil villain."

"Um, doggie kidnapping?" said Irena.

"And by the way," she continued, turning to look at Nycci, "you don't actually know if your copper bands and urine drinking will protect against whatever this is."

Nycci made a face and started tapping her wristcomp.

"Don't worry," Nycci said before anyone could ask. "I'm just looking up contact information for the Swedish Security Service and the Folkhalls... aw, damn, the Public Health Agency of Sweden. We can't just rely on the police, the councils, and the newsblogisphere."

Cosmo swerved left and right. The van tilted and creaked.

"Uh, oh!" he said.

Traffic was rapidly coming to a halt not far ahead at an unlit intersection. Self-driven vehicles were facing off against some minor confusion about intentions and right-of-way.

There was oncoming traffic, so Cosmo swerved around the jam on the right side. The van tilted with the right half of the van down a small slope.

Everyone yelled and pointed, seeing a tree coming right at them.

Cosmo swerved left at the last second, avoiding the tree but plowing right over a stand of direction signs and clipping a vehicle with the front left corner of the Fujmobile. There was a loud bang and a shimmy. Cosmo swerved right again, avoiding collision with oncoming traffic and putting the Fujmobile back in its lane on the other side of the intersection.

It was sheer luck they avoided a disabling collision. The pursuing vans behind them activated their strobe lights and swerved through the intersection on both sides of the stopped traffic, forcing the oncoming traffic to stop, too.

"Merde," said Cosmo. "Shit," said Uncle Bode and Nycci, all at about the same time.

"Yahuh," said Irena.

Everyone inhaled, stretched their legs, and moved their necks and shoulders to settle down.

Nycci noticed a flash on her wristcomp. "Check this out," she said.

She swiped something onto the display for all to see.

It was Ronja's show, her ad.

There was thumpy music as the Solid Cold Dancers shook their booties and their other inny and outy bits. The drone camera rose above the dancers and turned, opening to a wide view revealing the avenue, buildings, and costumed inhabitants of Ronja's snow globe.

Snow was falling inside the wonderland.

Titles zipped in from the sides to overlay the scene:

Welcome to Ronja's
Winter Wonderland
Nostalgia Experience

The view dropped and the titles remained in place, rising out of view. The view turned as the music changed to a nostalgia-inducing drum-and-chimes accompaniment, perhaps with a gently played acoustic guitar in the background. It was hard to tell over the road noise.

There at the end of the avenue were the extras, including Annika and Hugh Borg, standing right about at the spot where Uncle Bode had zapped the lead security guard into unconsciousness. All of them were all singing, or at least lip-synching, that winter folk song that was sung by Ronja's guards in the V-290 during Squad Fuj's kidnapping.

In moments the song reached the "la la la" stage and the music and voices faded out. The view turned again, now showing Ronja on the avenue, with the Solid Cold Dancers in her distant background hip-pushing and toe-tapping, left and right, over and over, as Ronja spoke impeccable Swedish into the camera.

She was as effervescent as anyone could be who was holding dogs and people hostage and preparing a nasty smear campaign against concerned citizens.

It ended with her stepping aside and gesturing back toward the Winter Wonderland, just as she had done in her last recorded message to Squad Fuj. The Solid Cold Dancers were once again central as the thumpy music returned. They performed that final flourish, with a twirl ending in the splits. The view moved past their beautiful, smiling faces and ample bosoms and flew down the avenue, showing off the scale and attention to detail of the Winter Wonderland with its real snow and real icicles. Then it faded to black.

"Let me see if I can find an English version," said Nycci.

After some tapping, and some Fujmobile swaying as

Cosmo passed slower traffic, Nycci displayed the same video, starting with Ronja's presentation.

The English subtitles said about what you'd expect based on the ad. Ronja was hawking her Winter Wonderland Nostalgia Experience as a place to go to bask in the memories of what cold winters used to be like. She promoted it to children, adults, and especially older adults who had childhood memories of such winters.

There would be real snow you could shovel, hot cider to keep you warm, playful snowball throwing, real icicles to marvel at, and so forth. It would be open through March, so book your visit now. Then it would re-open in November for the next season. And best of all, Ronja would be opening her snow globes in major cities across the world in the middle and upper latitudes.

Finally, Ronja reminded everyone in the Stockholm district to attend one of her numerous, rare and expensive, blue-colored fireworks shows at midnight, where random attendees would receive a free pass to the Winter Wonderland Nostalgia Experience.

The newsblogisphere went wild. The video was going viral. Comments were piling up indicating extreme enthusiasm for this latest realism-based, time-traveling theme park experience. People were asking if they could move into these snow globes in exchange for shoveling snow and doing other support work. Others were attempting to coordinate groups who would attend as many of Ronja's fireworks shows as possible in an attempt to collect those free passes.

Ronja was selling an idealized past to people who felt powerless to create a viable future.

"Let's get to work on the plan," said Uncle Bode.

They removed, broke, or torched off all of the van's central console cowling and front underpanels.

They cut wires and unbolted the front right seat Irena had been using, moving it to the rear of the van.

Irena and Keiok were cutting chunks of foam out of the seat to tape onto pieces of the cowling. They also bolted sharp bracketry onto the cowling pieces as makeshift tire rippers.

Uncle Bode and Nycci were scraping Magnesium and Aluminum shavings onto the sticky side of strips of duct tape, along with torn pieces of the flammable Winter Wonderland costuming and some plaster powder from standard issue canisters in their "mobile technical team" toolbags. They were making igniter strips to help ignite and burn the foam.

Irena and Keiok half-covered the igniter strips with chunks of foam before securing the foam to the cowlings.

Along with the seat itself, which would be doused with standard-issue flammable cleaning fluids and/or some of that alcohol Cosmo stole, all this junk would be ignited and dumped out the back of the van at a time of their choosing.

The pursuing vans might roll right over this stuff without any ill effects. But it might spook the drivers, tear up some tires, and/or cause some distraction. If it has any of those effects at just the right time, it would be worth it.

At the very least it would unclutter the floor of the Fujmobile.

They were entering a stretch of road that had no shoulder on their side, just a heavy guard railing. Cosmo had no room for error in his steering.

Nycci was lying on her left side under the dashboard, sticking her head into the lefthand side of the van's forward compartment. She was under Cosmo's legs, which were propped up on the dashboard.

Uncle Bode was lying on his right side under the dashboard on the right-hand side, where Irena's seat used to be.

"Are you sure that big-name repair manual is right?" said Nycci, her voice muffled by being neck-deep in the forward compartment. "Mine says it should be here, next to the converter."

"It can't be next to the converter," said Uncle Bode, also muffled. "That could cause too much interference."

"Oh, wait," said Nycci. "Is this it here? I see a small, silver box next to the controller."

"Why can't we just cut the wire at the antenna?" said Irena, having a realization.

"It's dead center on top of the van," said Uncle Bode. "and it would take more time to rip out the reinforced side walls to get to the wire, or to cut the reinforced roof. We don't have demolition power tools. And if we used a torch, we'd probably set the whole van on fire.

"Here it is, Nycci. I see it," he said. "That silver box on your side is the display controller. The transponder is here."

"Can you do anything with it?" said Nycci, backing out from under Cosmo's legs.

"Hand me a mirror," said Uncle Bode.

Nycci extracted from Uncle Bode's bag a telescoping rod with a mirror on the end, like the one Irena used at the grating in the tunnel. She started moving toward him when Cosmo yelled out.

"Merde!" he said. "Police!"

Irena jumped up and turned to look, then instinctively threw herself onto the bench seat and started strapping in.

Everything went into slow motion.

Ahead of them was one of the last isolated intersections before Tungelsta. The guard railing on their side of the road tapered down, then there were buildings on the left and right sides, then the tiny side road came in from the right, and not far beyond that intersection the guard railing tapered back up.

Except hidden just past the building on the right was an

Enforcer vehicle, and hidden behind the shrubs and fence in the lot on the left was a Watcher vehicle. There was an unknown number of laneblocker units like the one that was blocking the lane on the Centralbron when Cosmo ran down the Swedish Nazis. These were already in the road and also rolling in from the field on the right.

The Enforcer vehicle had the standard blue, white, and lime "Polis" Enforcer paint job. The Watcher vehicle had the standard olive and orange Watchdog paint job, with a smiley face emblem on the door. Enforcers called it "spyafärger," meaning "puke colors."

But it was two different paint jobs on the same vehicle, the venerable old Volvo ZQXG9000 Interceptor. It was bulletproof, fireproof, and electric shockproof. It had scanning radar and fancy display systems, allowing the driver to see through smoke and fog. It could do 200 kph for two hours straight on batteries alone. And all that was just what the public was allowed to know. The 9000 was a fearsome machine.

Irena could see all this now because suddenly the intersection was full of light.

No one had time to offer suggestions. It was all Cosmo now.

He jerked the joysticks in different directions, decelerating hard and turning sharply to the right.

Nycci lost her footing while reaching for the safety belt for the front passenger seat that was no longer there. Her foot landed on Uncle Bode's crotch, and then she swung onto her bench seat, gripping the belt.

"Aaowwww, Jeeesus Chriiiissstt," Uncle Bode's muffled voice yelled into the forward compartment.

Cosmo continued maneuvering.

Nycci looped her arm through its safety belt. The loose chair was fairly heavy, but it shifted around, threatening to jam Irena's and Keiok's feet. The cowling pieces shifted around on the floor.

The Fujmobile cut right just before hitting the nearest laneblocker unit but thumped down a drop in the terrain and when Cosmo turned left again it started fishtailing.

The right rear corner swung into the front of the Enforcer 9000 with a loud bang.

A laneblocker changed direction and started rolling down the slope to block the Fujmobile's way forward. Cosmo had to brake hard.

Things were not looking good. Everyone gasped in slow motion. The 9000's siren began to wail.

Cosmo reversed into the 9000 with another loud bang, then went full forward, hitting the laneblocker's wheel shield with the front left corner of the van. The collision was already in the direction of the laneblocker's motion, so on the grass, the two vehicles mostly careened off each other.

But the van was faster than the laneblocker, and Cosmo pulled ahead of it. The laneblocker's wheel shield scraped along the left side of the van but soon the Fujmobile was free.

Nycci jumped and pointed ahead, down the side road that led to some greenhouses.

"Greenhouses! Road!" she blurted.

The Fujmobile was bouncing hard over the uneven terrain of the field, and Cosmo had to dodge another laneblocker before he was able to get onto the farmer's side road leading to the greenhouses.

"Are we trapped?" Cosmo said with desperation in his voice.

"No, it rejoins ahead!" said Nycci as she plopped back down onto her bench seat.

Irena and Keiok were busy using their feet to keep the loose seat from moving, but now there was time to look at the rear camera display.

Behind them, the pursuing vans were doing what they

always did. Most of them followed Cosmo's pathfinding, and others rammed their way through tighter openings.

But it looked like some of the pursuing vans had experienced disabling collisions with the boxy laneblocker units, especially the ones on the road with dig-in stabilizers deployed.

"Holy shit," said Irena.

"Putain de merde," said Cosmo, catching glances at the display.

"Colorful metaphors," said Keiok, blinking placidly in the corner.

Cosmo cut left and then had to swerve again to avoid local onlookers.

He and Nycci exchanged looks and made wooo sounds with pursed lips. They were sharing a moment about barely missing those pedestrians.

Cosmo stayed with the side road, keeping to the left until it rejoined the main road not far from the roadblock.

The police had chosen a very good spot for an ambush. But they had underestimated Janitor Squad Fuj's desperation, Cosmo's new driving skills, and the Fujmobile's capabilities.

Not long after getting back on 257, the Fujmobile started to vibrate and then there was a loud bang at the front left wheel. Irena noticed that a crack was growing at the bottom of the front window, near the center.

"Oh, no, the motors," said Cosmo. "We've blown a pod."

"What happened?" said Irena.

"We've lost the front left pod," said Cosmo. "It will slow us down, and I don't think we can do any more crazy off-roading." Irena wasn't a mechanic, but it was fairly common knowledge that if a pod motor seizes, its drive axle disengages, thus preventing the wheel from locking up while the vehicle is still in motion.

"What the hell is going on," said Uncle Bode, still on the

floor and breathing heavily, but now uncurling his body.

"Sorry about that," Nycci said to Uncle Bode. "I'm sorry I stepped on your…"

"Never mind," said Uncle Bode, lying on his right side and looking back into the cabin.

"Would someone hand me another mirror rod?" he said. "Mine is gone. I dropped it."

Irena extracted her mirror rod and tossed it to Nycci, who handed it to Uncle Bode.

"It was a roadblock," said Cosmo. "But there's no time for details. We're not far from Tungelsta and we're still being followed on the road and in the sky."

It was action time.

Chapter 24

MacGyvering

"Merde," said Cosmo. "We're only making forty now." Headlights could be seen behind them. They were getting closer.

Irena and Keiok were strapped into the aftmost bench seat positions, equipment in hand.

The map display showed their planned route and current position.

Uncle Bode had his head and arms in the forward compartment.

"I'm ready to kill the transponder whenever you say," he said. "Just please don't crash into anything on my side of the van."

"Oui, oui, mon ami," said Cosmo. "Okay, that's Skogs Ekebyvägen," he said as they passed a turnoff to the left.

"Yeah," said Nycci, "if we're lucky, some of them will go that way and try to cut us off near Nedersta."

As they rounded the first bend past Skogs Ekebyvägen, they could see in the rear camera view some headlights arriving at the turnoff, and some headlights right behind those turning off 257. So far so good. Some of the pursuers were peeling off.

But the other headlights were gaining fast.

"It's too late," said Cosmo. "I'm turning right."

Cosmo veered right onto Kvarnvägen, an unmarked road with no shoulders.

"Uncle Bode! The Transponder!" he said. He had waited until they were straight and level to ask Bode to do the deed.

Soon afterward, headlights turned down Kvarnvägen to follow.

"How many are there?" said Cosmo, tension creeping into

his voice. Irena couldn't imagine the strain he'd been under since they started driving. It must've been hard enough to drive continuously using that thumb joystick controller, but Cosmo has had to do extreme driving multiple times, and that's on top of the responsibility he's carrying for everyone, for everything, the whole plan, Stockholm itself.

"I only count two," said Irena.

"Same here," said Nycci.

"We should assume others stayed on 257, to our left," said Irena.

"Yahuh," said Cosmo.

Bode extracted himself from the forward compartment and started moving aft. He handed the mirror rod back to Nycci, but Nycci gestured toward Irena. So he walked back and handed it to Irena, taking a seat beside her and strapping in.

The pursuing vans caught up with the Fujmobile shortly before the planned left turn that would keep them on Kvarnvägen.

Bang! They had rammed the Fujmobile, but it wasn't enough to make Cosmo lose control. Not yet.

"Now!" said Cosmo. "The chair!"

Irena kicked open the already-prepped back doors as Keiok lit the chair's exposed foam on fire. They both shoved it out the back of the van as Uncle Bode kept the cowling traps in place. The entire operation took seconds.

The van behind them had nowhere to go. It started swerving and braked, but the chair went right under it and became lodged.

Cosmo veered left at the planned turn.

There was a terrible scraping sound as the pursuing van drove the metal frame of the burning chair into the road surface. The frame collapsed, but so did the steering linkage it was lodged in. The van's front right wheel turned sideways and the whole van turned and tilted, out of control. The van

behind it smashed into it while trying to veer around, causing the front van to roll onto its side, bouncing as it slid off the road to its right. The one in back left the road on its left side, fishtailed in the grassy field, and rolled onto its side, sliding into some trees.

"Yes!" said Nycci, pumping her fist in the air.

"Haha!" said Irena.

Irena and Keiok pulled the rear doors closed and shifted some cowling traps into position for release.

Cosmo was double-checking the map and the plan.

Their destination was at the end of Kvarnvägen.

But as they approached the Tungelstavägen crossroad, two vans zoomed in from the left, from toward 257. They would reach the intersection before Squad Fuj.

There was a field to the left in front of the Kyrka, the church, but there were trees on the other side of Tungelstavägen.

"Merde!" said Cosmo.

Everyone knew Cosmo was trying to avoid off-roading again. Plus, two vans were approaching. Depending on how they blocked the intersection, if Cosmo tried going around them, he might simply crash into them, or the trees just beyond, ending Squad Fuj's flight and possibly their lives.

Cosmo screeched to a stop and started executing a 'K' turn. In moments, they were driving up Kvarnvägen again, toward the two crashed vans, with two new vans behind them.

"We need to get out of visual range," said Uncle Bode.

As they approached the previous intersection, with the two rolled vans, Ange-Mariam stood on the righthand spur of Kvarnvägen, in front of her rolled van. She had her rifle propped on her hip.

Cosmo froze. The Fujmobile kept rolling toward the intersection.

"Ange," said Cosmo.

Apparently, Ange-Mariam was just waiting for visual confirmation that this was the Fujmobile approaching her. She lowered the gun and fired one burst. One burst only.

"She's out!" said Nycci.

Ange-Mariam could be seen in the Fujmobile's headlights repeatedly pulling her rifle's trigger.

Then everyone realized that Cosmo was slumped in his seat and the Fujmobile was coasting.

Irena unbuckled herself and hopped forward, avoiding cowling traps.

She took the controller out of Cosmo's hands and sidestepped to let the others extract Cosmo. She found space to take a knee and tried to brace herself against the exposed central console frame as she began learning how to drive.

Irena took the Fujmobile left at the intersection, away from Ange-Mariam and the other survivors of those vans. As they passed, she thought she saw a horrified look on Ange-Mariam's face and the rifle on the ground beside her.

But there was no time to gawk. Vans were coming up behind them.

Irena tried hard to ignore what the others were saying about Cosmo. She slipped into his seat and braced herself against the dashboard with her legs. There was no time to buckle in. She looked at the map display.

She had to cut down Vädersjövägen a short distance and then turn left down Ålstavägen. Both were thin, residential streets. All other routes were cul-de-sacs.

"If possible, get ready with cowling traps," she said, speaking over the blurry conversation behind her.

She hoped there would be no pedestrians or animals on these thin streets. She hoped both vans would continue chasing behind her rather than doubling back to cut off their only routes of escape from this side of Tungelsta. She hoped

the unseen drones overhead would begin to lose them.

She turned off the van's lights, relying only on house and yard lighting.

Down Ålstavägen she drove, seeing the two vans turn to follow. They were spooked or something, because they were only following, not attempting any tactical ramming.

Or perhaps they, too, didn't want innocent casualties and were content to maintain visual contact.

Irena didn't plan on making it easy for them. She took another look at the map and decided on a plan.

When the thin road veered right, making visibility more difficult for her followers, she turned right down Vretalundsvägen. She zoomed up a block and turned left.

At the next side street, she found exactly what she was hoping to find, a right-of-way alley between buildings. She turned left down the alley just as headlights lit up the corner behind her.

This would either save them or it would end them. She was gambling. But simply driving in the headlights of their pursuers would never work. It was time to rely on their lack of a transponder and lights.

Halfway down the alley, she slowed down. It was not a long alley. Either one van would end up behind, or one behind and one ahead. If both were behind, she could zoom away. If one was ahead but didn't stop at the alley, she could zoom away after it passed. Only if both turned down the alley would all be lost, or probably lost. She planned her desperate escape through the backyards of the houses around her.

But she only saw headlights behind her, growing.

Irena began to roll forward again, slowly, quietly. The streetlamps ahead were not helping matters.

She decided to go before the van behind her arrived at the alley.

In seconds the Fujmobile was crossing Ålstavägen and

zooming down Tungelstavägen.

Irena didn't have time to peer into the rear camera view to try to determine whether her pursuers had seen her exiting the alley this way.

She veered right, down Blomgårdsvägen, which was also tree-lined and house-lined, and it veered left near the end. She merged onto Kvarnvägen again and was back on the original plan, heading south.

Now terrain was on her side, at least relative to anyone farther up Kvarnvägen looking south. This part of the road was going downhill, and she was below the hill's crest.

"Why am I the one who always gets shot?" said Cosmo in the back of the van.

The others cheered and clapped.

"Hang on," said Irena.

She reached the end of the road. They were at the railroad tracks, blocked by fences. This was the plan all along. Across the tracks was Söderbyvägen.

She turned right, at the entry to the service road, turned the van around, then rolled a short way back up the road. Now she buckled herself in.

"Here we go," she warned everyone.

Then she yanked the joystick backward. The Fujmobile sped backward toward the train fencing and crashed through. She had to do some jiggering to get the van over the tracks, but it made it. Then she had to do some more back and forth to take down the fence on the other side.

But they were through. She continued backing up into the train station parking lot, made a 'K' turn, and sped away down Söderbyvägen.

In moments they were away from the train tracks and away from Tungelsta. There was not a lot of tree cover, but they had no transponder, and they were still driving without lights in the dark. Drones would have a hard time spotting them unless they knew exactly where to look.

Irena kept the Fujmobile at its new top speed, a painfully slow 40 kph. At this speed, it was hard to imagine surprise obstacles being an issue.

Down Söderbyvägen they went. After reaching an area with taller trees, Irena put the headlights back on.

"What's his status?" she asked.

"Keiok is some kind of trained medic," said Nycci.

"Yeah, eh?" said Bode. "It was a through-and-through in the shoulder. Keiok sewed him up even with all the bouncing you put us through."

"Whew," Irena vocalized. "Glad to hear it."

"Me, too," said Cosmo quietly.

"Go to sleep," said Nycci.

Söderbyvägen took them all the way down, across 73, and then right onto Nynäsvägen. From there it was just a few turns onto the Östnoraberget WPPPS access road.

With the clock reading 1726, they saw the facility just ahead.

Irena wondered what had become of the Swedish Nazis. She'd lost sight of them somewhere in the fog of Tungelsta, but they worried her. In a sort of panicky moment she imagining them suddenly appearing behind the Fujmobile, chasing them all the way to the parking lot, her team throwing burning junk at them and sending them over the cliff at the end of the lot.

Irena was snapped back into focus by Nycci sliding open the side door and jumping down, two of their toolbags on her shoulders. Irena had parked the van near the service door completely unconsciously.

Keiok and Bode helped Cosmo out of the van. Irena grabbed the remaining two toolbags and stepped off the van.

Out of habit, they slid the side door closed. When it slammed shut, the Fujmobile slumped toward the ground, the front window shattered, and various side panels fell off the van with clangs. Some buzzing electrical sounds could be heard coming from inside.

Irena gave the van the Janitor Squad salute, which resembled the squeeze of a spray bottle followed by wiping with a cloth. The others attended for that moment, silently thankful.

Then they all resumed their walk, or groaning hobble, toward the WPPPS' mid-stage chamber service entrance.

Chapter 25

San Vicente

Their access code had expired, of course, but Nycci knew how to run a bypass and had the right equipment.

Once inside, Nycci said, "Seal the door. Hurry." She and Bode pulled out their hand torches and began welding the metal door to its metal frame.

Keiok all but carried Cosmo into the facility, but even for him, it was slow going. He was taking great care not to rip open Cosmo's wounds.

Irena knew she couldn't wait. She hurried toward the lab.

Once inside the lab, she locked the door.

Then she crouched under the computer desk and found the main network cable. She used a knife to slice a hole in its sheath and then used her standard-issue fiber cutter to cut the key, outgoing fiber line. The local network would still work, but she had severed their connection to the outside world.

All that waiting in the back of the van while her team was chasing scapegoats paid off. She'd had time to research the molecular analyzer as well as this espernet cable.

She pushed that section of the cable back into the passthrough grommet in the back of the desk to hide it. Then she sat at the computer and navigated to the network drivers folder. She double-clicked on the main network hardware driver and breathed a sigh of relief as the system opened that file in a hex editor. Thank you, computer nerds of the SVOA I.T. department.

It was just in time. Keiok and Cosmo were just reaching the top of the metal stairs, and from the clunking footfalls behind them Nycci and Bode were probably on their heels.

They started banging on the door's window after discovering the door was locked.

Irena conspicuously pretended to make edits to the network driver.

When she heard Nycci and Bode talking about breaking in, she stood up, went to the door, and opened it.

"What the hell?" said Nycci.

"Yahuh," said Cosmo.

"Irena, what did you do?" said Uncle Bode.

Irena walked to the molecular analyzer.

Nycci and Uncle Bode inspected the computer screen. They swapped to other windows and discovered they could not connect to the outside world.

They checked their wristcomps. No outside network connection, just the internal network.

"You edited the network driver to disable the outgoing network connection," said Bode. "Why?"

"I can't take the chance that," Irena paused, "someone might have been lying about agreeing to redo the molecular analysis. Or changed their mind along the way. We can't report to the authorities or be caught and interrogated without first cracking Ronja's secret. We can't!"

Everyone stood in silence, except Cosmo who had been set down in a chair. Keiok walked to the back of the lab. The others looked back and forth at each other.

"Yeah," said Nycci. "That was probably a smart move."

"I suppose so," said Uncle Bode.

"Yahuh," said Cosmo.

"Okay, it's 1734," said Irena. "Let's get cracking."

Irena pulled up the instruction manual on the molecular analyzer's screen.

"Damn, it stinks in here," she said.

"I'll get a fresh sample," said Bode. He started trying to lean over the bioreactor again, but his cracked ribs disagreed. "Oof, maybe not. Nycci, would you take a fresh sample, please?"

Uncle Bode handed Nycci a fresh, sterile, urine sampler tube and then eased himself into the chair at the desk, with a hand on his rib cage.

Nycci collected a sample while Irena ran the analyzer's self-cleaning cycle and pulled the calibration samples out of the cabinet.

Loud bangs were coming from the freshly welded entry door. This was it. The end of the road. Everyone inhaled and pressed on, except Cosmo, who seemed to have fallen asleep, and Keiok, who was in the back of the room with his hands up again.

This time they skipped the centrifuge step with the urine sample, so they weren't artificially removing anything from the sample. They just set it aside for a few moments.

Irena showed Nycci how to run the calibration cycle, then she realized something was happening at the computer.

Uncle Bode was stealthily trying to do something at the computer.

"Aha!" said Irena, pointing at the computer.

"I just want to send the data and get this over with," said Uncle Bode, evenly. "But I can't seem to find what you changed in this driver. You cleverly cleared the edit buffer."

"We're doing the analysis," said Irena. "Just wait for it. There's time." She had been watching Nycci, too, making sure Nycci was doing the calibration cycle correctly.

"Nice," she said to Nycci. "Looking good. Now we tie in the general chemistry analytical support software."

Nycci had the manual open to that step and was following the called-out steps. A second screen lit up showing the software was loaded and ready.

Irena and Nycci stirred the sample and placed three separate draws into the analyzer's three independent feeds. They pressed the go button.

The clock said 1746.

"Damn!" said Uncle Bode. "I give up. You've covered your tracks too well." He pointed at the analyzer. "What does that thing say now? We're running out of time."

"It's analyzing," said Nycci.

They tapped their feet.

There was more frantic banging at the facility entry door, plus some scraping. Bode casually walked to the lab door, closed it, and locked it.

The analyzer beeped. The support software screen reported its results.

After asking it to hide all entries related to what one would expect in an average WPPPS urine sample, they had to also ask it to filter out the virus. That left what was inside the virus.

There were trace amounts of Thallium, but it was not the bulk of the virus' payload. It was some kind of custom-designed, liquid-crystalline molecule.

The software was using chemistry terms no one in Squad Fuj understood. Near-infrared and UVA radiation would cause photodissociation of the doping moiety, which would essentially open a door in the molecule's casing. There was something else inside this custom molecule.

They instructed the software to filter out the "container" molecule so they could see clearly what else the analyzer found.

It was P.A.

"We didn't contaminate the sample, right?" said Irena. "You didn't touch your P.A. after putting on the gloves, right?"

"I did not," said Nycci. "Gloves were clean."

"Well, there it is," said Irena. "Polyamour."

That was Ronja's plan. She was going to get thousands, maybe tens of thousands of people, maybe more, to attend her special, blue-themed fireworks shows, which would subject audiences to higher than usual doses of near-infrared

and UVA radiation, which in turn would open the container molecules and dose everyone with P.A.

"Oh, eh?" said Bode, reading the results summaries. "Does she not understand that some fraction of the population will have bad reactions to that stuff?"

"And even if they don't have toxic reactions," said Irena, "having that many people on an uncontrolled dose with no sober, caring people to act as guides through the trip, who knows what wild and crazy things people might do? And it was warm during the day, but tonight's getting cool already. There could be exposure deaths, too."

Cosmo was awake and listening.

"She probably thinks she's doing everyone a favor," he said. "opening hearts and minds. I know people like that, who secretly dose their friends. But it's always done when friends are there. Mass dosing would never even occur to them."

"She could kill thousands, maybe tens of thousands," said Nycci, looking at the copper bands on her wrists. "You don't dose people without their permission."

"Send the report to the computer," said Uncle Bode. "Irena, please fix the network so we can send this to Nycci's list."

"Yahuh," she said. She closed the editor, making sure no changes were saved. Then she knelt down again and pulled that cable out of its pass-through grommet.

"Uncle Bode, would you please hand me a fiber-optic coupler?"

"Hehe, you tricky, tricky mop-pusher, eh?" he said, pulling a coupler out of his bag.

Irena spliced the cut fiber lines together with the coupler. The network returned.

Together the team composed their summary of the analysis and of their time held prisoner by Ronja, adding their e-signatures. They attached the molecular analyzer's report and Irena's bodycam footage from their time at Ronja's. They addressed it to the Stockholm police, the city, district, and regional councils, the SSS, the Folkhälsomyndigheten, and the newsblogisphere. The time was 1757.

Then the lab door slammed open and into the room spilled a dozen or so armed guard types in the black clothes and body armor that was now familiar to Janitor Squad Fuj. The one in front was that lead guard Uncle Bode had zapped at Ronja's snow globe.

Irena lifted her finger, completing the 'send' operation. She had a huge smile on her face.

Chapter 26

Upplösning

No longer distracted by their intense report writing on a deadline, Janitor Squad Fuj could see through the lab's window that the hatch was open at the top of the ladder on the rear wall valve-access platform. They could see a regularly flashing light through the hole.

"Come with us," said the lead guard. She was dead serious. This time they were pointing their shotguns and tasers at Squad Fuj.

"No," said Keiok from behind his squad.

Squad Fuj turned in surprise.

"The time has come for me to reveal myself," said Keiok.

"What the?" said Squad Fuj.

There was a click. Everyone turned to look at the lead guard. Her finger pulled the trigger again. Click.

"Technology?" said one of her underlings behind her. She exchanged her shotgun for his. She aimed at Keiok and pulled the trigger again.

Click.

Several guards tried to fire their tasers.

Click Click Click

The lead guard slung her gun and stepped toward Keiok, pulling out handcuffs.

Keiok said, "No." And started walking forward. The lead guard simply stood in place in the back of the room.

All the guards now had confused looks on their faces. It became clear to Squad Fuj that the guards somehow were experiencing motor muscle paralysis.

Keiok used one hand to beckon his squad. He had a hint of a smile on his face, something no one had seen before. He walked toward the door, lifting and moving a guard out of the way to clear the path. Then another.

He walked down the metal stairs. Squad Fuj followed.

When they were halfway to the service entrance door, they heard clangs on the lab access staircase. The guards behind them were no longer paralyzed and were following.

Keiok walked to the welded service door. He touched each weld bead with his fingers and the welds started to crack. That's when Irena noticed something odd about his skin.

He opened the door. There was a brief surge of motion outside, but then the crowd of vigilantes in the parking lot stopped moving.

In the facility's lamp lights Irena saw several vans parked in the lot, including two news vans. Small drones hovered around the area, presumably camera drones. There were also police 9000s, and police here and there around the lot, and behind the Fujmobile.

Keiok walked out and stood to the right of the Fujmobile, where everyone had a clear view of him, and he of them. Squad Fuj stepped forward and stood behind him.

There was another Click behind them. The lead guard had tried another shotgun. She threw it aside in frustration.

Now everyone could see Keiok's skin had become shiny and iridescent. Irena leaned around him to look at his face.

His facial features were getting smaller. In a few moments, his face was gone, replaced by a bluish light.

"Who remembers the Icebergers?" it said, the voice projecting from the 'head' as if from a loudspeaker.

"Who remembers the Iceberger probe in the Labrador Sea?" it said.

Nycci bumped elbows with Squad Fuj, showing them the video feed on her wristcomp. They were on all the news vids.

"I am that Iceberger probe," said Keiok, its 'hand' gesturing toward its 'chest.' By now, Keiok's hair had melted

into its head. Its clothing had melted into its body. It retained a generally humanoid shape, but its skin was a grey metallic color, not unlike all of the day's utility vans.

"Until now, my mission has been to understand humanity," it said.

Ronja's guards had circled around and were now looking at Keiok from the parking lot. Their weapons were now holstered and slung. It became clear that all the other people in the lot were no longer paralyzed but were simply rapt.

"This team," it gestured over its shoulders toward Squad Fuj still standing behind it, "has unknowingly assisted me, to your great benefit." Now it gestured toward the cameras and the crowd.

Nycci pointed at the vid feed on her wristcomp. It showed a zoomed-in view of Keiok-probe's 'face,' which now only had a dark, rectangular band across it, with a light that moved back and forth within the dark band.

"My new mission is to offer something to all of humanity," it said. "Something wonderful."

There were some exclamations from the crowd.

"Anyone who wishes to live in peace with us on the moon you call Umbriel is welcome," it said. "Sustaining you on Umbriel is trivial for us. And I understand that many of you will enjoy the colder temperatures we can offer there."

Another round of exclamations from the crowd.

"We have access to your communication networks. Anyone who wishes to come to Umbriel need only reply to the message you are about to receive…"

Everyone received a text message from a new phone number. "**This message is from the Icebergers on Umbriel. Reply 'YES' to accept our invitation.**"

"…and we will come to you," said Keiok-probe. "This probe's mission is now concluded, and it will be retrieved." The probe began to lose its remaining features. Legs, arms, and head melded into the body, which stood motionless in a rounded cylindrical shape before them.

While that was happening, a purplish dot moved across the sky above them. Some people in the crowd exclaimed and pointed upward.

The dot grew ever larger until it resolved into a spherical spacecraft that came to a stop and hovered about ten meters above the Fujmobile. The sphere was about as wide as the parking lot.

With it this close now, Irena could see its surface had a fluidly moving iridescence.

A cylindrical pipe extended from the sphere toward the thing that was Keiok. When it reached the probe, there was a brief slurping sound. The probe post became liquid and was slowly sucked into the pipe. The pipe finished off by tapping on the ground and slurping some more, then it withdrew into the spacecraft, and the spacecraft flew away into the night sky.

Nycci's wristcomp was already showing a video feed of Ronja being remotely interviewed on Focks. She was saying sarcastic things about the "Icebergians," suggesting that maybe they really wanted humans for snacks and that her snow globes were guaranteed to be safe and fun. Then the authorities arrived and took Ronja away from her camera, while Focks continued their smear campaign of the Icebergians.

For the sake of the historical record:

The remaining members of Janitor Squad Fuj were absolved of their crimes due to "extraordinary circumstances," although they were ordered to pay appropriate damages. Their earnings from books and appearances on the lecture circuit more than compensated.

Cosmo and Ange-Mariam got together again, and

Ange-Mariam's combat rifle appeared in a special display in a re-opened corner of the Armémuseum in Stockholm.

Bode was able to retire and move into a flat across the street from his daughter, who was happy to discover his true identity.

Nycci got Monty Hogue's job after using her bodycam to catch him playing video games on the job. Monty Hogue ended up working in the Stockholm SVOA I.T. department under the close scrutiny of Hugh Borg. Annika Borg continued to work at Stockholm SVOA.

Irena finally had a chance to open that message from Kekoa, which was a job offer in decontamination (cleaning vac suits at the Kyrgyz Moon Landing Museum). Irena accepted. On the way there, she kept sighing and thinking, "At least I'm not an attendant." Her sister, Bronya, healed up and recovered her mobility.

Contrary to the opinions of Focks and its followers, the Eisbergspitzisch were found to be honest, frank, and transparent about their motives.

When asked why they offered refuge on Umbriel, their answer was two-fold. First, humanity needed to get out more, for its own health and the health of its planet. Second, as they had told humanity decades earlier, all they really wanted to do was get high and watch tv.

And it turned out that the lateral frontal pole prefrontal cortex in the ventrolateral frontal cortex of the human brain formed just the right growth environment for an otherwise difficult-to-cultivate Eisbergspitzisch microorganism. This microorganism was entirely unharmful to humans, but it produced one of the Eisbergspitzisch's favorite drugs, which they'd named "Spok."

Also, the Rose Hip Neurons of the human brain formed an electrochemical lattice that was perfect for producing their other favorite drug, which they'd named "Makoi."

For the same amount of effort redirected to sustain a human population, their yield on Spok and Makoi harvests was many thousands of times improved. Their human visitors only had to undergo occasional spinal taps to harvest the drugs.

And to them, humans were mostly harmless anyway, so it was no skin off their noses to make the offer.

This, they said, was similar to humanity's relationship with mammalian pets, like cats or dogs. Having them around helped humans produce pleasing drugs within their own brains, and the cats and dogs didn't mind, as long as it was a good home.

And after this latest mass migration and peaceful exchange of information with the Eisbergspitzisch, humanity was able to actually reverse global warming and re-establish food production sustainably and efficiently enough to end the Give Them a Better Purpose campaign. Cats and dogs once again lived together in (usually) good homes with social primates.

No harm, no foul. Right? Check.

See X.HoYen's surprising bio and subscribe to his newsletter at https://XHoYenAuthor.com -- show your support for indie autistic writers, stay informed about future projects, or just stop by for the Ditties page, now with rabbit holes.

"Attendants of the Future" is X.HoYen's next book in this "of the Future" Un-series.

Even on the moon, someone has to shepherd the museum visitors. It's not a job for robots. When an impetuous visitor steals the Kyrgyz Moon Landing Museum's flag and jumps into a nearby crater, will VJ's fellow attendants come to his aid when he follows? And will the mysterious machines they awaken pose an existential threat, or will they just cause VJ's beloved, Silhouette, to finally leave him? Read this book to find out, and be grateful you're not an attendant. (If you are an attendant, FYI there are job openings at the Kyrgyz Moon Landing Museum.)

"It's hard to make predictions, especially about the future."

- Yogi Berra